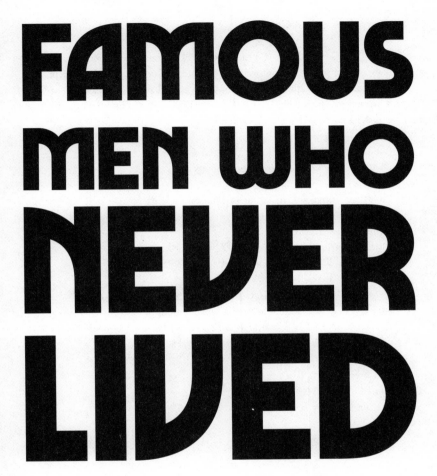

Published by Tin House Books, Portland, Oregon
Distributed by W. W. Norton & Company

Library of Congress Cataloging-in-Publication Data

Names: Chess, K, author.
Title: Famous men who never lived / by K Chess.
Description: First U.S. edition. | Portland, Oregon :
Tin House Books, 2018.
Identifiers: LCCN 2018041655 | ISBN 9781947793248 (hardcover)
Subjects: | GSAFD: Alternative histories (Fiction)
Classification: LCC PS3603.H4855 F36 2018 | DDC 813/.6—dc23
LC record available at https://lccn.loc.gov/2018041655

First U.S. Edition 2019
Printed in the USA
Interior design by Jakob Vala

www.tinhouse.com

FAMOUS MEN WHO NEVER LIVED

K CHESS

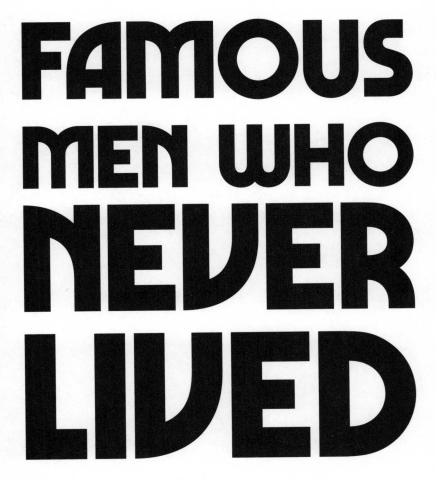 TIN HOUSE BOOKS / Portland, Oregon

To the brave and resilient refugees of the world.

"She had a houseful of books that she could neither read nor bring herself to use as fuel. And she had a memory that would not bring back to her much of what she had read before."

—OCTAVIA E. BUTLER, "Speech Sounds"

CHAPTER ONE

Hel stepped over the threshold from the sagging porch, squeezing her body between towers of junk. She fought off the tight, proprietary excitement that kindled in her chest. The cottage, marooned on a street of much newer semidetached row houses in the Brownsville area of Brooklyn, was smaller and shabbier than she'd expected. Dwayne Sealy, the owner, followed her in and pulled the street door closed behind them. As Hel's eyes adjusted, she saw shoulder-high stacks of newspapers and magazines, blocking even the windows. A narrow path wound through the canyons of disorder, a passage three squares of brown-and-gold linoleum wide.

"Bulb's out, I guess." Dwayne flicked the switch up and down. "Wait right here—let me see what I can do." He activated the flashlight app on his phone and maneuvered around her, making his way into the dim room beyond.

Happy to stay where she was, Hel breathed in the precious dust. Within these walls in another Brooklyn, the great writer Ezra Sleight had lived, rats under the floorboards, a pile of books in his bed. Within these very walls in a different Brownsville, he'd penned his best novels. His masterpieces. *The Pyronauts. The Pain Ray. What to Do with the Night.* But none of this was his. There was nothing worth discovering. Everything surrounding her here was an artifact of After, the time after the split.

This was not the Brownsville she knew. Just ten minutes ago, on New Lots Avenue, she'd witnessed a group of kids pretending to piss on a man slumped unconscious in an alley. She'd noticed melted vinyl siding fronting a building a few doors down, that ominous black smudge that marked a place where a car had burned hot. This was a different world, a world in which Ezra Sleight had died as a ten-year-old child. His life cut short, his genius never apparent to anyone, he never wrote the books that made him seem, to scholars like Vikram, worthy of attention. Perhaps a few had mourned the boy Sleight—his family and his schoolmates—but no one remembered to mourn him now.

No one but Hel. 1909. The date, when she'd learned it, stood out in neon.

Dwayne returned carrying a battery-powered camping lantern that cast a warm glow on the walls of old newspaper. "I forgot," he said. "They cut the electric. Come on back. I can't say it gets much better, but it does get brighter."

They passed through what might have been a sitting room, though no clear place to sit presented itself in the cramped squalor. They entered the kitchen, at the back of the house. Here, motes swirled in the sunbeams from the big windows.

Hel sneezed. She noted mismatched appliances, a rounded, monstrous Frigidaire, the type of stove that must be lit with matches, a front-loading dishwasher in avocado green partially hidden behind a mound of black plastic trash bags. The double sink was full—not with dishes but with dozens of back issues of some magazine she'd never heard of.

Dwayne jerked open a drawer. "My grandmother. I loved the woman, but she had a problem. Didn't know it had gotten this bad." He squinted at the clutter inside but did not touch. "I told you she passed away last week?"

"Yes," said Hel. "On the phone, you mentioned. I'm sorry for your loss." That, she'd learned, was what you said here when someone died.

"She practically raised us in this house—me and my brother—but the last couple years, she wouldn't let us inside. Now I see why." He stood abruptly, kicked at a cardboard carton. Whatever was inside tinkled as it broke. "Shit."

Traffic on the Belt Parkway two blocks away rumbled like distant thunder. Hel looked up high, up above the broken surface of this roiling sea of possessions. She examined the dirty wallpaper, fussy bouquets streaked with grime. A design from Before, from the shared history of her world and Dwayne's. She took in the dark wood cabinets, their old doors hanging crooked on the hinges, where Sleight might have stored his dishes.

Something reaching for her, making contact. Signs in the dust that most people couldn't read.

"Guess I should have checked things out before I brought you over," Dwayne said. "You're not interested now."

Within these walls, what might have been.

"You'd be surprised," Hel said.

○

Looking back, she wished she'd deliberated about what to carry through the Gate. One bag, the evacuation officials ordered, providing maximum dimensions, as if those thousands luck had chosen were booking seats on an airship for a vacation.

But Hel remembered her world history. As she packed, she'd considered the rumors about forced labor at America Unida's hidden education camps, and about what the Power Brothers in Ceylon had done in the jungles to city-dwelling elites. And she'd remembered the KomSos clearing the shtetls of the Pale from east to west. All of these regimes relocated citizens en masse by imposing arbitrary rules that encouraged compliance and complacency. Leave what you own behind. All you'll need is your identity papers. You'll see your neighbors on the other side. Then, the march into the caves, the group showers, the trenches to be dug. Docile victims unaware of what was coming: the suffocation, the live burial. The shot in the back of the head.

Stay calm, the Evac Commission instructed. And yes, it needed to be said. Order was just barely being maintained in those chaotic days, by the hope—a fiction Evac promoted— that everyone had a chance. Hel's name being chosen in a frantic lottery didn't mean she was going to get out alive. Anything could be waiting.

Thus prepared for the worst, Hel brought practically nothing. Packed in her padded shoulder bag: her portable ordinator and its charger (not compatible with anything here, of course), the medical journal she happened to be reading at the time, her allergy medication, two liters of water. And just to be safe, inside a plastic folder, her passport, birth certificate, and a copy of her New York State medical license.

In the other pocket of the folder, she'd tucked a drawing her son, Jonas, had made for her in pre-form, years ago, back before her ex-husband took him away to California. It depicted a tiger with a red-crayoned mouth and blood-dripping claws. On the other side of the page three crude human figures smiled, representing Raym and Helen and Jonas himself, all three of them drawn with the same scribble of hair. Hel could tell which one was meant to be her because of the earrings sticking straight out from her head—as big as hands—and by the mole next to her nose, which her son had been careful to add in brown crayon.

That bag. All she had left of her home.

That fall/winter 2018 issue of the *Journal of Clinical Insights* with its drab cover. Nothing special about it. The report of a study on a radical new treatment for Albertson-Huhn syndrome in immunocompromised patients whose methodology had once seemed to her positively irresponsible. In the years since, she'd read and reread the piece, along with every other article between the covers.

Because the issue was the last, the only. Because the *Journal of Clinical Insights* did not exist here. The study did not exist here. Albertson-Huhn syndrome was named after someone else entirely.

Everything was like that. 1910 was the magic year, as far as anyone could prove. Before that was a known quantity. It was

After—after 1910—that things slowly started to unzip, one set of possibilities uncoupling from another and veering off, gradually at first, but then more and more drastically.

Without exception, when UDPs like her gathered in groups, they asked each other what they'd brought through. It was almost a party game. People laughed at Hel's practicality when she answered this question, when she described the water and the charger and the antihistamines.

The knife—that flick-blade she'd always carried—she'd concealed it in her shoe, but the sticks found it at the checkpoint, confiscated it before she passed through. She'd had to buy a replacement, later. She knew better than to mention that, even to UDPs. None of them would have found it funny.

Vikram, the man Hel lived with, had his own regrets. In his hurry, he'd brought only books, his backpack straining with them. Now, he mourned the loss of the picture albums from his New Jersey adolescence, photos from family vacations. Most keenly, Vikram rued his hasty abandonment of his mother's bangle, an heirloom etched with Mughal designs passed through her family for generations. It could have fit right in the front pocket, he often said, where he'd made room for one more paperback instead.

Hel was glad he'd chosen books; UDPs who'd taken objects of more tangible value found themselves disproportionately likely to have that property missorted by the authorities during Debrief. She teased him, though, about his choice of titles. Why just literature—no science, no books on technology? (Because Vikram probably hadn't owned any nonfiction at all, before he lived with her.) Why so many older books, books from long

Before, which turned out to be superfluous? (Because he didn't know—none of them had any way of knowing—and because he didn't think he could live in a world without Rumi or Tolstoy or Jules Verne.) On the whole, Vikram made his selections with wisdom and luck. He'd saved novels by Darby Kenyon, by Grant Wilder, by Samara Vaugh. He'd preserved poetry by Nakamura Hideki rendered into luminous English by renowned translator A. J. Butler. These bestsellers, prizewinners, and canonical works existed in unique volumes on Hel and Vikram's shared bookshelf in the Bronx. And he'd rescued an electrostat draft of his own unfinished dissertation, as well as the novel it treated. A slim paperback.

The Pyronauts by Ezra Sleight.

Why, Vikram lamented aloud sometimes, in moments of self-punishing sorrow, had he thought only of his job? Of his stupid life's work, meaningless now.

"You weren't thinking of work," Hel would say, to comfort him. She could hear in her own voice a fierce protagonism. "You didn't make a mistake. You were thinking about the persistence of our *culture*."

○

In *The Pyronauts*, the world was cleansed by fire.

The aliens arrived in shield-shaped ships made of shining crystal on a mission of peace. They had monitored Earth's communication broadcasts, so they already knew how to speak human languages and how best to solve earthly conflicts. Tall, wise, and graceful, with long appendages, the aliens were brilliant scientists as well as natural mediators. They went to the Council of Nations and disinterestedly fixed all the looming problems of Sleight's early twentieth century. They gave the Jews of Europe a permanent homeland in Polithuania, convinced Japan not to attack the AMFR, introduced a hardier and faster-growing strain of millet to the starving Chinese, eliminated smallpox and the battle flu, and brokered a peace between the warring Dominico-American and Voudon armies. Humanity hailed them as heroes.

But then, to the chagrin of the aliens, the world they'd gone to so much trouble to save began to wither and die around its inhabitants. An extraterrestrial organism, a microscopic pirate from the homeworld that clung undiscovered to the hulls of their crystal ships or stowed away in the folds of their flowing robes, proved toxic. First to the trees, large and small, and then to the crop plants, and finally even to flowers, grasses, and lowly weeds. The pollinators starved and the animals famished and in their turn, the people of Earth began to suffer privations, suffering quickest and worst in the lands the aliens had visited personally. The blight spread, ungovernable, moving through water and air. The visitors invented a vacuum-canning process that would enable the beleaguered human population to preserve what was left of their stores, showed them a subterranean cultivation method for edible mushrooms, and then, with profuse apologies and vague promises to return, got into their shields and left Earth's survivors to their own devices.

In North America, survivors formed scattered fortress-settlements underground or in those rare valleys whose natural topography provided some shelter from the killing winds, imposing quarantines to keep travelers from spreading the aliens' final gift. Only the pyronauts—men and women in special suits whose job it was to burn all infected plantlife in the Neverlands, the abandoned world beyond the settlements—were given license to move freely.

Apparently, it all stood for something bigger. Hel remembered that from the high-form classes she'd taken against her will as a teenager. It reminded her of the Truth deck, of spreading the cards out in horseshoes on the bedspread and interpreting them for her sister. Literature always seemed to have some hidden meaning that a normal person wouldn't guess. According to Vikram, most critics understood *The Pyronauts* to be an anti-colonial narrative and an anxious exploration of the possible consequences of the atom bomb. It was read and taught as a parable, warning its readers of the possible unforeseen results of harnessing a power greater than man to influence geopolitical affairs. Now, Vikram saw the novel as a trauma narrative speaking to the varied ways in which individuals cope with adversity. "What a conference paper I could write about it today!" he would say.

Or used to say, two years ago. Back when he still cared about Sleight.

In the book, pyronaut John Gund and his patrol-partner, Asyl, walked the hills of ash together in the waste-state of Pennsylvania with their tanks of fuel and their fire-spewing hoses. John Gund, a former cardsharp and all-around wastrel, had been serving a long prison term for shooting a rival gambler at the time the aliens arrived, and was let out by mistake in the ensuing upheaval. He found that he preferred the scorched Never to the flashy Philadelphia of his youth but felt he must keep this judgment, like all of the details of his personal history, a closely guarded secret from Asyl, young enough to be his daughter and born in a bunker city, who often asked him what the world had been like Before. (They used that term too; "the capital *B* audible in speech" was how Sleight's narrator described it in the book.) John Gund and Asyl walked through the floating cinders on their endless patrol of the Never, checking every stalwart new blade of grass that poked its way out of the charred ground with their alien-provided test kits, always finding unacceptable traces of the microbes, inevitably having to burn each sprout. Together, they crouched in their fireproof tent in the evenings, the helmets of their suits removed so they could eat their miserable vacuum-sealed ration packets of fungal protein, and John Gund entertained Asyl with tales of Before, full of self-aggrandizement and lies of omission.

Lovely, innocent Asyl in the tent, her face framed by curtains of dark hair, who said her prayers every night and harbored stubborn illusions—she touched Hel in a way Hel didn't really understand. Asyl, whose very name meant shelter.

○

Vikram heard Hel's voice, strained, but measured, from his place on the edge. He listened without understanding. "I found it," she was saying, and then he was coming, so he lost contact with the world for a moment, squeezing his hands into fists by his sides—trying not to touch her, because she didn't always welcome it, not when she was on top like this and she was about to come too.

When it was over, she flopped next to him on the mattress, dug her sharp chin into his chest, staring into his face, wanting something. He closed his eyes, listening to her breathing as it slowed. He wrapped an arm around her and they rested.

She'd been impatient for hours. Earlier, when he got home from his shift, she'd been waiting for him on the bed wearing a T-shirt, reading the dog-eared Sleight book. "You know, this is so great," she'd said then, closing it gently. "Really great. How could the world do without this?"

She never read for pleasure; she'd told him as much when they met. He remembered how they'd been when they were first together, both of them disconsolate with grief and loss. They'd ride the subway trains for hours. Underneath the earth was the only place where Vikram's pain felt sufficiently muffled; how jarring it had been to emerge. Once, when the G train they were riding climbed unexpectedly from the tunnel—the tracks running aboveground for a few blocks in Brooklyn to cross the Gowanus Canal—the sudden pain of it, of that slice of dark sky and the spreading landscape studded with lights, had cost him the last of his fragile control over himself. He'd cried for his mother, then, for his two sisters. His boyhood best friend, Keith Chen, whom he hadn't talked to in years. His job. His city—the real one—with its velocabs and duple buses, its efficient elevated tramways that looked so much like this short stretch of track.

Hel never cried, not even in the first months. Instead, she walked around all day, picking vicious fights with the people who didn't seem to be real to her—the trainee social worker, the assimilationist housemates she'd lived with before moving

11

into Vikram's apartment, the junior agent with the tape recorder who'd questioned the UDPs from her entry group, even the tired old men sitting out on their stoops. When Hel wasn't arguing, she was obsessing. At a certain point, Vikram had felt obligated to take that old medical journal away from her for the sake of her sanity, removing it from her custody before the pages softened to illegibility. "Careful," he'd joked. "Someone else will want to read this artifact someday."

That remark might have been the start of it. Her preoccupation with documentation. Her conviction that some outsider might actually care about their stories.

"Wake up," she said, after a time. She nudged him. "I was telling you, I found it."

One by one, Vikram stretched out his limbs. He flexed his fingers and toes. "What? What did you find?"

Hel threw a leg over him, then sat up, obviously ready for more. "Sleight's house. You won't believe it when you see it. It's full of junk."

"You want to switch?" Vikram asked. He still felt spent, inebriated, unable to think clearly, which put him at a clear disadvantage; she never seemed to have that problem.

"No, I don't want to switch." She rocked on top of him. "The house where he would have lived, if he hadn't, you know, died."

"You know, that's not remotely sexy."

She leaned close, breathing in his ear. "It should be a museum, Vikram. I'm going to make it happen." Now she moved his arms, positioning them above his head and pinning his wrists in place with one hand. She knew what he liked. "What do you think?"

The ends of her hair tickled his shoulders. "No one would care," he told her. "Who would want to go to this museum? Literally no one."

She leaned forward, increasing the pressure on his wrists. "Why not?"

Helplessly, he bucked up with his hips. "Because everyone who isn't a Bible Numericist hates us. You know that UDP who's all over the news for cutting up the old lady and then stabbing her thirty-seven times? That's the association people have. They think we're unhinged."

Hel had released her grip; he began to bring his hands back down to his sides, intending to risk a touch, to stroke her thigh, but she shook her head, admonishing. "No. You don't move. Stay still." Her warm, dry palm on his erection. "1909. You *know* why I think it's important."

"You're a doctor. You're supposed to be a scientist." He was finding it difficult to maintain focus. "Just because two things happened doesn't make them related."

Her hands roamed up and down his chest as she shifted her weight on top of him. "Shh." She twisted his left nipple. "I told you to stay still."

"Hel. That hurts."

"What else explains it, if not Sleight's death?" She guided him inside her. "What else could it be?"

"Chaos theory," he said, the words coming out half-choked.

"What did you say?" she asked. But he couldn't answer. They moved with each other, then against each other. She rode him with head thrown back and he knew her eyes were closed. She always closed her eyes. He watched a muscle in her jaw jump. Experimentally, Vikram released one of his hands from its imaginary bonds and placed it on her hip. This time, she didn't say anything, so he moved the other one up too, slowing the pace.

"More rain," he forced out. "More rain in Asia breaks a dam. Crop prices go up. People starve. Births decline. Population dives. And the person who was going to invent flying pods never gets born."

"Shut up," Hel said. "There's still no flying pods."

Afterward, he lay in her arms, her face right next to his. He could see the clumps of mascara in her eyelashes. Taste her breath, that mint-and-Helen taste. "What's your biggest regret?" he asked. "Your biggest regret in life."

What did he expect? For her to jump out of bed. For her to slap him, for her to rake her nails down his chest. For her face to go slack, or tight. For her to say something about Jonas, whose name was taboo, spoken by her only when she was asleep. To say nothing at all.

What he didn't expect. Her hand moving up to pet his hair, and her answer: "The books. All the books I never read."

And after she left to shower, he lay alone in the bed and he couldn't fall back asleep. He rolled over and opened the window to smoke a cigarette. At home he'd used sniff, but they didn't have that here. Hel, who used to be an otolaryngologist, said sniff was also bad for you, but at least it didn't reek like smoking. So he leaned his whole head out.

He watched the beginning of the October day unfold for the kids down on the street walking to the subway with their school backpacks on and for the store owners unlocking and rolling up the metal gates over their premises. A shirtless guy wearing some kind of head covering with long ties that looked like it was made of black panty hose was trying to shake the dirt out of the floor mat from his enormous car. Vikram wondered what the head covering was and why the man wore it. He wished there were a way to look that kind of thing up on his phone. The guy banged the mat against a sickly tree. The tree shook. Synched traffic lights on Jerome Avenue flicked to green, one after another—green lights to eternity.

She was back from the shower, a towel around her hips, her breasts rosy-tipped. She took her comb from the dresser. "The kid who owns the Sleight house? He's maybe twenty-five. The place was a bequest. He would love to have it taken off his hands."

Vikram threw the cigarette stub out the window. "Leave it alone. OK?"

"I can't. What dam, Viki? Find me the dam that did it."

He grabbed her right hand and kissed it, tracing with his lips the mysterious scars that crossed all four of her fingers. "I don't know what dam. I made the dam up."

"There is no dam. There's just Sleight. His death."

Every UDP agreed that something had gone wrong. Only she had it narrowed down to a day, a minute. A singular event, dividing Before from After. Her fascination and her talk about another world worried Vikram. Next thing he knew, she'd take out those Tarot cards he'd bought her in the Village as a joke.

How torn Hel always seemed, between the rational and the mystical. He sank back down on the bed. "There are plenty of causes more likely than some science fiction writer falling out of a rowboat as a kid."

"*Some science fiction writer?* Really? That's all he is to you?"

What was he supposed to say? "I never knew him, Hel. You never knew him either. He's not even real anymore."

CHAPTER TWO

It all ended in a rush nearly three years ago now, when the first lots of lucky people moved through the hole into this world. Groups of one hundred at a time—men, women, but no children—stepping dazed into the spaces between the grave markers of Calvary Cemetery in Queens. There were ten entry groups per lot, lots coming at precise hourly intervals, the hole closing up behind them each time like a wound healing in time lapse. Emergency crews had their hands full, moving the newest arrivals out of the way to make room for more. All of the newcomers told the same story—coordinated teams of domestic terrorists, young men radicalized by pro–America Unida messages hidden in visor games from the south. The power plants in Poughkeepsie and Richmond and Escondido simultaneously sabotaged, all timed to the minute, and the sulfur-yellow radiation clouds blowing with the prevailing winds. Then retaliatory strikes across the Caribbean, backup from allies. Old promises called in and standoff agreements abandoned.

And that miraculous escape hatch, shining in the air above Calvary. Their Calvary—the one that corresponded. All these people, the gathering crowd of onlookers realized, were New Yorkers, too.

Finally, another hour passed and a 157th lot did not come through—it just never showed up. An unexplained end to the exodus. Of course, that spurred further media coverage and more speculation about what might have happened on the other end to halt the evacuation.

At first, public curiosity had been intense, the attention not unfriendly. The scientifically inclined and the religious were equally fascinated by this miraculous proof of the existence of a version of creation other than the one they knew. Multiple universes seemed likely, each one fully formed and somehow held apart from the others until now. It made great copy. It took a while to dawn on the amazed people of this New York that they had 156,000 new citizens to feed, house, and somehow integrate. Individuals diverse in their needs but all propertyless and homesick, some of them elderly or disabled, some trained only to do specialized jobs that did not exist here, many suffering from PTSD or immobilized by grief.

The newcomers, whose reality had betrayed them. Here they all were, crash-landed. Resented and resentful. Universally Displaced Persons.

Meanwhile, everyone who hadn't gotten through the Gate had died. That was a given. The Gate was a prototype. One of a kind. One-way.

◯

The logbook didn't mention anything unusual, so Vikram left the guard shack for his first tour of the perimeter in good time, by 23:15. He liked working late tours, knowing that the self-storage warehouse would be quiet for hours. The last person he'd talked to was Kabir, in such a hurry to leave for a date that they'd barely exchanged two words, and Vikram, if all went as expected, wouldn't see another living soul until 06:00 or so, when the front desk worker arrived for the early shift. Sometimes, adventurous teenagers snuck into the parking lot behind the building in search of a wall to tag or a dark corner to hide a tryst. Sometimes he found a homeless person huddled by the fence like wind-sent trash. But most nights he spent entirely alone.

He took the keycard-operated elevator up to the top floor of the old mattress factory. Some entrepreneur had gutted and retrofitted the whole building back in the '90s, converting it from three stories to five. During the retrofit, most of the old windows had been sealed up; only the ones in the hallways remained uncovered. They no longer corresponded properly with the stories of the building; on some floors, hazy illumination from the parking lot came in near the ceiling, but on five, half windows disappeared into the floor.

Vikram made his way down the narrow corridors between the rows of locked doors, pointing his light into every corner. He walked in a winding pattern that took him past each unit on his way to the fire stairs, then pushed through the heavy doors and walked down a flight, where he swiped his card to access the next floor. On four, he followed the same pattern. The beam revealed nothing but the narrow corridor, the faceless doors of the units, the sprinkler heads up above and smooth cement floor below. He found the routine comforting; the pleasant indistinct scuffing of the rubber soles of his own shoes on the cement and the intense prickle of watchfulness he felt on each new level when he pushed open the door from the stairs. Would someone be there waiting?

He'd held this same menial job since the early months of his displacement. The only real duties were the rounds, but video monitoring of the guard shack made it impossible to read a book or sleep without getting written up. Kabir had warned him of this. Kabir, a fifty-five-year-old Pakistani, had been standoffish during the half-hour overlaps of their shifts at first, rushing off to the bathroom to wash his hands at any accidental touch, as if Vikram were the carrier of some unquarantinable disease, but as the silent weeks wore on, the older man's natural pedantry won out and he began to spend their overlap time instructing Vikram, delivering heavily accented lectures on such diverse topics as John Grisham, Cher, *The Fresh Prince of Bel-Air*, and the Brooklyn Nets. Kabir had explained the concept of online poker and what an "ass-load" was. The information he provided was far more essential to Vikram's education than anything he ever learned in his Reintegration Education group. In return, Vikram confided in Kabir about his loneliness. Fat Kabir, with his bad teeth and bad advice, rocking in his wheeled desk chair. Vikram felt sheepish about how much he'd revealed, back in that period of his life. He looked at it now as his adjustment period—a time when he believed he was too good for this work. Vikram had complained until there was nothing left to say, sharing far too many of his disappointments. He preferred the loneliness of the storage company after Kabir was gone.

The layout of the first floor of the old factory differed from the floors above because of the placement of the centrally located reception/security desk, and because of the larger, more expensive units. Vikram peered into the cage that enclosed the vacant desk, sweeping his light across the blank-faced monitors, the row of hooks on the back wall, the dangling keys as yet unassigned. Then he checked both first-floor hallways, holding his breath as he turned the corners. His radio hung from his belt, tugging at the waistband of his trousers, and his big flashlight was solid in his hand.

Sometimes, he imagined what it would be like to hit someone with it. An action he'd take only in extremity, of course, only if the intruder seemed dangerous.

Gravel crunched under Vikram's shoes as he toured the inside perimeter of the high cyclone fence to check the rest of the property. The locked gate and, next to it, the shack, lit from inside, which when seen from a distance reminded him inevitably of the watch post on the frontier of Victory City in *The Pyronauts*. There was the parking lot, yellow lines dividing it up into spaces for trucks or moving vans, all empty—Vikram himself having taken the subway to work. There were the concrete ramps. The low sad bushes clotted with dirty leaves and plastic bags where Kabir had discovered, one shift, three nervous high school girls with a sack of rocks, out on a window-smashing dare.

All clear.

A full two decades and a universe away from here, sixteen-year-old Vikram and his friends once broke into the partly burned-down and abandoned New Jersey State Lunatic Asylum, prying the plywood off a boarded-up side door. The boys intended no vandalism. They were dizzy with the excitement of exploring the time capsule that the decommissioned children's ward had become, untouched by modernity or the fire that had taken the north wing of the building in the '60s.

After half an hour inside, scaring themselves silly, they'd heard the crash and the raised voice from downstairs: "Police! You're all consigned for trespass!" The area must have been on the department's regular patrol; they should have thought to park their borrowed pods and motorbikes off the access road instead of right out front.

The sticks were coming up to find them. No time, nowhere to run. The boys' only option was to shut off their electric lantern and freeze where they were, crouching in the aisle between two rows of diminutive beds. In the pitch black, Vikram listened to his own quick breathing and to the sounds of his friends' shifting bodies, listened for the footfalls of the officers two floors below and their gruff stick-voices calling out to one another as they searched. He imagined where he was and what was around him unseen, what the lantern had just revealed piece by piece in the minutes before: the line of rusted metal bed frames, the dusty sheets, the spiderwebbed glass of the nurses' station. The peeling, amateurishly executed cartoon mural of Rocket Pig and friends. Rocket Pig, so familiar and so desolate in his bubble-shaped ship, painted there to make these sick children of a generation ago feel at home in a place without parents, a place of needles and drugs and restraining straps. Electric lantern near to hand, he fought himself not to turn the dial that would give them away, just to see it all again.

"I'm scared," Keith Chen whispered into the dark, barely audible.

"Shut up," the rest of them hissed back, all more intently alert than they had ever been before. Listening for sounds of the police coming to find them, yes, for they were obedient boys, good students from hardworking immigrant families. They hated to break the rules. They were not superstitious. But they listened for more, for some sound, a cry. They were waiting for a sign of an otherworldly presence, for the breath of an extra set of small lungs.

Rounds completed, Vikram made his way back to the guard shack, tossing his Maglite in the dark so that it flipped once in the air before he caught it. He knew its balance intimately. He'd lived through the death of his world and everyone he'd ever known and escaped to start anew. He wasn't scared of flesh-and-blood intruders. In fact, he was ready.

If there was a noise in the dark. If it was a man—a full-grown man with ill intent, a thief wielding a weapon. How the halogen lights mounted on the side of the old factory building might glint off a blade. Vikram would yell an order to freeze, but the intruder would ignore him. He would rush at Vikram with that blade extended and Vikram would bring down the flashlight hard on the top of his attacker's head, cracking his skull.

Self-defense. The knife skittering away on the blacktop.

Take that.

Imagining scenarios like this might have made some people jumpy. It made Vikram feel prepared. He would never admit it to Hel or even to Kabir, but he liked it. He liked it.

He took out his cheap Bic—its precarious mechanism different from the steady-burning lighters at home—lit up, and began to walk back toward his comfortable chair for an idle hour. He was thinking about the logbook and about the unfamiliar oldies he would play on the old radio in there. Thinking about what would be on the grocery list he should probably make for tomorrow. He inhaled deep; though it was more inconvenient and far unhealthier than sniff, he secretly enjoyed smoking, the act of firing the lighter as pleasurable to him as the nicotine. And just then, Vikram became aware.

Later, he would wonder about this, second-guess himself a bit, but it really wasn't a noise that made him turn around. No clink of chain-link, no rustle in the bushes that might have been rat or cat. It was a feeling.

He looked behind him—still no one there—but up ahead, a line that bent two corners glowed distinct on the side of the building, an upside-down U, vivid blue. It hadn't been there before. It took Vikram a minute to recognize the phenomenon as light—blue light—escaping from one of the units on the third floor, a glow from inside seeping around the two sides and the top edge of the boarded-up window that corresponded only partially with that floor.

Based on its placement, he knew it couldn't be coming from the hallway, but from beyond one of the doors he'd passed. Somebody *inside*.

Should he call the police now? Should he check the security recordings? The front-door-mounted camera would have caught anyone who wasn't supposed to be present. Vikram sprinted back to the building, let himself in a second time, rushed past the empty cage, the vacant desk. The elevator doors were secured as always, the floor indicator as quiet and dark as it ought to be. He went to the fire stairs making as little noise as he could, conscious of a strange and gratifying calm suffusing him. Outside the thick steel door he paused to listen, though this was futile, of course. Then he counted to ten, bursting through in a sudden movement. The stairwell interior remained as black as a mine shaft until he pointed his beam up. No movement but the shadows cast by the light in his own moving hand. "Hey," he said in a quiet voice. "I'm coming up."

Blue light. He knew that color.

He turned off the flashlight and followed the railing, his heavy shoes patting the stairs in a steady and deliberate rhythm, not quite a run; he didn't want to be out of breath by the time he reached the door.

The lock on three clicked as he swiped his card. He looked straight down the first corridor, bathed in the dim glow of the security lights. Nothing, but then, the unit in question must be on the other side of the building—the side that faced the parking lot. He moved forward. Yes, his heart was beating faster than normal. Yes, he was frightened. But he didn't mind.

The weight and balance of the flashlight in his hand, a cudgel.

Around the corner now, moving as silently as he could. One of these units then, on the left, but which? No light leaked from under any of the tightly fitted security doors. It was impossible to tell. He satisfied himself by tugging on the padlocks, one after another, first the three belonging to the doors he most suspected might lead to the unit he'd noticed from outside. All locked.

He advanced methodically down the corridor, checking every single lock. All held fast.

How could a light turn itself on within a locked unit?

The most sensible answer was a timer, one of those devices that could be set for a certain hour to give a home the impression of occupancy and deter thieves. Some common appliance in this world that glowed blue, something that he'd never heard of. That was all it was. Vikram felt his breathing slow a bit and he was glad that he hadn't called the police, but he still felt himself on edge. For there was another answer, one he wasn't allowing himself to think about. Keeping quiet, he retreated down the hall and descended the fire stairs back to ground level. He pulled the main door behind him, listened for the catch.

The parking lot looked just as it had before, as did the half-familiar but immutable skyline—low, workaday Queens with Manhattan ranged out behind, buildings he knew from his world and buildings he didn't, the angry sky bruised purple from light pollution.

The old factory loomed behind him. The light that glowed the same color as the Gate he'd passed through was snuffed out. He hated to hope. And yet. What if there were more of them coming.

Or a door. A way to return.

In the guard shack, he settled back in the chair in front of the static monitors and pulled out the incident log. He licked the tip of his pencil. Checked the time.

Exactly 12:13 AM. He wrote *0:13* in the log, paused.

Back at home, where everyone used the twenty-four-hour clock, they'd called that bad luck time.

INTERVIEW TRANSCRIPT:
IMAN IBRAHIM, AGE 59, QUEENS

I set up the lottery system, and I rigged it in my favor. I'm a statistician, after all, not a martyr, not like Dr. Mornay, a captain who insisted on going down with her ship. Mornay herself patted me on the back and sent me through the Gate with the first entry group in the fifteenth lot.

Just hours after the meltdowns, as she and her department began to haul all that dusty equipment out of secure storage, I was in my office at Gaynor Tech, programming an ordinator to pull from military and Alternative Service records and sort out those with Extreme Crime convictions. Mornay and I knew each other from years back, when I'd done the mathematical modeling for the Gate prototype. I'd been surprised to hear she'd held on to her job, much less her machine. But I was happy to help her.

Half the stations had gone black by midafternoon on the day of the attacks. The newsreaders on the stations that were left were wearing paper masks over their faces, as if that could do anything against radiation, talking about containment strategies for Richmond. Poughkeepsie was already a lost cause. I don't remember what they were saying about the plant in Southern California at that point. Meanwhile, Mornay's team trucked all the equipment down to Calvary Cemetery and set it up there without permission. That was the best open space they could think of, accessible to the most people via tramways and with three major traffic arteries right there. She had people pulling on all their connections—research colleagues, old contacts at government agencies, anything—trying to get permission to do what she was already doing. And then they sent through old Dr. Cristaudo, with a transmitter, as a test. A second test.

The first test came years earlier, during the development of the Gate prototype. I remembered the rig, of course, that meter-and-a-half-tall unit they'd set up in the safety-shielded first-floor Applied Physics lab at Gaynor, cinder-block walls shivering in its light. I used to go down there and watch. They'd throw items in attached to strings, and reel them back home. They'd take pictures. They'd send various instruments through and run my ordinated probabilities, again and again. But none of those physicists knew what, exactly, the hole connected to. And then one night, someone left the Gate powered up, and a graduate student of Mornay's, a woman named Ree, stepped through.

At that point, their knowledge of what the device did was only theoretical. They had no idea the effect it would have on a living human being, or how much matter the aperture could accept at once. They'd tried a paper clip, an apple. Never a person. Now, they had proof it was possible for a living being to pass through—and a citation before the Human Subjects Board, to boot.

There was no way to call Ree back. She'd planned exactly what she was doing, though. Just before she ducked into the field, she looked up at the security camera and gave a little wave.

My escape was just as neat. By the time Homeland Defense set up their ad hoc Evacuation Commission, I was helping the army developers integrate the codes my lottery picks generated into an identity card scanning protocol. Once we were sure everything was working properly, I gave myself my promised reward. I fed my own code into the system.

The only person on this side who's ever appreciated what I accomplished was the agent. He found me at the coffeehouse here, in Astoria, where I do my contract work from my laptop a few mornings a week. They sent a Somali American in a skinny tie and expensive-looking shoes to sweet-talk me, as if our parents' distant shared ancestry could possibly make him feel like kin. In my own world, where the terrorists were America Unida and the Afghans drove out the Russian communists and the Jews never settled Cisjordan, I did not experience anti-Muslim prejudice. That only set me father apart from the midwestern-accented young agent, who must have suffered it all his life. A miscalculation. He was handsome. Maybe his handlers hoped I would find him sexually attractive. Or that I'd see him as a son. He sidled up to me, tried to buy me a bubble tea, and for a moment, I thought he must be from yet another government department. Another line of Debrief, a secret loyalty test. But no, it was much more sordid than that. He worked for a power delivery infrastructure company. His employers didn't care about refugees; they were looking for ways to incorporate Gate technology, specifically its amorphous metal power transformers, into the smart electrical grid.

"I'm not an engineer," I said. "I'm a statistician. What do you think I know?"

And his eyes went round in a gratifying way and he said, "More than we do."

That would have been enough for some UDPs. The interest. We so resent being resented.

What do I remember, from Calvary? I stood between the graves and saw the Gate swallow up the one-hundredth and final entry group in Lot Fourteen. This was the first time I'd witnessed the full-sized model, the imposing physical architecture of the Gate itself, the hasty welding of its base, its rattling generators and galvanic compressors and the snaking cords that powered them all. Not to mention the cough-syrup-blue light it threw up. I saw the machine power down. Then, the soldiers began to let the next group of strangers file in through the checkpoint near the generators. I joined them at the staging area, looking up at the lingering spread of the plasma dispersal, as awed and frightened as anyone else.

Mornay was still there, supervising the emergency patch of some tube in the coolant system—even the prototype had always run incredibly hot—and I remember seeing a new looseness to the very skin of her face and wondering about how many hours she'd been up. Somewhere else, fires at the three power plants still raged, and workers risked their lives to operate the heavy machinery that would bury the smoking hulks, though the tons of earth could not muffle or contain the radiation. Somewhere else, army ministers met in various chambers and halls and bunkers, trading dares and threats, counting their weapons. And here I was, abandoning it all.

I didn't want to distract her, but I felt the need to say something, to say I was sorry. I must have said something like that. Her response, I recall perfectly: "You did your part, Dr. Ibrahim." Then, she put her hand on my shoulder blade. "From each, according to her ability."

Insultingly self-congratulatory, really.

Still, I wish the agent from the power delivery infrastructure company had been as plainspoken, as realistic about my limits. He thought my brain was an ordinator, that I had blueprints stored in my synapses. All I could tell him was my own system. How I'd picked out who would go and who would stay.

"You were fair," he said. "You made it as fair as you possibly could."

"You're just trying to flatter me," I said.

"You could do good work again. Imagine if power were cheaper, if we could modernize. Wars, Iman, are fought here over oil. Help me stop that. Help me use what you know."

There's a lot of tech they don't have, that the Gate could potentially unlock. I'm surprised I haven't been asked for more. But I told him nothing.

Because Mornay was right about me. I'd already given all I had.

CHAPTER THREE

Hel found Dr. Carlos Oliveira waiting for her in James J. Walker Park in the West Village, deep in conversation with two little girls with hair the same shade of red, both under the age of seven or so, both dressed in immaculate playclothes. A sharp-eyed young woman who must have been their nanny sat on a nearby bench. As Hel approached, the girls dissolved into giggles—the little sister merry and daring, the older one reluctant, half-shy. Oliveira smiled benignly from under the brim of his hat.

Hel knew what they were staring at. Oliveira's area of study—the spread of disease—was as relevant in this world as in his own, and he'd redemonstrated his brilliance immediately upon his arrival. He'd earned an endowed chair in sociology at the CUNY Graduate Center. His new, rewritten book, a social history of cholera outbreaks in the nineteenth century and the birth of modern epidemiology, had won last year's Robert K. Merton Award. Now his celebrity spanned two worlds; he had the distinction of being the least-hated UDP there was. Consequently he'd become a generally recognized spokesperson for the whole community. It was crazy that he'd even responded to Hel's email when she'd written last year to ask for his theories about the workings of the Gate, unbelievable that he'd pursued a friendship with her.

But she doubted the girls recognized Oliveira from his recent *New York Times* profile. By anyone's standards, he stuck out of a crowd. As she stepped closer, she saw him open and close his pincers rapidly—first the left set, then the right. Amazed laughter burst from the younger girl while the big sister covered her face, peering at him through the gap in her fingers.

"There are two bones in the forearm," Oliveira told them. "Radius and ulna. You have them too. Mine were separated by surgeons after I lost my hands. They fixed the muscles so I can use them to pick things up. Like chopsticks." All the while he was talking he was gesturing with his maimed, modified arms. The children looked on, transfixed. Hel had been given to understand that the procedure existed in this world also, but having been invented by a German, it wasn't common in the United States, where bilateral hand amputees were much more likely to be fitted with prosthetics.

As she watched, he deftly picked up his high-tech phone from his lap and used one stubby digit to jab the voice-control button. "Call Helen Nash," he intoned, then said to the girls, "See? Very useful to me."

"I'm right here," she said, as her own phone buzzed from her pocket. "Sorry I'm late. These underground trains . . ."

"Whatever time you choose to arrive is the correct time, my dear," he told her with characteristically immoderate gallantry. "I must somehow have arrived early."

The nanny on the bench called to her charges. Hel glanced back at the children with dislike. No one had known exactly how the Gate would function. They'd deemed that only adults could be legally eligible to risk evac. If your name was chosen by the ordinator, you had to say yes or no immediately and then report to the site in Queens—no time for good-byes or drawn-out decisions.

Most parents of small children had said no.

"Let's walk," Oliveira said, as he always did. Silently, she handed him the bouquet of red carnations she'd picked up at a corner grocery on the way over, where she'd stopped to buy an energy drink for herself. Oliveira took the flowers. "Feeling wealthy, are you?"

"No." They meandered down Saint Lukes Place; without discussing it, they turned right onto Bleecker Street toward Father Demo Square. Hel squinted into the bright autumn sunlight at the people around them, slightly scruffier than the West Village denizens of her own time and place. She took a fizzy sip of her Rockstar.

Energy drinks were possibly her favorite thing about this universe, but the store where she'd bought this one displayed a NO ALIENS sign prominently on the register. She'd considered taking her custom elsewhere. Instead, she handed the proprietor exact change for the drink, then swiped the flowers from the stand outside the door without paying. "I just feel like celebrating," she told Oliveira now. "I'm making progress on a project."

"What project is this?" Every time they saw each other, the old man asked her about her recertification. The American Board of Medical Specialties had quickly established re-licensing protocols for UDP doctors, just as the American Sociological Association had helped Oliveira transfer his tenure, but she'd never looked into the details of this process—she lived perfectly fine on public assistance. Her focus was elsewhere now. "Ezra Sleight," she said. "Do you know much about him?"

"Ah. That's Dr. Bhatnagar's specialty, correct?"

Vikram, tossing around his damn flashlight like a cowboy. "Used to be."

"*The Pain Ray*," Oliveira said, eyes closed. "I read that one when I was a boy. How could anyone forget *The Pain Ray*? Yes, I know of Sleight. What about him?"

"His house in Brooklyn. He lived there from '35 to '57. After. I've found it here. I talked to the man who owns it."

"But Sleight *didn't* live there," Oliveira said. "He never existed." They had stopped in front of a green-painted bench. Oliveira handed the carnations back to Hel as, stiff-jointed, he levered himself to a seated position.

Hel sat down next to him. "No. That's not exactly true. He was born. He lived to age ten. 1909, Carlos. That's when he died. It's the oldest change I know about."

"Everyone says 1910, don't they."

"Exactly! But Sleight died in 1909. I'm sure of it. The *Brooklyn Daily Eagle* has some of its archives online; there was a profile on NorthKing Baking Soda, Ezra Sleight's father's company, that mentioned his son's recent drowning. It didn't say the date of death—just the year. I need to do more digging, to find the death certificate or something."

"It could have been a mistake. A typographical error."

"Yeah, I guess so. But what if it's not? If it *was* 1909, that's months before any of the other recorded divergences. It's got to mean something!"

Oliveira eased off his glasses. "Are you positing a causal relationship? Do you think Sleight's death influenced it all somehow? A ten-year-old child, son of a baking soda tycoon? That's what changed the world?"

"You sound like Vikram with the causal stuff. I'm not an idiot, OK? It doesn't matter if he's the cause. Him *being first* is still significant. There should be a museum. Can you imagine it? Right in that old house. A museum."

"To Sleight?"

"To the earliest of the deviations anyone's been able to discover. It wouldn't just be for him; it would be about all the others. A memorial to everyone else we lost, starting with the first. By the middle of the twentieth century, many of them were never even born, you know."

"Yes, yes. I've looked into all the vanished epidemiologists in some detail myself: Pascal Toussaint's mother died in a kitchen fire; Louise Stuart's parents had seven other children, but somehow they were all boys; Jin Fan-Wen was born, but never went to university—that set back the discovery of the causes of cardiovascular disease by almost ten years." Oliveira sighed. "And there's Christian Hassel. He was born too, lived to be a teenager, but was then killed by the KomSos—by the Nazis, I mean. They called themselves Nazis here."

"Wow," Hel said. "That's awful." To her, those born just Before whose lives had ended prematurely were the worst cases, the most frustrating. There was something especially poignant about knowing exactly what these men and women might have accomplished if only history had proceeded the way it ought to have. "All the things they should have done. They need to be memorialized."

The old man's eyes were cloudy, but his gaze pierced her. "Our community is so small."

"But it wouldn't just be for UDPs! This would benefit everyone! Only we know about these inventors, these discoverers, these artists. It is our duty to share that knowledge with the whole world. Don't you think? We can make them understand us."

"A museum dedicated to those who never existed." He said the words slowly, trying them out. "And what do you think you need to make that happen?"

A fair question. Three hundred and fourteen thousand dollars—that was how much Dwayne Sealy wanted for the house, plus it would have to be cleaned out. Exhibits would have to be created, information compiled from all the other UDPs she could find and cross-checked with the historical record here. The list of tasks was overwhelming. What did she need to make it happen? Money, certainly. Help applying for a grant, perhaps. And some string-pulling. What UDP had the resources? Not even Oliveira. And what non-UDP would possibly want to take on something so unpopular?

She asked herself: What did she really want? Sympathy? She had that. The old man's enthusiasm, his encouragement? Those couldn't be bought for a bunch of corner-store carnations. "I don't know," she admitted.

"In this life, each of us must find a single thing that we think is worthwhile and do it faithfully," Oliveira said. "For you, I think that could be practicing medicine again. You and I are fortunate. Like the method of finding proximate and distal causes of disease in a population, the basic laws of the human body will never change. You can work, just as you used to."

She thought of her years of training. The beautiful complex structures of the head and neck, presented on tissue-thin paper in the texts. And the impossible-to-anticipate variations. The actual flesh under her gloved touch as she cut a straight line from the brow down along the side of the nostril and through the upper lip to remove a paranasal cancer. Cutting the bones, removing part of the hard palate, the orbital, sometimes the eye. The care she'd taken to leave a clear margin. You needed a certain mind-set. A sureness and serenity she didn't have anymore. "No," she said savagely. "I don't want to."

"It doesn't have to be medicine, but I think you need to pick one thing. Focus on it. One manageable, attainable goal."

"What if this is it, though? My goal. This museum?"

They sat quietly for a minute. Hel watched young people in bad clothes kissing, arguing, and looking at their personal digital devices on the other benches. In the center of the piazza, one pigeon tried to mount another, the two birds waddling back and forth at her feet. The aggressor never got anywhere, but his intended victim couldn't seem to escape his attentions.

"At least help me try," she said.

Oliveira squeezed the flowers she'd brought between the opposing digits of his left arm, his grip crackling the green cellophane they were wrapped in. "All right," he said. "I'll do my best."

○

Hel stood in front of the open closet door in her bra, feeling faintly ridiculous. She wore no panties; she wasn't sure whether underwear would show through the delicate black silk, cut on the bias, of the only dress she owned that would possibly work. She didn't want to put it on yet; she'd bought the high-necked, unfashionable garment a year ago and worn it only once, to the funeral of a UDP from Vikram's entry group who'd shot himself in the head.

But tonight, she was headed to an arts fundraiser, and important well-connected people would be there, people Oliveira said she should meet. She had to look *formal*.

She stepped into her shoes. She wasn't used to heels—women didn't wear them at home—but something about the authoritative echo they made pleased her. Still bare-bottomed, she clopped into the living room, crossing to the single press-board bookshelf squeezed between the window and the radiator, and trailed her fingers down the spines of the titles on the top shelf, looking for an egg-blue cover. Vikram, at work for the night, kept the precious books he'd brought through the Gate on the top shelf, segregated from all of the other books he'd picked up since.

There. *The Pyronauts: A Novel* by Ezra Sleight. It was an edition Vikram had bought for himself in 2001 or 2002. It contained a foreword by some professor he used to know and an afterword, as well as a chronology of the author's other works. The cost code appeared on the back cover: $124, in their inflated currency. Priceless now. The only one of its kind.

She'd read the book for the first time just to make Vikram happy. Now, John Gund and Asyl and even Aitch, the stranger they met in the Never, were like old friends. She couldn't put into words the way the novel made her feel, her celebration of its beauty mixed inevitably with an exquisite sadness that there was no more. None of Sleight's short stories or other novels survived, no articles, no interviews. The man and the ideas he'd had were completely gone from the world of this After, persisting only in the memories of a few. She decided she would take the book with her as a sort of good luck token, tangible proof she could pull out if called upon.

If only they'd foreseen, when they packed for the cemetery. It was hard to put herself back there—not emotionally hard, though that was true too, but literally hard to remember those days. Traumatic amnesia, the psychologist who once came as a guest speaker to her Reintegration Education meeting had called it. If only there'd been a way for her to understand in advance what it would be like to be shipwrecked in a world populated by seven billion strangers with whom she had nothing in common.

She slipped the book into her capacious bag, and went back into the bedroom to put on the dress.

○

At Reintegration Education on Wednesday, they watched a DVD that promised to introduce them to the principles of the US criminal justice system. Vikram thought he would have trouble paying attention. He'd spent most of the last week dreaming of the Gate, strung in the sky above Calvary like

41

a loop of Christmas lights—trying to remember while trying to forget. But he found this video unexpectedly absorbing. It began with a reenactment of a witch trial. A young and beautiful white woman in colonial dress was herded to a riverside by a crowd of angry townspeople, who pulled the bonnet off her braided hair and tore at her clothes before pushing her into the water. The camera pulled away before it became clear whether she would float with guilt or sink to the bottom, innocent. The words *There Is a Better Way* appeared at the bottom of the screen, followed by a shot of the Statue of Liberty.

The members of Vikram's group sat in a semicircle, stonefaced. After nearly three years of enforced weekly meetings, it took a lot to provoke a reaction from them. Old Catalina, however, could always be relied on. "Do they really think we need to see this?" she asked Vikram in a highly audible whisper. She spat on the floor. "Reeducation horseshit."

"Hey!" barked Emily Sato, their Reintegration Liaison Officer, from her seat by the door. "Mrs. Calderón, we've talked about this! That's not sanitary."

"Bah!" Catalina muttered. Vikram watched her smear the spittle across the floor with the tread of her walking sneaker as the video went on to show a group of modern jurors—a group as racially and ethnically diverse as the UDPs sitting in this high school basement tonight, though much more cheerful and enthusiastic—as they listened to the evidence in a case presided over by a wise-looking judge. *Without Your Participation, No Justice Is Possible* read the caption.

The DVD ended and Officer Sato flicked on the lights. "So, what did you think? Mrs. Yee? Mr. Westmorland? Anyone?"

Vikram looked around; each member of the group seemed immersed in a private stupor. Several people covertly checked their phones. Was anyone else thinking of the notorious Debrief abuses? About the way assaults against their people were never prosecuted as hate crimes? About the phony charities that had raised money in their name but never turned it over? No one responded to Sato's question. "I thought this would be a good segue into a discussion of the type of justice system you guys had back at home!" she said. "Compare and contrast. Plus, good stuff to know if you ever get chosen for jury duty, right?"

"I don't think any of us have to worry about that," said a tall black man in the back whose name Vikram didn't know. The guy was new—he'd arrived from his original resettlement destination in another state when the graphic design firm where he'd found work transferred him up to its New York office. His boss must have deemed him good at his job, valuable enough to go to the trouble to sponsor UDP Change of Residence paperwork. Resentfully, they'd all kept their distance from the newcomer so far.

"Great comment!" Sato said. "Want to elaborate, Mr. Agnew?" Vikram knew Sato was an intelligence officer of some kind—she wouldn't tell them what agency—but she was certainly junior and low-ranking. Her questions had obvious right answers; any traps she set were easy to avoid. Still, seeing her take notes on her tablet, as she was doing now, always made Vikram nervous.

"I don't think they ever call UDPs for jury duty," Agnew said. "We're not exactly the 'peers' of most of our fellow citizens. And even when it's one of us that gets accused of the crime, it seems like they don't trust the rest of us to be on the jury. There were no UDP jurors on the Micallef trial, right?" He looked around at the rest of them, shrugging. "Have any of you served on a jury up here? None of the UDPs I knew in Tampa ever got called."

Catalina shifted in her seat. "Oh, shut up, you ass-whore," she said, her words accented but perfectly intelligible to everyone in the room. She was from Colombia, first state among equals in the America Unida system. For the thirty years before the disaster, she'd led an ordinary immigrant life in their Brooklyn, but Vikram knew that before that, in her long-ago youth, she'd fought against the United States as one of a second generation of woman commandos in its on-again, off-again war against Capitalism. Once, Catalina had brought in her old uniform shirt to group and shown them the many medals pinned to it, explaining with pride what each one meant. A small condor emblem for her birthplace. A bee in memory of the fallen dictator, El Mero Mero. A purple hammer and sickle representing ideological purity. A double bar on a black chevron, awarded to Catalina for excellence in marksmanship.

"Mrs. Calderón!" Sato snapped. "That's enough! You need to leave, now."

This seemed to be what the old woman had been angling for all along. She stood slowly, shuffling away from the circle of folding chairs toward the corner, where her mobility scooter was parked. She showed a triumphant, broken-toothed grimace. "I'm just trying to help him."

"How are you possibly helping?"

"I'm giving this little gootch some extra Reintegration Education." Catalina pointed a shaking finger in Agnew's direction. "Trying to show him what's good for him. Why you didn't learn to keep your trap shut in Tampa?" she scolded as she sank down into the scooter's seat. "You can't say stuff like that. You should know they put in your file. Never criticize them, dummy."

"What about you?" Agnew asked. "You're not exactly staying quiet."

"Ha! I don't gotta worry. I be dead soon. What they gonna do to me? But the rest of you. You wait. The government, they gonna put UDPs in camps." She tilted her head back to look Sato in the eye. "Camps, just like your America done to the Japs. I read in my textbook. How you like that?"

"Christ, just get out," Sato said. They could hear the whine of the motor fade as Catalina moved down the hallway to the elevator. "Can the rest of you just take out your Citizenship Workbooks?" Vikram checked the time and settled back into his seat to live out the rest of the session. Fifteen minutes left. Fifteen minutes.

CHAPTER FOUR

Hel skulked around the edges of the reception room on the fourth floor of a SoHo hotel that should not even exist. This ought to be a park. She remembered it: Palast Park, with its fountain, its lion mural, its hobs for games of quoits. She stood where it ought to be impossible to stand, twelve meters above the surface of the earth, her own displaced self displacing nothing but air, floating in what ought to be empty space high above the benches and the tops of the elm trees and, a block away, on Broadway, the elevated tracks of the K train. But here, in this New York, there was no Palast Park. A blight had killed off most of the elms and relegated the survivors to cages. Even the trains, most of them designated with different letters and numbers, routed underground. It was all wrong.

And Oliveira was nowhere to be seen. Again, she checked the clock above the bar, where two white-jacketed servers mixed drinks for a throng of partygoers, the servers working together without speaking or even looking at each other. It was 20:15 already. He was not here.

How would she ever find the person he'd sent her to meet, the museum director? Hel considered asking the efficient young employee stationed at the door, but before she could decide whether this was reasonable, a fashionable stranger in a sequined jumpsuit and heels whirled away suddenly from the group she'd been part of. The contents of the woman's cocktail splashed deliriously outward, soaking the top of Hel's dress.

Hel shuddered from the cold impact and felt a flash of irrational fury, the way she felt when someone stepped on her shoe on the crowded subway platforms here. Ice cubes clattered against the polished floorboards.

"Oh my God!" the woman said, her cheeks flushed and eyes wild. Her male companion began to laugh at her. "You asshole! Why didn't you tell me someone was standing right there!" The woman glared for a second, seeming to look straight through Hel, then turned abruptly and loped toward the bathroom without offering an apology.

The drink dripped between Hel's breasts, cold and sticky. Her anger faded; she felt foolish instead. What was she even doing here?

"Hey." A round brown-skinned woman with short-cropped hair now stood before her. "Hey, are you all right?" She held out a wad of cocktail napkins. "You want to take care of that yourself, or do you want some help?" She winked, and Hel noticed bitterly that she wore trendy sneakers and a flannel shirt, the sleeves rolled up to her elbows—unlike Hel and every other woman in the room, she was dressed for comfort.

Hel took the napkins and dabbed at the damp fabric. "Thanks."

"I'm Angelene," her rescuer said. "I'm an industrial chemist. Are you an artist?"

Hel shook her head no.

"See, that explains it. That's why you look so surprised. We're just, like, normal people. You and I sit at desks and answer to bosses and shit. Whereas someone like Leslie over there, consumed by her muse, operates under conditions so rarified we're not even capable of understanding them." Angelene leaned forward. "Leslie makes sculptures out of split telephone cable. My wife's a fan."

Hel was taken aback by the terminology, but tried not to show it; at home, verts could only legally partner, not marry. "Really?"

"Yeah. My wife says the work has to do with communication and with representing the electrical impulses in our brains, *mapping the threads of the unconscious*. Sounds super-important, huh?"

"Hey, don't be like that," said a regal woman in a silver sheath dress. She might have been annoyed. Or she might have been gently amused. It was hard to tell.

"Am I not getting it right, babe? Isn't it electrical impulses?" Angelene slid an arm around her middle. "Or is it synapses? Neurons?"

Ignoring her, the regal woman turned to Hel. "Hi. I'm Ayanna Donaldson." Her hair, elaborately coiffed, rose in a crest up the center of her head. The fabric of her sheath glittered in the light.

Hel felt unbearably frumpy in her death dress. "I know you by reputation. I'm very pleased to meet you."

Donaldson shook her hand. "How are you enjoying the party?" she asked. "Have you checked out our silent auction, by the coat check?"

"Yes, the items are . . . yeah, great. I'm sorry—I'm Helen Nash." She should have said that during the handshake. "Dr. Oliveira put me down as his plus-one."

"Right, Carlos. He collects nonrepresentational line etchings, doesn't he?" Donaldson sipped at a clear, still liquid in her narrow champagne flute. "Are you interested in contemporary Asian, too?"

At a party like this at home, with nothing to prove, Hel would have just said no and moved away. Here, she was conscious of the strap of her bag on her shoulder and the weight of the book inside, and she thought of all the other books, big volumes on the coffee tables of her vanished friends, books left behind on bookshelves and on library shelves and in extinct bookstores. Thick volumes with their pages of photographs. Photographs of canvases, sculptures, and assemblages that no longer existed in physical reality, which had no home anywhere outside the memories of her people.

The picture books she'd read to her son.

"I'm not a collector. I'm a doctor, a medical doctor—by training, anyway—and I don't know much about . . . I'm not really . . . It's sort of hard to explain. I was hoping Dr. Oliveira would be here. He said he'd introduce me to you. I'm like him—one of the Hundred Fifty-Six Thousand." Behind her, Hel heard Angelene release an appreciative gasp. The others in the group quieted. Even the laughing man, caught in the middle of a story, finally shut up.

"That must be very difficult," Donaldson said after a minute. "To be so far from home."

"Yes. It is."

Donaldson put down her drink on one of the small tables scattered around the room. Hel felt the weight of the woman's full attention on her, all at once, as if Donaldson were a sleepy cat and she a squirrel who'd just been noticed in a nearby tree.

"Usually, people expect me to be grateful," Hel said. "And I am. I'm grateful for my life. But everything is different here. People ask me what I think. I want to be able to tell them, but there's so much, and I'm only one person." Donaldson was nodding along; this was Hel's chance. "I want to teach them. I want to be able to *show* them. I know you're the director of the Museum of Modern Thought. A lot of us, we have things. Things we brought through the gap. Things like this."

She opened her bag. Thankfully, the leather flap had protected the volume inside from the spilled drink. She hadn't really intended to show *The Pyronauts*, but here she was lifting it into the light with careful hands. Around her in the room, the party seemed to have gotten even louder than before.

She flipped to the title page, then turned the book so that Donaldson could see it. Angelene and Leslie and the man who'd laughed moved nearer so that they could see too. "I'm not a literature person, but where I'm from, Sleight is canonical, like Poe. Like your Lovecraft. He wrote five novels, all of them gone now except for this. This is the only copy of any of his work that anyone has, as far as we know."

She and Vikram, disalike in every way. When he was going through his hardest times, she would come to his apartment, where they'd lay themselves out on his duvet together like corpses, holding hands, the cold wind blowing in through the open window. She was just a visitor, she told herself—a visitor to this grief, this building, this street, this world. The two of them would share a benzodiazepine, bought from a kid down the hall and cut in half, and once the anti-panic drug took effect, he would relate to her, in detail, the plots of the four missing novels of Ezra Sleight. *Chinese Whispers. The Pain Ray. What to Do with the Night. The Poorhouse.*

He did them all, in order. He did them each more than once, over the course of months. This was their ritual. They were strange to her, these novels she could only ever know through Vikram's words. In his former life, he'd been an adjunct, assigned every semester to teach introductory survey courses on American literature in general. Only once had the department head deigned to allow him to lead a final-year seminar on Sleight.

Here, Vikram was the world's de facto expert.

"Look at the publisher," she said now, pointing to the title page. "That imprint doesn't exist here. This isn't a hoax."

Was she boring her audience? Maybe Donaldson didn't like books. Hel herself never had. "I mean, there's other stuff, too." She shut *The Pyronauts.* "This is the tip of the iceberg. People saved all kinds of things, carried them through. Thousands of people and their keepsakes. Statistically, some of it must be art."

"You have access to these things," Donaldson said. "To people's treasures. And you want to put together an exhibit."

"I want to make a museum. Not just for the stuff itself. The stories. There are so many memories behind each physical object. A museum of vanished culture."

"A museum," Donaldson repeated. "Do you know very much about what that would entail?"

"No, I don't. But this is the hook, I think," Hel said. "Sleight. I think he is the perfect focus for all of this."

"Why?"

Hel reached out and took a drink from the tray of a passing waiter, buying herself a minute to think. The drink tasted not unfamiliar. Champagne and peach. Maybe something harder underneath. She wasn't going to say anything about 1909 this time. Every time she did, people said she was crazy. She had to win Donaldson over more cleverly than that.

She could tell it like a story. If she had a son still—if Jonas were here, if he'd somehow magically remained that tale-craving age he'd been when she last saw him—she might have told it to him as a ghost story.

○

Once upon a time, there was a little boy whose mother died. His father, a busy and important man, loved him very much, but did not know how to raise a child on his own. He arranged to send the boy to a large estate in the country. Years before, it had been a rich man's house, but now it was a school. There, the boy would learn to become old enough not to frighten adults.

In the grand entranceway of the school hung a painting in a heavy gilt frame, the centerpiece of the dead rich man's collection. Actually, there were half a dozen paintings displayed there, but the boy only ever looked at this one, the biggest.

The sky took up the top two-thirds of the canvas, a morning rendered in transparent layers of blue and gold and white and pink. Sun shone behind pillars of dramatic cloud, the brushstrokes of the master hard to see. The boy might have been immersed by that sky, if that were all there was to it, but his eyes were always dragged lower, where two icebergs sat at the horizon, much smaller than the cloud towers. Even smaller, at eye level, a ship floundered, broken in an Arctic sea, its masts tilted at a horrible angle. Men in sailors' clothing crowded the deck of the sinking vessel.

When the boy looked at the painting, he imagined what these men were doing, imagined their hurry as they ran from stern to bow. He imagined how they must be trying to remain calm. But that wasn't what scared him. In the water in the foreground, in front of the ship, a hand extended out of the water. It was tiny, in relative scale, but it was the most important thing in the painting, the most important thing in the whole big sea. The skin was very white against the dark water. That pale hand and part of the forearm were all that showed, the rest of the man invisible beneath, groping blindly for a rope the others had tossed futilely in his direction.

The boy knew the passive reaching fingers would never find it. The man would freeze. He would drown.

But why? Where was his other arm? Why was he not thrashing to save himself, where was his gasping mouth? Why couldn't he struggle up to the surface?

Every morning, students assembled in the wood-paneled foyer. They ordered themselves by age, oldest in the back. Short for his age like his father and slightly built, the boy could usually only just see over the top of the head of the younger boy who stood in front of him. Each year, his part of the line moved back to make room for the new class of pupils. Each year, the boy stood at a greater remove from the place where the painting hung. But he always remembered what it looked like at close quarters. He always remembered the small, harrowing tragedy of that hand amid the greater disaster.

On the grounds of the school was a lake, calm and warm and not very deep. In the springtime the lower forms splashed and paddled by the shore while the larger, stronger adolescents rowed about in boats. The few boarders who remained over the summer holiday—as the boy always did—took swimming lessons by the wooden dock. The murky, opaque green water was perfectly safe, everyone told him, but thinking of the painting, he never dared venture farther than the bank. He bore the others' teasing with patience.

How did Helen Nash know all this?

In letters home to his father, the boy would write about the painting and the thrall of fear it held him in. And he would grow up. He would leave the school, but he would never forget. He would tell his fiancée about his shipwreck dreams, and she would note this in her personal journal and someday, when he was famous, every scrap of paper that documented his life would be scrutinized by others, and those entries and letters—true stories—would be a part of the story told about him. People would say they explained why he turned out the way he was.

Always, the boy who became Ezra Sleight knew better than to enter dark water. Out there, something could pull you down.

As a man, he returned to the school and found the painting, which still hung there. He was shocked to see how small the hand was. It did not stand out starkly in the composition the way he remembered. Some onlookers would not have even noticed it. Still, it remained important to the man Sleight.

He didn't know it, but the hand had saved his life.

○

"It's art," Hel finished. "It's history."

"But Ezra Sleight did die," Angelene said. "So, the painting was never painted in this world, or what?"

"No, it was. It's called *The Shipwreck* and it was done by George Lowery, a sort of obscure British artist living in Denmark in the 1820s and '30s." There was murmured acknowledgement from those listening. They were art people—did they recognize Lowery's name? Hel continued. "The painting was completed and exhibited in Paris in 1828. It's well documented up through the turn of the twentieth century, but as far as I can tell, no one knows where it is now." Right around the time of Sleight's death. She didn't know how to end her story without placing an emphasis on Sleight and her theory of the first divergence that might make them write her off as a crackpot. "*The Shipwreck* is the kind of thing I'm talking about, for the museum, if it could be found. Not just artifacts from UDPs, you know. Things from here too, that relate to there."

"It's a good story," Donaldson said. "May I?" Hel nodded her consent and the other woman lifted the book out of her hands, riffling its pages delicately. "You're going to need to have more than an anecdote. Here—will you come with me?" Donaldson turned, heading toward the door.

Hel followed along in her wake, wondering if this was some kind of brush-off, if Donaldson meant to escort her out of the party, but no, Donaldson still had the book. Surely she would have passed it back if she wasn't interested. They stopped in front of the table at the front. The flow of incoming guests had slowed; the employee at the table was now doing something on her phone. She seemed to sense Donaldson coming and looked up alertly. "Ayanna."

"How's it going up here?"

"Not much action. Hotel guy says the dining room is all set up. The silent auction ends in ten—they should be giving everyone a reminder in a minute—and then the cater servers will start herding everyone in to their tables."

"Good work. Do you have a moment? I want you to meet Helen Nash. Helen, this is Teresa Klay, my intern. Teresa, Helen has an idea for an exhibit that I'd like to explore, in preparation for a presentation to the board. I thought you could help her do some research."

Teresa Klay raised her eyes. She had dark hair that curled wildly, tied back from her face, and the style of eyeglasses that Hel had learned was worn by people who wanted to signal that they were serious. "Of course," Klay said. "What's the concept?"

"Ezra Sleight. He's some kind of a cult UDP author who died as a child."

"I wouldn't say cult," Hel broke in. "I mean, he was kind of a household name."

57

"Helen's a UDP," Donaldson explained. She looked back over her shoulder at the people dancing and drinking and networking on the ballroom floor. "I'll need you after the auction, Teresa, to supervise packing up the stuff. But for now, I'll leave you two to work out the details."

"Fine."

"Hello," Hel said. "It's nice to meet you."

The other woman didn't respond. She was busy giving Hel a searching look, taking in, Hel imagined, her odd dress, her short-bitten nails, and probably the bags under her eyes—looking at her intently and unselfconsciously, as though, if she stared hard enough, she might find some bigger warning sign on Hel's person, something on the level of Oliveira's pincers that would demonstrate how radically she didn't belong here.

Alien. That's what they called people like her.

Don't treat everyone like an enemy, her liaison officer told them at Reintegration Education.

Breathe deep.

"How do you feel about meeting at the Brooklyn Public Library?" Klay was saying. "I have an archivist friend there. I could do Tuesday morning, next week."

"Tuesday would be fine." Hel noticed that Angelene had joined them and was standing at Klay's elbow with two more of the fizzy pink drinks, waiting for a chance to join the conversation.

"The library is in Grand Army Plaza," Klay told her.

The worst thing about her displacement status, Hel sometimes felt, was being treated like an out-of-towner, a tourist in her home city. "Yeah, I know where it is. I can meet you at the main entrance, right outside the terminus."

"The terminus?"

"Where the trolleys . . ." As soon as she began to say the words, she knew they were wrong. But it was too late.

"Girl, they really did a number on you, didn't they." Angelene extended one of the flutes to her.

Klay didn't laugh at her mistake. Didn't even look up. She sat at the table, entering the appointment into her calendar app, as if nothing had happened.

Hel decided to interpret this as a courteous gesture. She drank deeply. "I know where it is," she reiterated. "I'll see you there."

INTERVIEW TRANSCRIPT:
JOSLAN MICALLEF, AGE 22,
RIKERS ISLAND

Sure, I got wild and I did all those things to that old lady. Beat her. Made her eat salt. Cut her on the breasts. Then stabbed her and stabbed her till she died. I admitted to it in the trial, and I'm admitting to it now. I take full responsibility for my crimes 'cause I know I belong in the juice. I deserve it.

My lawyer is the one who wanted me to file a civil complaint alleging police misconduct. She keeps telling me I'm "on trial in the press" right now and that we need to fight back. Her name is Shevita Young and everything I know about the laws here, I learned from her. I've been found guilty of murder and multiple counts of aggravated assault. No matter, says Shevita. If we can show the world the ways that I've been failed—by inadequate support from the Reintegration Education and Adjustment Counseling Authority and by the ineptitude of my therapist, by a shitfoot of a dealer who preyed upon my ignorance of the potency of street drugs here, by anti-UDP bias against me in my initial trial, and by simple mishandling such as is evident in my encounter with the police—all that can help me. She seems to think that if she can get a jury to see how pathetic I am, they'll feel too bad to pin me.

Pin me. Where I'm from, that's slang for getting executed. Because they use the firing squad method there, and that means they shackle you to a chair with a hood over your head and literally pin a paper target to your chest first before they hand out the guns. So, pinning.

Shevita loves it when I mess up my idioms like that, especially when there are reporters around, but they don't have the death penalty here. Not in *this* New York State; what I'm looking at is life in prison.

I understand that, and I also understand what "on trial in the press" means. I'm not dumb. They do get us newspapers here in the Rose on Rikers.

It was a couple of hours after I'd killed Ms. Kravitz when the sticks came by my place. I wasn't a suspect yet, just the last person who would have been expected to see her alive, being scheduled by the care agency to get her up and do her meds and all. I let them in when they buzzed—thought I had to. I was coming down by then, but I was still pretty out of it. I'd cleaned myself up, but not well enough. I guess there was still a lot of blood on my clothes, and I couldn't really control the way I was talking. Also, I had her dog, Mimi, with me in my apartment.

The two police asked me questions. Shevita says there's some statement they're required to read—*anything you say can and will be used against you in a court of law*—and I don't remember them saying that to me, but I'm not mad about it. The state I was in, I bet I would have incriminated myself even if they had read it like they were supposed to. It only took five minutes or so of us talking for me to confess, in detail, to what I'd done, and then they were placing me under arrest, radioing for backup. I was put in those zip-tie handcuffs—I didn't try to stop them from putting them on me—and I sat in my apartment alone with them, waiting for their backup to come.

"You're one fucking remorseless bitch, aren't you?" the smaller of the two sticks said.

There's only one person in this world who knows the person I used to be. Shevita dug her up as a character witness at my first trial; a former classmate's older cousin who happens to be another one of the Hundred Fifty-Six Thousand. What are the chances, right? The authorities resettled this woman in Seattle. She's got cancer now from the rad exposure, like most of the people from the final lots. She knew me before, but all she remembered was me playing Dusty Peach dolls on the carpet with her cousin fifteen years ago, so it did me no good.

I allowed that I probably was a pretty remorseless bitch.

"We never should have let any of you through," the stick said.

I told him that I could see his point. I'd made a mess.

Personally, it's the salt that bothers me, more than the stabbing.

I want to blame the drugs, but it's my brother back home who had that weakness. They do brain scans on everyone at eighteen there, which is the legal drinking and smoking age, before they assign you to your military or Alternative Service unit. My scans came out fine, but he was found to have the propensity for dependence. Of course, it already was too late for him; he'd been wilding for four years with older friends and he was well and good addicted. When they did the aversion therapy on him, it didn't work the way it was supposed to. They just stamped NO CONTROLLED SUBSTANCES on his ID, so he couldn't buy legally. Within a year, he'd moved on to the hard stuff you can't buy in stores anyway—to grind and H and dross.

He used to hit his wife, my sister-in-law. He'd threaten her with pliers, say he was going to pull out all her teeth. Made her eat salt by the spoonful until she vommed all over the kitchen. Who knows why.

I would have said I hadn't thought of that in years, but it wasn't true. I must have remembered.

Spoonful by spoonful. Why did I do it?

I sat on my own couch, hands zip-tied behind me, trying to figure it out. To recap, at that point, the two police officers still hadn't read me my rights (which is a violation of procedure, Shevita says, classified as Abuse of Authority) and the smaller officer had just called me a remorseless bitch (a curse word, which is therefore classified Discourtesy). Then Mimi, Ms. Kravitz's little dog, climbed into my lap. She is a hairy, mop-looking thing with an underbite and a sweet temperament, and she'd been there for the whole thing that happened earlier, walking through the blood. Hadn't put up any resistance at all—really, she should have been embarrassed to let me treat her owner like that. Now, she got in my lap, curled up with a little sigh.

I wouldn't have hurt her. With my hands restrained, I couldn't have even petted her, like she probably wanted. But the smaller stick came rushing over, picked Mimi up real quick, like he was rescuing her.

"You fucking aliens," he said to me. "You're worse than animals."

Shevita argues that, used as an insult against a whole category of people, the term *alien* is similar to an ethnic slur or a racist or homophobic remark and should be considered Offensive Language.

I solemnly affirm that all this happened. The Abuse of Authority, Discourtesy, and Offensive Language. But who cares?

I don't. I knew—I *know*—that I deserved it all. I didn't start out wrong, like my brother did. I always did fine at home, never got into fights, never drank more than a few Mack Bullets. And then I'm here for a year and somehow I'm drinking every morning and in another year, I'm doing drugs I never heard of and wiping some old lady's ass for minimum wage, and the next thing you know, I *am* my brother. I'm worse.

"They're animals," the big stick said. The partner, this was— the quiet one. He said it sadly and he wasn't talking to me, so I knew he wasn't trying to goad me. He meant it.

I wished I could have agreed, but I didn't. "Animals don't do that," I told him. "Only people."

CHAPTER FIVE

On Tuesday, Hel arrived more than half an hour later than she'd said she'd be. The library building—different from the one she remembered—was a white wedge decorated in gold, like an Egyptian tomb. She spotted Klay right away camped out at a small metal table, one of several set up in front of the entrance, each one shaded by its own beach umbrella. Klay's bare legs extended beyond the shadow, stippled with goose bumps.

"Hey," Hel puffed, breathing heavily from the walk from the subway. "I'm sorry, I would have sent you a message but I couldn't get signal underground."

Klay offered a bemused smile. "It's fine, really." In the bright morning light of Grand Army Plaza, she looked younger than she had in the dim midnight reception room. Her wide face, her shorts, her impatient manner, her clunky plastic watch that re-sembled what a schoolgirl would wear in Hel's world: the overall effect was of an adolescent summer camp counselor, or the di-rector of a standard five play—someone insecure in her power yet exasperated by its limits. But Hel would have to swallow her doubts and make peace with this flunky. She'd left the precious book in Donaldson's hands, a hostage and an act of faith. Klay stood, gathering notebook and tablet from the table. "Ready to go in? We can do some digital searches of the archived newspapers for Ezra Sleight and William Sleight. And if there's anything on paper in the Brooklyn Collection—letters or photos or whatever—I can get us access. The archivist here owes me a favor."

Hel took in the people at the other tables around them—prosperous-looking families, women with strollers engineered with as much sophistication as the one-person pods adults drove at home. The green and maroon awnings on the buildings along Prospect Park West stretched out bravely in the sun, crisp and bright. A vendor sold organic ice cream from a cart. The Victorian-era urns flanking the park entrance—cast-iron vessels with twined cast-iron snakes for handles—stood at even intervals around the edge of the plaza. In her world, these were defaced by graffiti and several of them were missing. "You know, someone slipped me off here once. Robbed me at knifepoint. Practically right on this spot."

For the first time, Klay seemed interested in her. "What was it like?"

What it was like. "In the '60s, they routed the BQE through here, and it really tore up the neighborhood. Prospect Heights went downhill after that. It wasn't nice like this at all. I'm not sure whose idea it was to put the highway so close to the park—maybe there was some graft or bribery involved—the Queens triads, I don't know." How might Sleight's visiting aliens have viewed it, in their wise detachment? "It's better the way you have things." She gestured at the treaded tires of a nearby stroller. "With all the coffee shops and the dog biscuit bakeries and stuff."

Her neighborhood under the overpasses, the way it used to be. Run-down brownstones and Hispaniolan restaurants and old Irish bars alongside newer spit clubs and payday advance shops. All the trash, trash everywhere. Cherries loitering on the street corners and young gangsters casting their nets, pinching their sniff, smoking their dross and their crack and their H. But she'd loved that first apartment she and Raym bought together. Her neighborhood.

There had to be a way to observe without being brought down. Oliveira accomplished it beautifully in his articles, noting the differences in the worlds and making them amusing for an imagined audience while remaining untouched himself. Skating the surfaces: this was the key to remembering without remembering. She understood intellectually, but she'd struggled for three long years to master it, and she was ready to give up.

"Actually," said Klay, "what I meant was, like, what was it like to get, uh, slipped off."

"That's a personal question." Hel felt the knife, heavy in her pocket. A new blade was the first thing she'd bought, once she had her own money. She realized that her other hand had risen on its own to cover her mouth. She put it down in her lap.

"OK, I didn't mean to make you uncomfortable. I was just interested. I grew up in this neighborhood."

She was waiting. And Hel needed her, needed her help. *This neighborhood.* Hel tried to imagine where and how Klay had grown up, but she didn't have the imaginative empathy at the moment. She didn't care. She held her silence.

At last, Klay broke eye contact, checked her watch. "Let's go inside and get a computer."

○

Vikram and Kabir waited together in the shack across the parking lot from the storage warehouse, watching the second hand trace its way around the circle of the clock mounted above the door. Vikram, the assigned guard for the third shift, occupied the only chair. Kabir, who was killing time before his occasional second job, collecting the change from all the machines at his cousin's chain of laundromats, leaned against the file cabinet, cleaning his nails with a toothpick. His body blocked most of the output of the space heater.

"Why don't you get out of here?" Vikram asked.

"By the time I get home, it'll be time for me to leave again. It's a wasted trip. Plus, it's warm in here."

"Well, I'm not doing my tour until you leave."

"Why are you so concerned?"

"The boss will see you on the camera." Vikram felt his irritation like a stomachache, low in his abdomen. "You're not supposed to hang around if you're off-duty. Waiting for you to leave is putting me behind."

"Please," Kabir said. "Do feel free to go anytime you want, Professor. I promise to behave myself perfectly while you are gone. Or if you like, I'll come along on your tour. Just give me one of the hand warmers."

It was Kabir who'd introduced Vikram to the miraculous shake-to-activate chemical hand warmer packets. Vikram had recently bought himself a family-sized bag of them at Costco. He threw Kabir a packet and grabbed his flashlight from the desk. "Fine. Let's go, then. Now."

Kabir pulled the door of the shed closed behind them and followed. They walked across the smooth blacktop, laid the week before, its aggressive black-hole blackness evident even in the dark of this moonless night. The burned-rubber smell filled Vikram's nostrils and he found himself humming a song he'd forgotten, one that had been everywhere a few summers ago, the last summer he spent at home—constantly on the radio and over the speakers in stores and blasting from the portable players of kids walking down the street—a song he'd wished never to hear again and now never would.

Every summer, when he was growing up in Jersey, they would repave the parking lot of the vacuum depot near his parents' place. Vikram and his sisters would hike there in the middle of the night, the laces of their roller shoes tied together for ease of carrying, slung over their shoulders. The lot sloped downhill. They glided down the smooth surface, shouting at each other. The three of them raced, or sometimes they would make a train, crouching low to build up speed and then, at Vikram's count, standing tall.

"Have you seen any strange-colored lights in the warehouse recently?" he asked Kabir as he swiped them into the building. "Lights that go out?" He'd written up the incident a few weeks ago in the shift log like he was supposed to, but he'd tried hard to keep the notes as brief and as sane-sounding as possible. Anyway, he was pretty sure Kabir never checked the log.

"Lights? Do you mean the green flash? It's a common illusion, when the sun sets over the ocean or any unobstructed horizon. Some people think it's aliens, but actually, there's a scientific explanation having to do with the refraction of light."

"Yeah, thanks, but that's definitely not what I'm talking about."

"Don't be offended," Kabir said. "I didn't mean *aliens*, like the slur. I really meant extraterrestrials."

"I know. Besides, sticks and stones. Come on." They entered the elevator, and Vikram put in the keycard and pushed the button for the top floor. "It sounds crazy, this green flash thing."

"To be honest, you sounds a little crazy, too. What are you talking about, strange-colored?"

"Never mind. Nothing. You'd know what I meant if you'd seen it."

"Come on, tell me."

"Not lights in the sky. Lights in one of the units. Blue. But when I tried to find the room, it was just gone. And no one was in there."

"Please tell me you're making things up to frighten me. Because this job already gives me heartburn. I'm thinking about going to the laundromats full-time. I'm not a young man. Only, I don't like night work. I need my eight hours." Kabir sighed. "I would not be at either of these jobs if I was qualified to do anything else."

The elevator dinged and the doors slid open. "Yeah. Me neither."

"You're not fooling me. You're an educated man. I think you love this job."

They walked together to the end of the corridor, their footsteps echoing. Vikram shined his beam in a pattern of arcs up ahead of them, like someone on the beach marking the sand with a long stick. He felt bolder in Kabir's presence than he did when completing these rounds alone, but he missed the up-prickle of the hair on his arms, the tingle of alertness.

Kabir opened the door to the fire stairs and waved Vikram in. "After you, Professor."

They cleared four in silence.

On three, Vikram said, "This is where it was coming from last time. You didn't see any glow from out in the lot, did you? I know I didn't."

"No," Kabir said.

"Then you can relax. We would have seen it already."

They left the stairs and entered the third-floor corridor. "It's so dark," Kabir said. "I should have brought my flashlight too."

"Are you always this jumpy?"

The last days of any month meant lots of renters all over the city moving in and out of their apartments. In the self-storage business, that translated to new tenants getting units and old tenants emptying them out. Sometimes, people just stopped paying; after the deposit ran out, the storage company hired someone to haul away the junk, selling whatever looked valuable first, disposing of the rest. During the day, this hallway they traversed would be crowded with customers hauling boxes, pushing dollies, fumbling with padlocks, yelling at each other to hold the doors of the keycard-operated elevator. These people with their *stuff*—an amount, a sheer volume of possessions none of the Hundred Fifty-Six Thousand had yet had time to accumulate. During open hours, the doors would be open, some of the units packed tight with neat boxes or jammed full of black plastic trash bags. Other units held instrument cases, collections that took up too much room in tiny apartments, antiques people didn't want but couldn't bear to sell, shrouded canvases belonging to artists who couldn't hang all their work.

As they approached the bend in the hallway, he thought he saw it. It was as tenuous as the horizon in the east an hour before sunrise. They rounded the corner, and it was unmistakable now, emitting from a center unit on the left-hand side. Kabir clutched at Vikram's arm and they stopped, still yards away. The light seemed to reach toward them from the crack under the door, blue like the phosphorescence of some eerie deep-sea organism. Blue like the Gate itself.

Kabir began to speak, but Vikram shushed him before he could get out any words. He clicked off his Maglite and they waited together in the glow. There was no sound, besides the creak of Kabir's shoes as he shifted his weight and Vikram's own rapid breathing. No sound from inside the storage unit.

They waited there until the light turned off, dropping them into darkness like a bucket into a well. Vikram remembered the silent children's ward inside the old mental hospital.

"I'm going to break the door down," he whispered.

"No."

"I'm going to do it."

"You can't," Kabir said. "It's against the rules. It's against the law. It's trespassing."

Everything he said was true.

Equally true was this fact: part of Vikram didn't want to
know what was on the other side.

○

Klay drove them to the boarding school. Defunct for three-
quarters of a century, the estate had been sold at auction, then
passed from owner to owner until a group of weavers and ce-
ramics artists took it over for a gallery and studio space. Klay
hadn't been able to reach anyone on the phone, but the gallery's
website confirmed that the house was open to the public today,
still appointed with its original, historic furnishings.

Klay's SUV was an older, boxy model of Buick called a Rendezvous and its interior, which could seat seven, seemed cavernous to Hel. One hundred thirty klicks north of the city on the
Taconic Parkway, a yellow sports car swerved into their lane without signaling and almost ran them into the ditch, then zoomed
ahead. "A cancer on you, you fucker!" Hel yelled after it. She'd
been told repeatedly that this was not an acceptable way of curs-
ing in this world, but she hadn't stopped saying it. She fumbled
for the button to roll down the window, but was too slow to
make the gesture she intended; the car sped off in a cloud of dust.
Across from her in the driver's seat—enormously far away—Klay
smiled. Her two front teeth were very slightly crooked, one overlapping the other in a way Hel might have found charming under
other circumstances. "Your people can't drive," Hel told her.

"That's exactly what everyone says about UDPs, you know."

"Really?" The Rendezvous's general shape, its blocky angles,
reminded Hel of a huge version of her own beloved pod, a

two-person 2010 Kusama Kinetic with a forward hatch, bought new. It got twenty-one kilometers to the liter. She'd kept the Kinetic clean, swept the upholstery once a week. It never even lost that new smell. She wondered who was driving it now—whether it was sitting in the rented parking space where she'd left it, hopelessly irradiated, or whether an enterprising survivor had gotten it started and driven it west. She hoped so. West toward California. How far might they have traveled?

"How did you afford a car, Teresa?" Where Hel came from, even a used pod would have been out of reach for an unguilded young person without a proper profession.

The GPS on Klay's phone spoke. She followed its directions off the Taconic and onto US 44 toward the Connecticut border. She tapped impatiently on the center console with her free hand, in time to nothing. "Let's get in there and get this over with."

"I'm not trying to waste your time."

"I'm sorry," Klay said. "I guess I'm being rude. It's nothing personal. I just have other things to do. Meeting with Ayanna at three."

"What's she like to work for?"

"Smart, organized, it's a great opportunity. I don't know. How about that guy with the pinchers? What's he like to work for?"

"Oliveira? They're *pincers*, not pinchers." She stared through the window. "He knows how to get things done. And I don't work for him."

"I thought he sent you to the party."

"No. It's my idea, this whole thing. He's actually not very into it."

"But that article that quoted him, last month. That *Ostalgie* thing."

Hel remembered. A reporter covering the adjustment of UDPs as a human-interest story for the upcoming third anniversary of their crossing had published an article in the *New York Times* blog. The reporter compared the feelings of the Hundred Fifty-Six Thousand to the mourning of some East Berliners for their lost culture after the fall of the wall, whatever that was. (Despite the lack of a physical barrier in her own divided Western Europe, some of the same things had happened—a phone call between the AMFR and the Germans, the visit of an American president—but it had all unfolded at a much faster pace. The Latin American communists had stayed out of it for once, and everyone from Braunschweig to Bucharest had been wearing blue jeans and listening to Detroit-crafted pop music as early as 1974.) "UDPs are refugees from a place that no longer exists," the *Times* piece read. "Many of these people still think of their true home as the past, a past that is so utterly inaccessible, it exists now only in their memories." Then, the reporter had quoted his words directly: "As Dr. Oliveira puts it, 'There is nowhere for us to go back to.'"

"I guess you think it wouldn't be that hard, huh? Adjusting to this world?"

"What? I never said that."

"You'll never understand what it's like. Yes, I'm a mess. I admit it. But you would be too, if you were in my position."

"Sure," said Klay. "I'm sure I would be."

A billboard outside the town limits named the sites of historical interest—the mansion among them. Hel looked out at the ranch-style houses on the outskirts as they gave way to the grander, older houses of town. They followed the automated directions of the GPS into a dead little town center: a movie theater with a marquee that had been turned into a shoe store, a specialty shop that sold hiking equipment, a tattoo and piercing business, and two insurance offices. The remaining storefronts stood vacant. None of the metered parking was taken.

Klay guided the Rendezvous down a side street and into a gravel parking lot. Ahead, the old house loomed, unexpectedly large—a tall, half-timbered Tudor with a stone foundation and jutting stone chimneys. Squares of shake in overlapping patterns like fish scales clothed the upper stories. Leaden Xs held diamond-shaped panes in place. "This is it."

Finally here, where all signs could not have been expunged. "Wow," Hel said. "Where's the lake?"

There were two other vehicles in the lot—a van and the yellow sports car that had passed them fifteen minutes before. "Behave yourself," Klay said.

The biggest sign of all, in its gilt frame just inside, waiting to be documented. She took off for the house alone, already seeing it. She knew just where it was supposed to hang. Up ahead, the formal entrance in its portico, double doors made of carved oak, a modern placard with gallery hours detracting somewhat from the grandeur. She left Klay on the slate path, pushing her way inside, stepping into the foyer, high-ceilinged and grim, just the way she had imagined it. Like a child, she wanted to run. Hel crossed the room with eyes half-closed, making herself wait until she stood at the bottom step of the grand stairway before looking for the painting. She had imagined the ship, the sky, the ice so many times, and it shouldn't matter to her—it was a pale substitute for the things that actually mattered to her—and yet her breath came short with the anticipation. The rope. The hand. She turned around. Someone was calling to her, a woman's voice was speaking, but she shut it out.

Eleven decades—four long generations. 1910 was so frequently discussed as modern, recent, as if the dawn of the twentieth century and the era of the first divergence were barely out of reach, but placed in human terms, one hundred years ago seemed distant. Even Hel's great-grandparents were slightly too young to be Sleight's contemporaries. Still, all the history that stretched before that, and everything that hadn't happened yet—provided humanity could avoid the kind of disaster that Sleight had always predicted, the kind that had wiped out the world in which he'd predicted it—dwarfed that hundred years to the point of unfathomability.

Maybe that explained why young Ezra, dead and gone and separated from her by a raft of years, could feel so immediate here in this gallery of thirdhand memory. How he could feel so close, as her feet echoed on the parquet of the hall.

Once, over a year ago on a street in Midtown, Hel had thought she saw him. She thought she saw Jonas. She'd been on her way to Vocational Retraining, a few blocks west of Grand Central Station, the bright street sleepy and dusty through the lenses of her sunglasses, and she was thinking of nothing in particular as she walked the familiar route. She'd passed a building from which twin American flags dangled garish in the blinding sunlight, backlit like stained-glass windows, glowing blood red and electric blue. A bead of sweat trickled down the small of her back as, up ahead on the other side of the street, she observed a workman crouched in the middle of the sidewalk, polishing the gold Siamese head of the standpipe to a spotless gleam. A woman Hel's age walked a dozen paces ahead in the same direction, and Hel noticed the way she pulled on her child's hand to steer him around the obstruction. The woman wasn't anyone she recognized, of course—no one was, no one ever could be—but as she saw the boy from behind—gangly and tall for his age, the hem of his pants just a little too short, ankles exposed in white socks, the slight and fragile back, the thin brown arms, the messy thick hair—she knew it was her son. It didn't make any sense, but she knew it.

"Jonas!" she called out, but the woman was still hurrying the boy along; he didn't turn back. "Jonas!" Without looking, Hel dashed into the street. Two cyclists and a car swerved to avoid hitting her and a motorized cab laid on the horn. She dropped her bag right in the middle of West Fortieth and ran on. "Hey! Stop!" She was on the same sidewalk with them now, dodging other pedestrians. She swerved around a man with his dreads in a big stretchy cap and two punk girls walking arm in arm; she was right behind, yelling, "Jonas!" but the woman and child didn't stop. Hel reached out and tugged at the boy's shoulders, bodily turning him around.

Even from the front, even from inches away, he did look a little like Jonas. He had wide brown eyes and caterpillar eyebrows and even the same kind of chin with a sweet cleft in the center, but that didn't make him the boy Hel knew. *This* boy also had unwanted specificities—freckles across his nose and a scar on his forehead, provenance unknown. He was ten years old, a bit younger than Jonas would be now, Hel realized. The boy's mouth hung open in surprise. She had grabbed him roughly, had confused him, hurt him, this stranger. Hel experienced regret, so much stronger than nostalgia, so strong it nearly made her sick.

She could cope with distance. Almost five thousand klicks from New York to Palo Alto. After the divorce, she did it, exchanging strained and polite words with Raym, waiting for him to call their son to the ordinator link. She would see Jonas's face then, blooming sometimes in digitalized squares that froze and then sprinkled themselves across the viewer, but other times clear: his beautiful face. His missing front teeth and then, some months later, the big teeth that grew in their place, too big for his mouth, white and strong and unimaginably dear with their fine, sawlike bumps. He showed her the comics he drew, his school report, the visor Raym bought him to play the newest game mods, the dirty skull of a cat that he'd unearthed in his California yard. Always cheerful, always so generous to her. He must have resented the divorce, her absence—of this she'd been certain, on some instinctual level—but he'd never let her feel it, her beautiful son.

And then, the final two school holidays, he was old enough for cross-country airship travel alone. She remembered picking him up at Geoffrey Lyons Memorial Terminal from the steward and the ride back from Hoboken together on the ferry, his small suitcase in her lap. Both times, she was amazed at how big he'd grown. Both times amazed at the smell of his hair, his private and specific scent unchanged from the days of his babyhood.

But being with him again full-time during those visits felt like a departure from the single life she'd rebuilt after Raym left. She loved Jonas more than anything, but perhaps, some small secret part of her admitted, she didn't love him the way she ought to. The way other mothers loved their sons.

She'd felt herself pulled in two directions. Her practice in New York, her friends, her home. Her son in California, her blood. It was hard to be apart from Jonas, but she believed she could do it. She'd believed it when she brought him back at the end each time, hugging him tight outside the terminal and letting him go. She could go on like this.

But the Gate taught her a distance, a way of being apart, that was greater than kilometers, less permeable even than years. *Ostalgie* wasn't the word. There wasn't a word for what it was. An unmeasurable quantity, an unbridgeable remoteness. Her love, still oriented toward her son as a needle to magnetic north, an arrow permanently halted in flight.

And there she was on the ground on the sun-heated sidewalk on West Fortieth, heaving for air with something hard pressed against the small of her back. Someone shouted at her and it wasn't the woman, the boy's mother. No, the shouting voice was a man's voice. Hel's sunglasses had launched off her face and skidded off somewhere; bright light assaulted her. Her cheek pressed against the pavement; she turned her head to the side as much as possible and saw a person in a uniform crouched on her back, the workman she'd noticed before. Not a stick—an apartment building's door guard, maybe.

"It was an accident," Hel said then. The pressure on her back felt far greater than it should have. She sensed the weight of her whole creaturely existence pressing down upon her, the mass and heft of a missing world. A tiger was standing on her, digging rueful sharp claws into her skin. "I didn't mean it," she gasped. "It was an accident."

How could she have believed—how could she have forgotten—how could she have gotten it so wrong?

The grand entryway of the former school opened around Hel, ringing with noise. A showpiece for a rich man, a gathering place for groups of pupils on their way out to the grounds for games lessons—now, the foyer served as reception area and gallery. She saw piles of vibrant fabric, folded and displayed on plinths around the room, and a roughly loomed shawl draped around the shoulders of a mannequin, its price tag dangling. The shelves against the wall were stacked with bowls and vessels of different sizes made by the potters who worked now in the studios upstairs. Their modern asymmetry, their intentional primitivism looked incongruous next to the mannered paintings that hung still on the walls.

Stiff family portraits in oils, and still lifes of fruit and fowl. Hudson River prospects. Even other seascapes, a whaling scene. But none as tall as a doorway that a little boy could step through.

No hand. No rope.

○

In the Rendezvous an hour before, Teresa Klay: "When we get there, I have a suggestion. You can ask as many questions as you want—about the old boarding school, its history. About the drowning—though I don't know what a bunch of hippies will know about that. About the painting. Whatever. But maybe don't tell them your whole story, OK? I would appreciate that."

Hel, turning in her seat, fought the feel of the unaccustomed shoulder belt. Trees flashed by outside on the verge of the Taconic. "What?"

"I'm not trying to be cruel. Your displacement status can just be . . . distracting. Polarizing, you know? You're running a risk when you disclose it—some people are really bigoted. And even when they're not, it stirs things up. Remember Daniel? Remember how that went?"

"Yeah, sure. Daniel." The archivist at the Brooklyn Public Library, Klay's friend. He'd shaken Hel's hand with such zeal, once he'd heard what she was, that she took him for a Bible Numericist who believed that the initial lots of UDPs were in fact the 144,000 members of the tribes of Israel predicted in Revelations. But no, he was just excited to interrogate the differences. He'd spent the next twenty minutes testing Hel's memory and her patience with subjects she remembered only distantly from lower school. Who discovered mechanical flight in her After and how did it evolve? What were the Inter-American Wars?

"Don't get me wrong," Klay said. "I understand. It must be nice for you to have the chance to talk about that stuff, if you don't often get to."

"I get pretty tired of it, actually—"

Klay wasn't listening. "And the attention must be flattering."

Daniel, at the library. Was he good-looking? Sure. He was attractive enough in a bland, floppy-haired way. A good person? Who knew? Daniel, pumping her hand, giving his meaningless condolences. A face, a set of fingers to grip, a heart, a penis. An unlikely collection of atoms, assembled in a unique and different way, utterly unspecial to her. A rock among rocks on a beach she wished she'd never visited. A man whose name she would be glad to forget, right now, if she could. Daniel, who didn't—shouldn't—exist.

"No. I don't care about that. I don't like it."

"Oh." Klay's hands loose on the wheel, casual. "Cool. Then it won't be a problem, this time."

○

In the foyer of the mansion turned school turned artists' space, Hel looked around her. At the elderly woman in a patterned woven scarf, coming toward her to see what was wrong. At the greasy-haired visitor scrutinizing tiny vases in the display case, that same shitfoot from the yellow car. At Klay, behind her, bent over her phone, no doubt sending a dismissive text message to Donaldson. A picture of the picture that wasn't there, a lack-of-progress report.

With a howl, she sank to her knees.

She would trade them all. She would let them all drown if only she could go back.

CHAPTER SIX

"Next stop York Street stand clearatha closing doors." The announcement echoed through the car, the voice on the PA distorted and barely intelligible. At home, Vikram recalled, NYAT used a recording—an anonymous lilting robot—on all trolleys and streetcars and the few underground trains that ran through Midtown. He couldn't recall the substance of the precisely expressed message anymore, though he'd heard it countless times. Doors are closing, exercise caution. Something like that. "OK," he decided aloud. "Next stop."

"We're getting off?" Hel asked.

"Yep. I called it. Those are the rules." They'd started their game in Lower Manhattan, taking the 4 train uptown and switching to a 7 that brought them to Bryant Park before catching this Coney Island–bound F into Brooklyn. Vikram knew Hel had given a presentation to some museum people today about her idea. She wouldn't tell him anything about it, but her mood now was brittle, a veneer of cheerfulness he didn't think would stand up to much.

"Can't we change again?" she asked. "At least one more change."

"No. I'm the leader. It's my turn to choose. Anyway, I thought you hated being underground. We've been riding long enough. Let's get some air."

"Fine." Hel slid closer to him on the bench and reached across his body for the bottle-in-a-bag he held in his other hand. She took a long pull. "York Street it is. You're the leader."

"I missed this game. It's more fun than I remember."

"That's because you used to be depressed all the time when we played it. That's why I invented it. To cheer you up."

Hel passed the bottle back. A woman sitting across from them tsked audibly. "We're visiting from another country," Hel told her. "We're from a civilized land, where alcohol is permitted for adults on public transportation. We don't know your stupid foreign rules."

"York Street," the conductor muttered over the PA.

"It's OK, ma'am," Vikram said to the woman, finding his feet. "We're getting off."

They climbed together up the cement steps to street level. Hel walked ahead, her arms stiff by her sides, then dropped back, as if she'd remembered that the rules she'd devised required her to let him choose the way. The sky, brilliant blue overhead, faded almost before their eyes to whitish gold in the west. Working nights, Vikram always wanted the hour before sunset to feel like daybreak, but it never did. No matter how established his nocturnal routine became, his body still knew something was wrong.

"Where are we?"

"I don't know. You're the leader."

They wandered downhill, away from the massive edifice of the Manhattan Bridge, past a fancy drugstore and a taqueria with a mural of a rooster. They looked in the windows of a specialty chocolate shop, closed today, and then wandered into a used bookstore where a live cat hissed at them from behind the register. "You can't drink on transport, but you can keep a domestic animal in a place of business?" Hel said loudly before Vikram tugged her back out the door.

"Let's get a drink."

They settled into a booth in a very dark, very hip bar across the street from the bookstore. Exposed brickwork and ugly paintings. Vikram chose a dark draft of some adventive style. He wished he had sniff with him, or that smoking indoors were legal. Hel ordered an energy drink, which came already poured into a glass. When the server wasn't looking, she topped it off with whiskey from their bottle. "That's disgusting," he said. "A disgusting combination."

"What's *disgusting* is to charge seven dollars for a beer during happy hour in Gairville, of all places."

Vikram already had the browser open on his phone. "The neighborhood's not called Gairville anymore. It's DUMBO here."

"Dumbo?" Hel scoffed. "Really? Who came up with that?"

"It's an acronym." He navigated to a related page. "It's also a classic cartoon movie from 1941 about a small elephant."

"Who cares?" She sipped at her drink, made a face.

She hated to see the gentrification of neighborhoods she'd known as poor. She also hated to discover formerly prosperous areas that had become run-down.

"Be honest," Vikram said. "You just hate change."

"At least the Manhattan Bridge is pretty much the same. I guess it must have been designed and built BS. That stands for Before Sleight," she explained, before Vikram could ask. "I'm hoping it'll catch on."

She had to be kidding. "Instead of just saying Before, you expect people to say BS?"

"They'll *want* to say it, when I've proved what I know about him. Let's walk over the bridge."

Vikram waited until she'd reached the door to leave a tip on the table. Hel never tipped. Outside, the sun had slipped in the direction of Manhattan, leaving behind desperate colors. There in the dusk stood the skyline, lit up and famous, right but wrong. They found the pedestrian access near Sands Street and began to walk uphill on the south side of the bridge. On the initial approach, over land, the highway passed below them and they stared directly into the windows of the buildings around them, people working in some and seas of empty desks in others. On their left, a sports club spread out its tennis courts below eye level. On the right, tracks carried trains from borough to borough.

The pedestrian walkway arched over the riverside park on the Brooklyn side and then they were crossing the East River itself, at last. Hel took his hand, but did not speak. A chain-link fence curled above them to preclude suicidal jumps. Through the grille, Vikram watched barges and boats far below, some carrying tourists. The watercraft parted the skin of the water in white-foamed cuts that closed seamlessly behind, scars that could heal perfectly.

One-third of the way across, they reached the first of the supporting towers and stopped to look out at the water. Vikram picked out the Statue of Liberty and the unfamiliar skyscrapers of Lower Manhattan. The space where the World Trade Center buildings had stood, built before his birth yet destroyed before his arrival. No trace of them now to see, their absence important to everyone but people like him and Hel.

"Remember, you're the leader," Hel whispered in his ear. "Turn around?"

"No. Let's keep going."

As they walked on, the suspension cables at their side dipped lower and lower. A jogger passed them right at the midpoint of the bridge, and a heavy MTA train rumbled past, its noise deafening. Vikram felt an unhelpful pang that he tried to suppress.

Every big city has its ghosts. A line from the climactic scene in *The Pyronauts* in which John Gund pursues a fleeing Asyl into the incinerated ruins of Philadelphia. Sleight's words wafting over from another world.

It was just the density of population in urban centers that caused this feeling, the way that living chockablock with others encouraged anonymity, each member of a crowd consciously shutting out everyone else until one felt surrounded by ignored strangers. It was the tangible history; the new layered with the very old. "Every big city has its ghosts." He spoke the words aloud. Someone in this world had probably said pretty much the same thing, only Vikram wasn't sure what to read to find it. He thought again of the destroyed Trade Center buildings. Of the light from the window in the storage facility, flashing out like a beacon.

As they walked, the suspension cables on the river side rose to meet the second support tower. When they reached it, Hel said, "Stop here. Is anyone coming?"

Vikram looked in both directions. It was really getting dark, but the sight lines were good. The jogger, a tiny speck now on the Brooklyn end of the walkway. "No."

"I was thinking," Hel said. "The bike path is on the north side, right?" She pointed across the tracks. "So, anyone who approached us, they'd be on foot. No surprises—we'd see them coming a long way off."

"I guess. What's your point?"

She pushed him up against the support, the cold steel painted dull blue, then spray-painted in pink and silver bubble letters spelling something he didn't know how to read—some other language, maybe—and tugged at his belt. "I wore a skirt," she said, low and throaty. "Help me. Quick."

She nipped gently at his neck and snaked her hand into his briefs, stroking him awkwardly from a cramped, restricted angle that somehow charged the movement with eroticism. The roundhead bolts pressed into his back like a sentence in Braille. Over her shoulder, he could see the water and, on the Manhattan side, cars on the FDR, the baseball diamond, the Chinatown projects where they once bought a huge bumpy-skinned jackfruit and didn't know how to eat it. He shimmied his pants and briefs down his hips and lifted her up onto him.

○

The first card Hel found after the meeting with Ayanna Donaldson was a Queen of Spades, scuffed and bent. Fate dealt it out to her on the sidewalk outside the old Domino Sugar refinery complex, whose large brick edifice now housed the Museum of Modern Thought. The loading chutes Hel remembered had been demolished and newer buildings joined the smokestacks protected by the Landmarks Preservation Commission. She stood in the shadow of those stacks, still reeling from the meeting, and felt the sensation of being watched. But no one was here. No one lingering outside the museum, no one in the landscaped open space that joined the new buildings to the old. The card lay faceup, showing itself. Waiting.

She bent to retrieve it, wondering what it meant. The suit of Spades—analogous to the Swords of the Tarot they used here and the Truth deck she remembered. Swords signified ambition, power, conflict, courage. And queens, of course, symbolized female authority.

"It's not going to work." That was how Donaldson had said it, just ten minutes before. And the worst part was Hel's lack of surprise. She had to admit that she'd expected all along.

The museum director met with her, not in her office but in one of the workrooms at the back of MoMT. A steel-topped table stood in the center of the room, its surface covered with what looked like half a dozen archaeological relics. Chalky white, each one the length of a thumb, they lined up in a neat row, waiting to be catalogued. Donaldson wore blue latex gloves; otherwise, she was dressed all in white. "Give me another chance," Hel said, aware of the artificial sound of her own words. Had she dreamed of this? Had she said them already?

"Give me another chance. I lost control in the artists' space. I shouldn't have expected the painting still to be there, but it exists. You can believe me. Whatever Klay said to you—I'll do better. I'll behave myself. We'll find it."

"I do believe you."

"Good. It can't be hard to track down a painting that big."

Donaldson snapped off a glove. "Helen. You're not grasping the issue here. I've given your concept more consideration since the first time we talked, and I've been taking the temperature. Asking some decision-makers—informally, of course. It's not as popular as I'd thought it might be. No one seems to want to know more about UDP history. There's actually a resistance, a hostility to the concept. You're going to have a hard time selling this."

She was saying *you* now, Hel noted, not *we*. "Since when do you care about what's popular? You're in the business of presenting art, not making people comfortable or showing them what they already know they want. You're supposed to broaden horizons, aren't you? Are you scared to do that?"

Donaldson's face remained serene; Hel had not succeeded in needling her. "I said hostile, but that was the wrong word. I meant—forgive me—bored. Your audience is tired of you. The records from the Decontam questioning and the commission report and all that went up on WikiLeaks, what, a year ago? Everyone who wants to know about UDPs has read it already. Let me be honest: it's frightening, to think about what happened to you. People prefer to keep it simple. To view you all as a problem."

"People can learn from problems."

"Only if they want to. Helen, I'm sorry."

And that was it. That was supposed to be good-bye.

Hel had never learned to swim. Seff, who'd had lessons in the crawl and the backstroke when their mother was still around, had no patience for her younger sister's caution around water. One summer, Seff pushed her under the line of buoys as they waded at Coney Island, right when a wave was coming. Hel's head went under for some count of seconds before she emerged, coughing and choking and spitting out dirty brine. "Don't be a baby," Seff told her. "I was about to grab you."

Even as her sister wrapped her in a towel and hugged her tight, full of remorse, Hel wasn't sure whether to believe her. But it didn't matter—she'd rescued herself. That was why some part of her blamed Sleight. She blamed him for not making it out.

Hel had looked around at the stark white walls, the polished concrete floor. In her world, the old refinery still operated, dirty and workaday, sometimes blowing sweet-smelling winds along the waterfront. She stared down at the table, realizing that what she had taken for archaeological samples were, in fact, small models. Trains? She picked one up from its place on the table to examine it.

"It's the lunar module *Eagle*, from Apollo 11," Donaldson told her. "That was the first spacecraft to land people on the moon."

She might have heard something about that, in Debrief maybe, or in a movie here. "So, they're all spaceships?"

"Each one carved from lunar rock the artist bought in an online auction. We're negotiating with NASA for permission to display them."

Hel turned the piece toward the light, somewhat awed.

"Would you put it down, please?" the director asked. "They're delicate. And it's time for you to go."

So when Hel saw the Sword card, just after that, she wondered: upright or reversed? She still had all the mystical significances of the Truth deck memorized. Depending on the card's orientation during a Truth reading, the Sword Queen could mean clarity, logic, matters of intellect. Or emotional bias, poor decisions. Which was it?

Hel put the first card in her pocket and kept walking, considering that question. Then, she spotted the second. Facedown, this one, and blown up against a construction barrier where it lay half-obscured beneath a grease-stained pizza box. Yet the card's old backing design was familiar, even from a distance. A gambling parlor card, the two cupids on their bicycles mirror images of each other, like someone riding through a reflecting pool or puddle, slowly, so as not to disturb the surface. She would recognize that anywhere.

Wonderingly, she picked it up. Flipped it over.

The Eight of Hearts.

Now she pulled the queen back out of her pocket. Its reverse showed a photograph of the Statue of Liberty.

Playing cards from two separate decks, then.

Hearts were the cards that told of emotional conflicts, corresponding with the Cups suit of the Truth deck's pips. Upright, the Eight of Cups signaled the desire to escape, feelings of abandonment, or voluntary withdrawal. When reversed, the card told of a drifting hopelessness.

Like it or not, the card said, it was time to go. As a message, it couldn't be clearer.

How might the cards have come to be here? She forced herself to think of a logical explanation. She imagined someone walking along Kent Avenue, two different decks of playing cards shuffling innocently in a pair of hands, the wind ripping these particular two away. Or two people, each with a separate deck. A massive game of war, played in the gutter by a brace of careless hobos. None of it made sense.

When she was reading Truth for her sister, when there was some kind of coincidence—all pips and no trumps, or all cards of the same suit, or the same face again and again—Seff said the cards were making urgent contact. Seff, who hadn't believed at first, began to keep the Truth deck in a silk scarf in the top drawer of her dresser, but Hel was the only one who could force them to speak.

She kept her eyes down as she walked. She didn't stop searching for other signs until she got to the spot where Vikram waited.

○

"I've been up here before," Hel said, after they disengaged on the bridge.

Caught up in wonder, Vikram didn't immediately understand her words. Fucking out in the open, like those teenagers he discovered every month or so in the sweep of his flashlight—it excited him. Normally, the idea of being watched held no sexual appeal, but it was different high in the air like this, with distant Lady Liberty and the ghost buildings and every anonymous soul in the tenements below. He felt as if he was the one who'd been

97

overlooking them. He felt as if their lovemaking could work a protective incantation, could keep these homebound sleepers safe and innocent.

"I've been up here before," Hel said again. "Just once, I think. Only I walked the opposite way, started in Manhattan and walked to Brooklyn."

"Way back BV, you came up here? That means Before Vikram," he explained, keeping a straight face.

"Yeah, I get it." Her warm shoulder, pressed up against his as they looked out in the same direction. "I did. I walked here BV."

Hel on the Manhattan Bridge, in the other world. Had she been by herself? With her friends, or some previous lover? With her ex-husband?

"Did you ever come here with your son?"

Why had he said that out loud?

She stepped out of his arms abruptly, ending their contact. With held breath, Vikram watched her shake out her hair and then put it back into its messy bun. Briskly, she began to walk toward Chinatown. He stood in place, watched the distance grow, the downward-sloping path toward the old-fashioned arch with its tribute to the Spirits of Commerce and Industry at Manhattan Bridge Plaza. She didn't answer his question.

She would leave him to go back, if she could. Of course she would. He would send her back himself.

○

After Hel was robbed, how she'd lain on her back in the black of Jonas's room listening to the thunderstorm. Her eyes were open and parts of her body stung—not the places where she was most wounded but other unexpected parts. Her bruised throat. Her left shin, where her attacker had kicked her. The corner of her mouth, where he'd demonstrated the sharpness of his blade by poking her. It was her hand that should have hurt, but she had no sense of her stitched fingers at all. Perhaps this was an effect of the drug they'd given her at the emergency clinic. Through the bandages, her hand felt warm against her chest, heavy, like it belonged to someone else.

At the time, she and Raym lived in the apartment in Park Slope on Fourteenth Street in between Fourth and Fifth Avenues, five rooms and a kitchen. Jonas's bedroom was in the corner, his child-sized mattress wedged in where the walls met. That night, craving comfort, her son had climbed up into his parents' big bed. Hel stole out.

The thunder did not come in bursts but expressed itself as a continuous growl, a giant, threatening dog, warning them all. In Jonas's room with the shades drawn, she didn't see the lightning itself as it came, but the covered windows flared white— first the one on the north wall and then, a fraction of a second later, the one on the east wall, by her son's pillow and his soft toys. She kept her eyes open and her tongue still and let it all roll by and let the room return to darkness. She was tired but afraid to go to sleep, and it was easy to pass time, awake.

Easy except for the stinging. She was a surgeon; she knew her living was her hands. Yet she did not worry about her bandaged extremities. Instead, she lay there and concentrated on that inconsequential but specific pain just below her lower lip. A sharp awareness, as if the blade were still there even now, the needle tip wiggling, digging around while she strove with all her energy to stay quiet and will him away.

Jonas. The fervent, unspoken messages she'd tried to send to him during the attack.

She realized, after some length of time, that the growling had stopped while she wasn't paying attention. The only sound was the rain falling and the heavy-duty trickling of water past that north window—the rain channeled into one particular path by an unseen system, no doubt, draining from the flat roof two stories above, the musical song and spatter below, no longer drowned by other sounds—and the shades stayed dark and the room stayed black and reluctantly, exposed and unprotected, she fell asleep.

○

What if you don't really love me? she wanted to ask Vikram. What if you love me because I'm the only one left to you? What if you love me, like Asyl loved John Gund, because I'm the only one you've ever known?

All the stories that were gone. But *The Pyronauts* survived.

She'd been so fixated on the painting that she'd nearly forgotten.

The Pyronauts. Donaldson had *The Pyronauts*.

INTERVIEW TRANSCRIPT:
GREGORY "WES" WESTMORLAND,
AGE 38, MANHATTAN

It would be funny now, if it hadn't been on my neck.

It took me a while to even realize what the problem was. I saw them all staring at it and I thought, what if people don't do body art here? This was right at the beginning. None of my lotmates knew anything about where we'd ended up, confined like we were in an old vocational school they'd converted into dorms. We never got to go outside, so the only people I saw who weren't UDPs, those first couple of days, were NYPD sticks they had babysitting us.

I noticed that although some of the officers were tattooed, none had cutting scars or cicatrization patterns like mine. So that was the conclusion I leapt to: that the marks themselves were what made everyone so concerned about me. I never considered that the design could be the problem. The swastika.

When it was my turn to get debriefed, it seemed like the investigators gave me extra attention. They kept asking me about my political beliefs and about what I thought of Jews and stuff.

They asked me what I thought of black people, too. They asked me what I thought of gays, which is funny, in retrospect—I didn't know that was the same thing as a vert, so I couldn't tell them I was one. None of us knew about the clandestine vetting built into the evac plan by its engineers, the way the supposedly randomized lottery was rigged to exclude anyone with an Extreme Crime convic or a gang affiliation. That secret only came out later. As far as my debriefers knew, I could have been any kind of antisocial monster.

One of the sticks finally cleared up the mystery for me as he escorted a couple of us back to our dorms after the daily questioning. Nice guy, PO Goncalves. He wasn't obsessed, like some of them were, with cuffing us while walking us from place to place. After all the bad trouble we'd been through, the realization that we were seen as maybe dangerous ourselves—that was like a whole extra kick in the eggsack. Anyway, I was at the front of the line and Goncalves asked me did I know what the symbol means, the one on my neck. I said of course. You don't just get an electrosurgical brand without thinking about it first, because for one thing, that shit is expensive. I told him about the swastika's history in ancient Asia, about how it was an auspicious symbol you'd paint on stuff you wanted to be lucky. I told him about the Santa Clara Swastikas, our national basketball champions four years running, and about the lotto tickets printed with the sigil. I told him that for Buddhists all over the globe, the swastika is a graphic representation of eternity itself. Goncalves got this blank look on his face. So then I started to explain to him about the Buddha, in case old Siddhārtha Gautama had somehow lost his place in the Western popular consciousness in this strange new world, but that wasn't the problem, of course—Goncalves waved me off.

He was like, "Don't you know about Nazis?"

"No," I said.

Then he showed me a picture of all these shoes piled up at Auschwitz. He called it up on his phone right then and there. Where I'm from, we thought that what the KomSos did to the Slavs was bad. We had no idea how much worse it could get.

I don't have an education or any particular skills, but I'm big and strong. When I was young, I never used to have any trouble getting a job guarding the door at clubs, or unpacking vacuum trains or work like that. Then, I met Bronson and we fell in love, and after that I worked for his family business. But here, the swastika problem made it hard to get hired to do anything. People aren't jumping to hire someone with the UDP designation on his or her ID anyway—they think we're stupid or damaged—but for me, it was even harder. The bosses didn't like my mark, and no non-UDP wanted to sweat next to me.

You can see where it used to be—right here? Positioned too high for a turtleneck to really cover, drawn too big for a bandage.

For a while, I worked at a liquor store owned by a guy who I think hired me because he was a bigot himself and got a sort of charge from it. Every once in a while, tough guys with their own tattoos would come in, look me over, say things to each other in Spanish. Every once in a while, one of them would get in my face and he would ask what the hell my story was.

Goncalves had prepared me for that. He told me what to say: *They did it to me in prison. They held me down and did it to me. I didn't want it.*

Shameful, but it worked. Worked every time.

It reminded me of when I was ten and I was messing around in the woods behind my aunt's house in the country and I got poison ivy on one arm and all over my face. Big angry blisters oozing pus. After a week, they deflated, leaving me with a scaly red rash on my skin like the surface of Mars. I didn't mind how it looked, not until I was at the food store, picking up milk, and this old pensioner came up, practically crying, and asked me if I was the boy who'd been in a house fire and if I was getting on OK. I didn't know what she was talking about, but I yelled, "No!" Then I turned and ran. I ran home and hid out in the chicken house until my aunt came and found me and asked me what was wrong, and I didn't have an answer.

So I quit the liquor store and my Adjustment Counselor got me a janitor job at a factory that made parody masks of politicians I'd never heard of. That's where I met Ari; he was at the end of the line, daubing color on the apples of Clinton's rubber cheeks, giving them that touch of life. I was still half in mourning for Bronson, but I couldn't keep from noticing him. Ari would never talk to me, though. When I said hello, he ignored me. If I smiled at him, he turned away. I thought maybe I was going about things wrong. I had trouble telling which guys were verts when the styles were so different. So I gave up. One day, though, Ari stayed late while I was sweeping up. He told me that both of his grandparents on his mother's side and all their siblings in Polithuania, in Vilnius, had been gassed in vans or machine-gunned in the woods. The swastika wasn't cool, he said. It was nothing to play around with.

I told him who I was, how and why I got the mark. I told him about myself at twenty-one, sitting in the red leather chair in the downtown burner studio, saying, "Here's the design I want." I told him about luck. I told him about free throws. I told him about eternity. His family had suffered directly, and yet he was the first non-UDP besides PO Goncalves who'd ever listened all the way through. And while Ari listened, I knew that I was finished. It couldn't wait till I saved up the money for a professional removal. It was time to be rid of it.

We went back to his apartment together, stopping on the way at a Rite Aid for antiseptic and bandages and tape and cellophane, then at a hardware store for a soldering iron. The bottle of vodka, he already had.

"Are you sure about this?" Ari asked, the hot iron in his hand. At that point, I guess he had started to feel a little sorry for coming down on me so hard.

I told him I was a Buddhist, and that after all, life is suffering.

Since then, I've spent a lot of time thinking about why it bothered me, having to tell those strangers about being marked against my will in lockup. I couldn't stand the pity, that was it, when in fact it was something I chose myself, something I used to be proud of. I couldn't stand people thinking they knew something tragic about me when what they knew was all wrong.

There actually was a fire in my aunt's township that year I got the poison ivy. A family lost their house and all their possessions, and the baby died of smoke inhalation, and the little boy was indeed very badly burned. Turned out the fire was the boy's fault. He'd been playing with matches.

I wonder about him, sometimes. I wonder what questions strangers asked him, all the rest of his life, when they saw his scars.

CHAPTER SEVEN

Vikram first visited the Sleight House Museum on a slow Sunday afternoon in the other world. He'd come down from Boston for the weekend expressly for this purpose with two other university students from the literature department—one a rival of his, one a woman he loved—as well as his flatmate, a well-read economist who happened to be a passionate science fiction devotee and had begged Vikram to let him come along. They arrived at New Grand Central and traveled to eastern Brooklyn by bus and velocab. They passed apartment blocks and shops and friendly 1940s-era concrete public buildings: a library, a community child-care center. Brownsville—this Brownsville—was a racially mixed working-class area where people kept their chrome railings shiny and maintained geraniums in pots on their stoops. The cabs dropped them at Sleight Park, a square of green across the avenue from a Moorish Revival synagogue. After paying their respects at the bust of the great writer, they walked the last few blocks to his house.

It would have been pleasant if not for the deluge of rain that suddenly caught them, curtains of water sweeping down the street, pooling around dams of leaves in the drains. The economist shared his umbrella with the woman student; Vikram and his rival were both soaked by the time they got to the address. For this reason, Vikram had no clear memory of what the exterior of the cottage looked like then. Clean white shingles and a green door with a brass handle, that was what he knew, and the feel of his cold shirt clinging to him and the worry that the dark hair on his chest was showing through.

Here, that door—the very same door!—was flaking brown paint, exposing splintered wood beneath. He'd spent a long time lingering on the steps after ringing the bell, so long he'd begun to wonder how much longer, given the dubious character of the neighborhood, it would be safe to wait, when a young man finally came staggering out with a bulky load in his arms—a box made of dark gray plastic with a dangling cord that threatened to trip him up. He kicked the door closed behind him before Vikram could get even a glimpse of what was inside.

This must be the owner Hel had mentioned. The kid.

"Hello. I'm Vikram Bhatnagar, Mr. Sealy."

"Dwayne is fine." He put down what he was carrying and took Vikram's proffered hand, looking like he was wondering what Vikram was even doing here.

Last time, there had been a guide, an unpaid intern from New Lots College who led them from the sitting room to the office, then to the half bath with its chipped pedestal sink and modest bidet. Initially morose, she seemed to warm to their group, growing more and more animated and departing from her usual script. Clear plastic barriers at hip height blocked entrance to the rooms proper, but the guide retrieved a screwdriver from somewhere and unscrewed the barrier from the doorframe in order to admit them to the kitchen, where Sleight, in fact, had done his real writing, over at the table by the stove. Sleight in a hurry, still in his wet overcoat, clothes and beard steaming as pen scratched paper.

They'd entered the rooms reverently, walked across linoleum Sleight had trodden. Indecipherable notes the man had scribbled to himself stood out on the molding. Vikram had touched them, though he'd known he shouldn't, with an outstretched forefinger.

"Where's the estate agent?" Vikram asked now. "The realtor. Will she meet us here?"

Dwayne didn't seem to know what he was talking about. "There is no . . . look, you can't go in there right now."

"But the woman I talked to on the phone said you were doing showings today. That you could fit me in, maybe, at four." The suggestion that the place was in demand had been welcome news. Vikram had imagined eager home-buyers with actual money who would snatch the place out from under Hel. Problem solved. Of course, that was before he saw the condition of the poor cottage, its sagging porch, its unlovable shuttered windows like black eyes. "I thought she was the estate agent."

"Eden?" Dwayne said with a laugh. "Shit. Eden's my girl. Not no realtor. I left my phone at her place, I guess. I don't know what she's playing at. Don't get me wrong—I'm glad you're interested—but the place is *not* ready. I can take your info if you want, give you a call when the junk is cleared out?" He stood there for a moment, waiting, and then, when Vikram did not respond, he picked up the appliance again and began to shuffle toward the edge of the porch. A paper note flapped, taped to the front of whatever it was, hand-lettered. The crooked words read FREE—WORKS.

"Hold on," Vikram said. "You need me to take a side of that?"

Dwayne turned. "Nah, man. I got it."

Vikram found himself picking up the trailing cord, just to get it out of the guy's way. He followed him down the three shallow steps, down the path to the street, like the maid of honor holding a bride's train. "What is it, anyway?"

"Old tube TV. They don't make 'em like this anymore. I tried to sell it on craigslist, but nobody wants it." He staggered, hugging the TV to his body with long skinny arms.

Growing up in the dangerous Jersey suburbs, Vikram had known guys like him—the baby of his tough family, a soft guy from a killer block. "What's craigslist?"

"What you mean? Are you another one of these . . . like that lady that came to see me?"

"Yeah. I'm another one of those."

"So, this place is pretty important to you?" Dwayne asked, dropping the television on the curb with a muffled bang. He adjusted the note, which had gotten wrinkled in its journey from the house. "Lady said it was some important writer's house."

Important. Work like *The Pyronauts*, ill bound between paper covers and sold for dimes to people who didn't know better, to dreamers and newcomers, paupers and children. Work like that explored realms of possibility, Vikram thought; not what was past and could not be undone, but an improbable future from which humanity was obliged to try to learn. Not that which seemed most likely to happen, but that which could teach readers the most about themselves.

He'd spent long hours at work last night in Jamaica thinking about it, alone in the guard shack as he watched the face of the old factory building, waiting for a message to light up for him on the broad brick side. He did his tours every hour on the hour and there was nothing to see in the corridors or in the fire stairs, no fear, this time, to keep him company. Disappointed— that was how he felt. And yet, if the timer explanation had been the right one, wouldn't the same storage space have lit up again at the same hour? It hadn't. All remained dark. As long as he watched, as long as nothing happened, possibilities existed, and the memory of the night before made his job seem less like a job and more like a vigil. Got him thinking about ghosts.

But there were no ghosts in this house. Or not ones he knew.

"Yes," Vikram confirmed. "A famous man who never lived. So don't start thinking you're sitting on a gold mine or something. Most of us wouldn't care. There's not even that many who had the chance to care. And some of us are dead by now."

"Then what are you doing here?"

"I'm here for Helen."

Dwayne walked back up to the porch and leaned casually against one of its supports. "She your friend? Your wife?"

"We're not married. But basically." Vikram stayed on the bottom step. He wanted to go inside, but he didn't want to ask and be refused. He didn't want to feel this curiosity about what might have endured the different years. Not the precious scrawl on the baseboards and the window frame, of course, but the kitchen table itself? The framed lithographs of partridges in the hallway and the old ornate radiators? It wasn't Sleight's history but his own, his twenty-four-year-old self, the incandescent excitement he'd felt, the contagious wonder. That was one reason for coming here today. The other was some half-formed desire to set Dwayne Sealy straight—to warn him that Hel had no money, that she was wasting his time, that she was obsessed in a way that was starting to make Vikram uncomfortable. To thwart Hel, to outmaneuver her, since she wouldn't listen to reason. Now that he was actually here, though, to do so seemed shameful, traitorous. "Did she tell you what she wanted to do with the place?"

"She didn't say, but I didn't think she wanted it for the view or the neighbors."

Vikram stared at the door. Where the newer paint had flaked, the old was visible. Green. Incredible.

He could imagine it easily here. A way back to the past.

○

It was midmorning when Hel finally spotted Donaldson emerging from the direction of the parking area into the sunny landscaped space that separated the old Domino Sugar refinery buildings from the modern residential towers across the way. She'd been waiting since dawn outside the leasing office. Newly planted bushes provided an imperfect screen; she'd had to sit on the ground to remain unseen and her legs were stiff and cramped when she stood.

"I have to have it back," Hel said, pushing through the shrubbery.

Donaldson's clothes were elegant, as always, but in her hand, she held an insulated plastic coffee cup with a cartoon cat on it. "You need what back?" She did not look even remotely startled by Hel's presence. But why would she be startled? She must have been expecting this.

"My book. The Sleight book, the one I showed you. If you're not going to work with me, I need it back."

"I don't have it."

Hel felt a thrill of panic; she hadn't expected staunch denial. "Yes, you do. I left it with you."

"Why would you have done that? That book must be priceless to you. You hardly know me."

Hel could envision it: *The Pyronauts.* That night at the party, the way she'd opened it to the title page and then to the table of contents. The pebbled texture of the paper, its brittle frangibility. Priceless, indeed. Donaldson and her wife and that other shitfoot with the braying laugh who'd been nearby, all of them bending their heads together to peer at it.

Many times over the past two years, in bed with the book in the Bronx while Vikram was at work, she had buried her nose in the spine. The scent of stale paper and ink would come to her then, as neutral as the body odor of a loved one. Age, faint acidity, dust. Reminiscent to her of nights studying medical texts in a basement carrel all those years ago. She could taste the book. She could feel its weight in her hand. Its worth.

Hel had difficulty sequencing. She knew other UDPs who had the same problem. In moments of panic or excitement, single impressions came back, shorn of sense-making context. Later, she couldn't always rely on her memory of the order in which events had occurred. But she remembered the suspended party. The hotel that shouldn't have been.

The expanse of pale wood, a dance floor hovering in air. The faceless serving staff in attendance moving around the periphery of the crowd. In her memory, the guests came together and drifted apart as in some choreographed dance out of a historical film, the kind of dance not popular in Hel's world or in this one for at least two hundred years. Strange men in collared shirts, narrow trousers, bright ties scattered here and there around the necks of the most conservative. No hats. Women in dresses with plunging necklines and floating hems; women held down only by the substantial jewelry in their lobes and at their wrists. All of them whirled at the center of Hel's memory, moving toward their partners.

And her own somber dress. Her stupid bag digging into her shoulder. Steps she didn't know, and the taste of peaches in her mouth.

That wasn't how it happened. The dancing didn't happen. But the feeling was right. And righter still was this firm memory: held in Donaldson's long-fingered hands, the paperback. Blue cover.

"You looked through it. I saw you," Hel said, brought back to the present moment by the breeze tossing the leaves of the manicured baby trees around them.

"I did," Donaldson admitted. "And then I put it down."

"No. I saw you take it away."

Had she? She'd wanted to give Donaldson a chance to look at it in detail: the verso and the number line showing the print run. To examine how it was bound and search its pages for familiar

passages and come up short. Hel didn't remember a conversation about these intentions. But Donaldson walked off the dance
floor with *The Pyronauts* in her grip. Of that, Hel was certain.
The hand. The book cover. The hand on the cover. It was as clear
to her as the smell. Clear as Jonas's smell. Clear as anything.

A scattering of sunlight shifted at her feet, one coin of illumination settling on Donaldson's brown forehead, like a sniper's
laser sight. Hel could smell her smoky perfume. "Call the hotel,"
Donaldson advised. "Maybe they picked it up. I don't have it."

Donaldson moved away but Hel remained. She sat down
on a granite bench, cold beneath her tights, and looked at the
decorative native grasses planted around the paths, the same
grasses that would have grown in a marshy place like this centuries Before when the land belonged to the Lenape and Mo-
hegan in every possible New York she could imagine.

Time passed, some amount of time Hel couldn't measure,
and she felt cold, and saw that someone's shadow had blocked
the sun. It was Teresa Klay standing in front of her, one hand
on her cocked hip, the other by her side, the call screen on
her cell phone glowing. Who had sent her—Donaldson or the
leasing office people? It didn't matter.

"Hel," Klay said. "Go home, will you?"

"I can't."

Klay put the phone away and sat next to her. After a minute, she tentatively raised her arm and looped it around Hel's
shoulder. Hel felt herself stiffen at the unexpected contact.

Klay muttered sympathetic words. "That's too bad. That's
too bad." It did not have the ring of a taunt. She sounded like
she meant it.

What was it like?

○

Helen was ten. Her mom was gone and her dad wasn't around—he was getting paid double for back-to-back overnight runs, which he took whenever he could get them—so her sister, Persephone, was left in charge. That was the year the three of them lived in an apartment over an osteopath's office in East Harlem—what would turn out to be the last Manhattan apartment. Their dad slept on the foldout couch so Seff and Helen could share the only bedroom.

Seff, who was sixteen, wanted a party. She wanted Helen gone for the evening, like their dad. "Don't you have a friend's house you can go to or something?"

"I don't have any friends," Helen said. "Anyway, I think I'm coming down with something." She hoped Seff would feel her forehead.

"You usually have one friend," Seff pointed out.

This was true. Since their mother left, they'd lived in half a dozen neighborhoods in four out of the five boroughs. Helen didn't fit in too well at any of the schools, but typically she had it in her to find a girl in her new class whom no one else liked much, discover something she had in common with that girl, and form a bond of mutual protection. That hadn't happened in Harlem yet. They'd moved in here only a month ago, but Seff was already popular.

"I don't have even one friend. And I'm sick."

"You're not sick."

"My throat feels funny."

"Fine, go lie down with your eyes closed then, cancer-face," Seff said. "I need to clean up in here." Helen knew that she was spoiling the orphan lie her sister liked to use at new schools to seem impressive. Seff would invite over her new gang, telling them that she lived all alone with no parents and that she could do whatever she wanted at her apartment. Indeed, the place would have been perfect for one person, with its fold-down table and miniature washer and dryer and the sweet little shelves under the windows.

But Helen existed. With pleasure, she considered the inevitable discovery of the lie. No matter what, her sister's schoolmates would find her out when they asked to use the bathroom, which could be accessed only through the bedroom the sisters shared. How did Seff expect to explain the two beds crammed inside, one of them outfitted with threadbare Rocket Pig sheets? How would Seff explain Helen's toys, her Pony Whisperer and Dusty Peach posters, unless she planned to tell those big high-form kids that they were hers?

Helen dosed herself with two tablespoons of the sapphire-blue cold medicine their father kept in a drawer in the kitchen, then went into the bedroom and lay on her own bed with the door cracked, where she could hear the angry scratching of the broom and the cabinet doors opening and then banging shut as Seff hid stuff inside and, under those sounds, the music playing on the player—a new band whose sixer Seff had just purchased with money from her cashier job at the public steam baths. The pink curtain over the window in the back wall made the light warm. Helen watched the leaves of the ceiling fan rotate, the motion slowing, blurring, until she slipped off to sleep.

When she woke up, the apartment was dark and noisy and a boy she didn't know was groping between the beds, trying to find the bathroom door. Helen waited until he'd gone inside, then got up and padded into the living room/kitchen. Seff perched on the edge of the coffee table, and her friends took up all the chairs and the couch too. They stood against the walls. Helen saw the twelve or fifteen crushed Mack Bullets lined up on the mantelpiece and an empty pouch of sniff drowning in a puddle of beer spilled on the counter. As she entered, the music on the player changed from a fast electro number to something slower, more nostalgic. Everything in the room moved in time to the new beat: the gesticulating motions of the kids who were deep in conversation; the cones of light cast by the twin table lamps; the upward-drifting bubbles in the empty fish tank; even the leaves of the philodendron their father kept on a chipped plate on top of the cabinet, which shouldn't be moving at all. Helen's own blood traversed her veins slowly, as sticky as the cough medicine.

All attention in the room was focused on a girl sitting cross-legged on the floor at Seff's knee, wearing a see-through dress. "I don't know how to do them," the girl said. "I just saw the woman do them for my mom a couple of times in Atlantic City. She was psychic. I'm not psychic."

"Just make something up," Seff urged, holding a deck of oversized cards that Helen had never seen before in her hands. "It'll be fun anyway." Then she seemed, all of a sudden, to notice Helen's presence in the bedroom doorway. "Hey, doll. What are you doing up? You look so tired—are you feeling a little better?"

Helen hated the fake kindness with which Seff always treated her when there were witnesses around. She didn't answer. Some of the partygoers turned their heads in mild interest. "Who's this?" asked the girl in the see-through dress, and Helen waited to see how Seff would lie, but all her sister said was, "This is Helen."

Helen went to the cold box and stood there patiently until the boy blocking it moved. She got herself a glass of juice and sat down on the carpet in the middle of the room to watch what would happen next.

"Done shuffling?" asked the girl in the see-through dress. "Give them here. Good." She began to deal out the strange cards. "This card is you, Seff—all right? This one I'm putting on top is your disguise—it's who you'd like to be. This card is your past, where you came from. Then, this one is your future, where your path will lead if nothing you do changes."

"Slow down," Seff urged. "You're going too fast."

The cards showed people with pale faces in bright, old-fashioned clothing. Animals and fruit. Swords and stars. They pulsed with life, too. The girl continued her litany. "This card is above you. It represents your influences. This card is below you. I don't remember what that means. Sorry! What you must overcome, maybe? It's something like that." She'd laid them out in a cross pattern without pausing to look at what they were. Now, she placed another card to the right of the cross, and piled three more on top. "Um, this card is your house, this one is your lover, this is your riddle, and this is its answer."

"Is that it?" Seff asked.

"Yes. I'm done."

From her spot in the corner, Helen examined the nearest card, the one on the far left of the pattern laid on the carpet, the one that the girl said represented Seff's past. It depicted a woman sitting up in bed, as if she'd woken from a bad dream, with nine swords lined horizontally behind her, all of them pointing the same way. The woman's hands covered her face. "What does that mean?" she blurted out. Seff shot her a look for interrupting, but Helen didn't care right now; she felt impervious to her sister's disapproval.

"I don't know," the girl said. She looked over with kind eyes. "What do you think it means? Maybe you can help me interpret."

"Something bad," Helen answered immediately. Seff glared, as if she'd told everyone a terrible secret, but Helen was sure she was right. "It stands for worry, too many worries."

"Makes sense to me," said the girl with the cards. "It's frightening, isn't it? What about this one?" She pointed at the Answer card, the last on the pile. A man in a turban whirled in place, unconcerned with the ships tossing on a rough sea in the background. In each of his hands, the man held a round loaf of bread. "The Two of Loaves. What do you think?"

"It's a happy card," Helen said. "He's juggling with only two things—easy. One for each hand. So he's not taking on too much."

"Cheating?" the girl suggested.

Helen didn't think that was right. "No. Balance."

"That's good!" one of the boys said. "Make her do more."

"This one," Seff said, won over. "Do this one." Her nail flicked the edge of the card that supposedly represented her future. "It's the prettiest."

"That's because it's a trump card," the owner of the deck said. She pinched a lock of Helen's hair between thumb and forefinger and tugged it gently, an odd, affectionate gesture, then let it fall. "Go ahead, little psychic. Do it."

Helen looked around her at the faces nodding with interest, the light pulsing out of them as they waited for her to speak. Their collective outward breaths heated the small apartment and the music buzzed dully from the player. Her sore throat stung and her head pounded.

She took in the card's details. Words along the bottom read THE CHARIOT, and the picture showed a male figure seated in a sort of throne with two sphinxes in front. The man held a scepter but no reins. Over his shoulders, small buildings stood on a hill, receding into the distance. Several human figures stood on the hill too, watching him drive off.

Helen thought she understood the card's warning. That was Seff in the chariot, leaving the city behind her in ruins. Helen had always suspected just this: that her sister would leave the world they shared. Not here and now, while the music played and the friends crowded close, but someday. Seff would escape.

She found her sister's eyes. "No," she said. "Stay."

Little did she know, she had it backward.

○

"Who is this?" Dwayne asked, eyeing the man Vikram had brought to his doorstep.

"This is Wes," Vikram said. "He's from my Reintegration Education group. I've known him for a while now—he's a good guy." He watched Dwayne take Wes in. A white guy in his forties with a short, reddish beard, Wes wore a short-brimmed trilby—UDP men who hadn't made a conscious effort to break the habit (as Vikram had) were likely to wear hats out of doors—and had tattoos and decorative scarring on his arms. There was also an ominous-looking burn mark, four inches square, on the side of his neck, its edges and corners too precise to be the result of an accident. Wes's right hand drifted up to the mark, half covering it. Then, as if it took effort, he extended it in a handshake instead. "Nice to meet you."

One room at a time until the job was done: that was Dwayne's plan. He would sort everything into piles—charity, sell, curbside, trash—then haul each off to its respective destination, load by load, in the wire cart his grandmother had once used for laundry. Hard work for a man with a full-time job, no car, and no help. "Don't you have any friends?" Vikram had asked, last time. "Neighbors? People from your grandma's church or something?"

Dwayne had covered his sweaty face with the tail of his T-shirt as he spoke: "She kept everybody out of here while she was alive. Seems like she knew what she was doing enough to feel ashamed of the way she lived. How am I gonna disrespect her by giving away her secret?"

Now, Vikram listed Wes's qualifications: his physical strength, his discretion, the fact that he was chronically unemployed and would therefore be willing to work for cheap, for cash under the table. Wes's most important attribute went unspoken: his very strangeness made him seem less intrusive. He definitely hadn't known Dwayne's grandmother, or anyone she knew. Wes was so out of place that he belonged.

"All right. Man, this place is just a UDP magnet, I guess." Dwayne turned back to the house. "I just picked up some Coronas. We can have us a drink and then we'll talk numbers. Vikram, want to stay for a beer?"

The yellow delicate-necked bottles that sat sweating on a pile of newspapers on the counter were some of the only things in the kitchen that looked like they belonged there. Unopened cardboard boxes with red *As Seen on TV* logos obscured the burners of the stove and blocked the cold box. Between those and the dusty magazines in the sink, Vikram guessed the old lady must have eaten takeaway or else lived on frozen dinners warmed up in a microwave that perched on top of a bale of plastic-wrapped toilet-paper rolls. Wes picked up a curious plastic vest with straps that hung down loose, attached by two tubes to a suitcase-sized machine that rested in front of the dishwasher.

"That was my brother's airway clearance system, for his chest wall oscillation therapy," Dwayne said, before anyone could ask. "It would, like, rumble, to clear out mucus clots from Shawn's lungs. He had cystic fibrosis. He's dead now too."

"I'm sorry to hear that," Vikram said. He put his palm on the cap of his beer and twisted, but it stuck fast, and he frowned as the metal cut into the skin of his palm. "Shit."

Dwayne tossed him his keys with a laugh. "Blue thing. It's a bottle opener. Here, let me. Beer bottles you're used to mostly twist-offs?"

Vikram took a swallow without answering. "Have you given any more consideration to what you're going to do with the place? I hate to disillusion you, but Hel's not going to be able to come up with the money you're asking for."

"It's a fair estimate! Got it off a realtor. Besides, I thought she had a hustle going to get some business partners to pay for it."

"She doesn't tell me much, but I don't think that's going so well. What about giving up your apartment and living here yourself? You said you rent in Bushwick now? You could save, moving out here."

"Nah, man. Nothing good's happening in Brownsville. I'm going to be a dad someday soon and I don't want to raise my kid in a neighborhood like this."

Vikram thought again of flowers growing in pots, of the yellow-bricked synagogue and the clumsy, vivid mural on the side of the child-care center that had once been. A small park with a bust of forked-bearded Sleight. "Your . . . Heaven? Is that her name?"

"Eden."

"She's having a baby?"

"No, I don't mean like that. We just planning ahead. Eden earned her degree already, and I'm bar manager now at a bowling alley in Williamsburg—and I book the live music acts." He pulled on his beer. "If I'm going to get more into entertainment, I want to sell this place and get out of here."

"Good for you," Wes spoke up. "I think that's romantic." Dwayne shot him a skeptical look, like he wasn't sure if he'd been slighted, but Wes shook his head. "No, I mean it. I think that's good. Really. It's good to meet someone who's not scared of the future. Don't you think so, Vikram?"

"Sure."

Vikram had a name now, the name of the tenant who rented the storage unit from which the light had come. L. Cristaudo was listed on the rental paperwork he'd pulled from the front desk records. So far, the name had proven amazingly uncommon—no hits when he searched online for addresses in New York, no listing in the rotting old paper telephone directory Sato brought in as a reference text for their unit on Using City Services—but Vikram wasn't out of ideas yet. He'd track the man down—or, if he had to, ambush him. Ask what he knew about the Gate. Make him open it again.

Years ago, in graduate school, Vikram had been plagued by a recurring dream. While his body slept in Boston, his mind returned to suburban New Jersey, over and over. Given the strict personal transport restriction system and the high fuel prices, the coveted areas in his world for middle-class families had been the convenient inner cities; his immigrant parents had finally worked their way into half of a duplex in prosperous downtown Trenton, a new town house off a nice courtyard with a clay pitch for quoits. But that didn't feel like home. Instead, the run-down split-level in Morristown where he'd grown up remained locus to his subconscious mind.

In the dream, which reoccurred at least a dozen times while Vikram struggled to write his dissertation, he rode on the back of someone's motorbike—the type of noisy rig held together with wire and luck that was popular with people his age who hadn't gone to university—as it moved through familiar streets. He could never see the face of the driver of the blazer, but certainly it was another man, a trusted man, with a broad back clothed in denim. Sometimes, Vikram knew it was Keith Chen to whom he clung, sometimes his cousin Sanjay. Other times, the driver was a complete stranger. It didn't matter.

Vikram wrapped his arms around that back as they sped down the Delaware Canal towpath together and bumped their way up onto Pennsylvania Avenue. They took the corners tight as they raced past the Keeper Hall, past the athletic club, past the two food stores and the gambling parlor. Poultry called out to them from backyards and dogs barked, but there were never any people in sight. It was as if everyone in the world had fled in the middle of the night. The doors of houses were closed, the robbery bars locked down over doors and windows. Sometimes in the dream—but not every time—vacant vans and pods scattered their path like obstacles, as if abandoned in some sudden evacuation. In those dreams, the driver skillfully slalomed around them without reducing his speed. Whoever he was, he never spoke to Vikram.

Bastard fuel fumes in his lungs, wind in his blinking eyes, Vikram would have the strong impression that he should know where they were headed—though, upon waking, he was never able to say where that was. He felt a sense of purpose and anticipation. He recognized every house, every food garden, trash heap, and ditch. Every hydrant was the same as it had been, every locked security gate. Each NO TRESPASS sign seemed to be placed just the same as it had been the last time he visited Morristown. This world—this teenage world—was static, preserved in amber. Nothing about it could ever change.

The dream wasn't frightening or threatening in any objective way, but it used to upset him. As he lay there in the bed in his student apartment two states away, it was the memory of that sureness—that it was all still there, just as he had left it, unchangeable and unchanged—that convinced him he could never escape where he'd come from. The past, the future—indistinguishable. At the time, it frightened him.

Now he longed for that return.

○

Seff's Truth deck had origins in the Before that were long and well-documented. For centuries, the leisure classes of Europe had used a deck with four even suits overmatched by a fantastic array of motif cards to play a trick-taking game. As the cards traveled across the continent, the *trionfi* became *triunfo*, *triomphe*, *tromf*, *Trumpfen*, and at last *trump*, a concept used in a variety of games, including the Italian *tarocco*.

At the end of the eighteenth century, enterprising fortunetellers began to use the special trump cards for cartomancy. A hundred and twenty years after that, the esotericist and mystic A. E. Waite commissioned English-born illustrator Pamela Colman Smith to bring to life a version better attuned to the spiritual frequencies he felt were inherent in the deck, which he would call Tarot. Throughout the summer of 1909 and into the fall, Waite described to Smith the images he saw in his head and she realized them, using for reference *tarocchi* like the Sola-Busca deck that was on display that year in the British Museum.

But something went wrong in the first tender months of the vanished epoch of Hel's After; instead of publishing the deck together as they would in this world, the two occultists quarreled, and Smith fled London. She brought the drawings with her to the city of Smyrna, where she showed them to her self-styled dervish lover, an Armenian convert to Islam, born

Hovsep Hovnanian. Yusuf, as he called himself, encouraged her to incorporate Mevlevi Sufi teachings into her next version of the deck; Yusuf imparted to it also a sort of lapsed-Catholic savor. She sketched the cards over and over, refining them. The two of them lived together in material poverty; Smith's journals showed that hunger inspired her decision to turn the European suit of coins into round Turkish bread. When it came to the deck's name, though, West trumped East; Yusuf urged her to call it *turuq*—a Sufi-Arabic word for "divergences"—but Smith preferred the resonance of another source, the libretto to an oratorio by Handel named *Il trionfo del Tempo e della Verità*.

The Triumph of Time and Truth.

So it came about that, when the artist traveled to the United States in 1915 and brought her finished designs to a Cincinnati toy-and-game concern, the printed boxes read *Smith's Truth Divination*. Pamela Colman Smith died a year later, crushed to death by a crowd after a freak theater fire, without making a penny. The cards proved equally unprofitable for her erstwhile cocreator; despite Waite's contributions, his pamphlet *A Key to Divining the Tarot* did not distinguish itself from the several unauthorized guides to the Truth deck written by other former members of his numinous order.

Not until decades later would Hel's father's postwar generation become fascinated by sibylic cards. Their children would buy copies of the Smith deck. They would create their own versions with images culled from various faith traditions and artistic styles, but always aping Smith's designs. (These clones were the distant cousins of the many Rider-Waite Tarots of this world.) Some, like Seff, would become true believers.

At last, Time and Truth emerged into the mainstream, victorious.

○

Hel stared down at the phone in her hand. The screen displayed the hotel's website: *Contact us*. The number uncalled. In her bones she felt a fitful disquiet. A warning. She wanted divine intervention, the God of Asyl's cult or the God of the Bible Numericists here or the God of the Keepers of the Covenant, that extinct sect from her world. Someone who could see all the possibilities from a distance and judge, for better or worse. All of it laid out like cards on a blanket, someone who could save them. A higher power to intervene inside the Beaverbrook Nuclear Power Plant that day in Poughkeepsie. To make the technicians among the banks of ordinators more attentive, to force them to heed the warnings. A grid controller who would shut down the reactors safely. Or a better, earlier intervention—security personnel placed up on the catwalk to tackle the saboteurs, to stab them or hit them or shoot them. A police detail tipped off, ready to pull the convoy off the highway before the saboteurs arrived at the targets. Teachers to admonish them, to take away the propaganda-laced black market sims they'd played. Mothers to love them more as children. Murderers to kill all their mothers.

Someone on the shore with Sleight, telling him no. Someone at the airship terminal with Hel as she hugged her son for the last time. Telling her yes, telling her to hold him tight. Someone who could warn her, at least, not to let the book out of her sight.

She tapped the screen to initiate the call and rolled onto her back on the bed.

There is no one else, she admonished herself. No High Priestess or Magician or Heirophant to order things.

There is no one but you and your own determination.

"Hello," she said. "Do you have a lost and found?"

CHAPTER EIGHT

Vikram took the fire stairs straight up. He could do it in the dark; he'd counted out the steps. On three, he eased open the door and held his breath before stepping forward as quietly as possible.

He halted around the corner from the Cristaudo unit and sank silently to the floor, pulled his knees to his chest, and settled in. Here he was again, waiting it out, just as he'd done all those years ago in the burned-out ward with Keith and the others—his friends, all dead now. All ghosts. This time, Vikram felt no fear, only a sense of the inevitable. This L. Cristaudo would come. He might not call open the Gate until he was sure he was alone, but he would come tonight.

After some time had passed—minutes? half an hour?—Vikram sensed a modulation in the absolute darkness. Granted, a little light came through from the parking lot, prying through the cracks around the edges of the badly sealed windows, and his eyes were adjusting. But even taking into account those factors, didn't the corridor seem less black than it should? He wasn't sure. He eased himself to his knees, then stood. He held the dark flashlight in front of his body.

Twenty paces to the end of the hallway, the ninety-degree turn.

And around the corner, he saw it, the source of the faint brightness. A glowing cobalt trapezoid halfway down the corridor. In his shock, he took a moment to realize what that meant. An open doorway, the same unit as before. The half-open door partly obscured light that emitted from inside.

He ran.

He ran toward the light. As he drew level with the unit, a shadow moved toward him from within and his heart caught in his chest and his fingers clenched around the flashlight as the woman—the shadow-shape was a woman—straightened to her full height.

"I'm so sorry," she said. "I must have mistimed it."

She was an old lady with a sallow, unhealthy look to her un-wrinkled face and straight gray hair. Vikram lowered his make-shift weapon, which he'd lifted above his head. He was glad she hadn't stepped closer or he might have brained her.

"Where did it go?" he said, helplessly.

For, other than the persistent blue glow, there was no sign of the Gate in the empty unit. He saw blank walls and part of a boarded-up window, the door, which opened in. No stuff in there but a rolled-up sleeping bag; nothing stored. The woman blocked the doorway. "If you'll excuse me," she said. "This is my space. Private. I've had it since the first of August. Everything's in order."

Vikram got up on his toes, trying to peer over her shoulder into the unit. Was there something on the floor next to the bedding?

She twisted her body, blocking his view. "I'm not stealing anything. I know it's your job to guard this place or what have you, but I have the right to be here. It's what I pay for. You can check the records—I'm Lida, Lida Cristaudo."

"L. Cristaudo."

"That's right. Will you take a step back?"

Vikram got out of the way and Lida followed him into the hallway. She moved quickly for someone who looked so ill, but as she exited the unit, she couldn't help giving him a brief glimpse of the machine that lay on the floor in the very center. It was palm-sized and had a portable, utilitarian look, like a small vid recorder or a Geiger counter. Coming from its pinhole, a shaft of pure Calvary blue. "What is that?"

Lida pulled shut the door. "Don't you worry about it." She produced a key from her pocket that fit in the lock and turned it, sealing the storage space. "I'll come with you. You can escort me out."

Was she from his world? Had she just come through, somehow? Only the other side had the tech. Hoping against hope, he imagined people alive there, a new passage opening. "I want to know what you were doing."

"What I do in the unit I rent is my own business."

"I'm a UDP too."

She stopped, gave him a critical look. "Are you."

"Entry Group 73-04. And you? What's your entry designation?"

"I don't have one."

Vikram's heart fluttered. "You survived the attacks. You've come here to help us back."

"Oh, no. No, I'm sorry. I've been here longer than you. I was their canary in the mine shaft, you see. I used the Gate two days before the first lot. Mornay sent me through during the panic."

"Mornay?"

"Dr. Mornay at Gaynor Tech. She was a genius of our field. We all thought it wouldn't work, but Mornay said she'd done it before with a prototype. Sent someone through—a graduate student. Only she had no way to know if Ree survived. So I volunteered to test the setup she'd rigged at Calvary with a vital signs monitor wired to a transmitter. The cemetery looked the same from the other side, though I couldn't see the Gate or my colleagues or anyone at all. If it hadn't been for that, I wouldn't have believed I'd gone anywhere at all."

"You're making this up," Vikram said, remembering the crowds that had greeted his own arrival.

Cristaudo pretended not to hear him. "I found my way to a road, where I saw those blocky passenger pods that people drive here. That's when I started to have an idea of what I was in for. I flagged one down and got a ride to a police station house. It was early morning, so there was no one in there but some hooligans, waiting for a friend to be released from a drunk-and-disorderly."

Vikram steered her toward the elevator and pushed the call button. He got his card ready to swipe them in. "Where was this?"

"Elmhurst, I think, or farther west," Cristaudo answered without missing a beat. "I'd been walking away from the river."

It struck Vikram that if she were a liar, she was that most effective type, the kind who can put herself under her own spell.

"I told the desk sergeant my story; I'd thought he would be amazed, but he just had me sit down on the bench and wait. One of the hooligans called me 'ma'am' and offered me a packet of snack chips. I remember the flavor, which seemed very exotic to me then. Cool Ranch. And the posters on the walls." The old woman rubbed a palm against the cement-block corridor, as if smoothing a notice only she could see. "One offered a reward to citizens who gave information that led to the conviction of any criminal who'd shot a police officer. I asked myself: Where would an ordinary person get a *gun*? And the reward seemed so slight, as if the printer had skipped a zero and misplaced a comma—off by an order of magnitude."

Vikram remembered marveling at that too, when he'd first arrived. But then the ding of the elevator reminded him what he was supposed to be doing. "I know you've been in here before," he said. "You sneak in late at night."

"I come before you close. I installed a duplicate lock that works from inside. Tonight, I mistimed your rounds. You were supposed to have passed by and gone already."

"I thought it was the Gate I was seeing," he admitted, a little sheepish. "Your device."

"It emits a signal."

"A signal for what?"

The elevator arrived at the ground floor. He let her step out first.

"Did you know this is the site of Gaynor Institute of Technology?" she asked.

"I never thought about it."

"It is. My office and Mornay's—they were in the Sciences building. Just where the parking lot is, as far as I can calculate. There should be a direct sight line. I'm following the protocol."

Two days before the first evacuation, she'd said. She was claiming to have passed through the Gate on the very same day of the plant attacks! If this were true, it was the secret history of a heroic last stand. Hel would say someone should preserve it, ask questions, write it all down.

"What protocol? What did they want you to do?"

"I was to signal to Dr. Mornay's team. To let them know I hadn't had a stroke or an aneurysm and died on the spot."

"Did they get it?"

"Well, I would assume so," Cristaudo said, drawing herself up straighter. "After all, the evac rolled on. The first hundred people came through, all at once. Would Mornay have risked their lives, without my transmission?"

"You don't think so?" The old woman had more faith in the humanity of the evacuation's designers than Vikram had. "And what were you supposed to do after that?"

"We never really worked that out, amid all the panicked planning. Warn the authorities here, I suppose. And I tried. I remember at the station house, a female officer took me into a little room and gave me coffee in a white cup made of foam. I told her all the same things I'd told the sergeant."

"Did she listen?"

"She tried to talk me into checking myself into the psychiatric ward at Elmhurst Hospital Center. She was very polite in the way she went about it, and when I refused, she told me I would have to go home to the address I'd given them when I signed their book. I didn't know yet that my apartment building had been torn down or never built."

"They just let you leave?"

"The female officer and her partner walked me to the door, and even the hooligans waved good-bye. I walked out into the cold."

"So, you were never debriefed?"

"Oh, I was. I turned myself in when the rest of you came through. They detained me at the National Tennis Center."

Vikram winced; he'd heard about rough interrogations at the Flushing Meadows site where all UDPs deemed to be important were brought.

"I wanted to do my duty," Cristaudo said. "But I never brought them the transmitter. I'd hid it, and as soon as I got out, I took it back to Calvary. Nothing. No response. I tried for almost two years before it occurred to me that I should be more strategic. The worlds correspond perfectly. Who would be in that spot—in a cemetery—on the other end in the middle of the night? Now, I'm trying here at Gaynor instead. After I signal, I just sleep in my storage room till open hours." Trailing behind Vikram through the reception area, Cristaudo stopped to point. "The fabrications lab was just about there. Always someone in the lab, working late."

"Have you ever thought that maybe everyone there might be . . ." He hesitated, unwilling to finish the thought. "That it might be sort of futile, after all this time?"

"Weren't you the one who thought I was operating the Gate, ten minutes ago? Didn't you hope to go back?"

Kabir had explained the Schrödinger's cat thought experiment—the cat that could be living and dead at the same time. It worked only while the box stayed closed. Was Vikram the kind of person who would lift the lid? For Hel he would. Even if it meant he would lose her.

He keyed in his passcode and the front door buzzed. Cristaudo followed him out into the parking lot through the dappled halogens but then stopped, craning her head to look up at the building looming above them. There—faint blue lines from whatever it was that she'd left running in the room. They watched together as the light blinked out. Darkness.

"I think about the time I spent waiting to talk to a stick, back when I was not sure what would happen next. That fragile hour. When my colleagues on the other side saw me walk through, they witnessed an escape. They must have thought they'd saved the world, and I certainly thought so too. Everything still seemed possible while I sat on the bench in the station house. I still thought they would find me. I didn't know anything about this world—the ways it was different, or the ways it was the same. The ways it would disappoint me." Cristaudo took Vikram's arm. "The only sensible conclusion," she said, "is that they're all dead. Think about all that radiation. Poughkeepsie's not very far, after all. And the likely escalation, the retaliation . . . but even if they're not dead, it's been three years. The Gate will never open up again. Not for us."

"What was that, then, just now? The signal—what's it for?"

"It's just the visible portion of the electromagnetic spectrum. A pyre, maybe. A votive. I don't know."

"OK," Vikram said, feeling gutted.

"Maybe it's silly, but I'm going to keep trying."

O

Hel had no intention of swimming, but the only way into the pool was through the ladies' locker room. Women clutched at their towels as she passed by the rows of lockers, their backs turned, their hands covering breasts and genitalia in the brief interludes between street clothes and bathing suits, their eyes deliberately averted from one another. The immodest cut of the typical two-piece bathing suit and the confident nudity on display on billboards and in magazine ads belied women's actual reluctance to be seen by each other naked, even those who were friends or mother and daughter. If Hel were an anthropologist, she'd have a lot to say about what this signified about the culture.

But no one would want to hear about that either.

The pool area itself smelled tangy with chemicals. Oliveira was already here swimming laps. His stroke—a fierce, clumsy face-out-of-the-water crawl—moved him through the water with surprising proficiency. When he noticed her, he cut across lanes to the ladder, gripping the metal bars deftly with his pincers, levering his body out of the water.

He wore nothing but a pair of baggy trunks and a foam flotation belt, and she found her eyes drawn to the human frailty his bathing clothes revealed—not just his mutilated and reformed arms but his skinny bowed legs, his barrel chest, the white hairs that grew around his liver-colored nipples.

She wished that Oliveira had invited her to his apartment instead of suggesting they meet at his health club. In his home, which she had never seen, she would not feel so out of place. There, she would know the rules and understand the eccentricities. Things looked a certain way; it was a shared cultural taste developed over a century. UDPs typically loved rugs, carpets, and patterned linoleum—the bare, shiny hardwood floors fetishized here by the rich were almost unknown—and a visitor knew she would have to remove her shoes upon walking through the door. UDP families preferred shelves for everything over end tables. Any room without windows would be equipped with square, wall-mounted light banks to simulate natural light. (These were harder to find here, but people had them. A specialty photography store in Lansing, Michigan, in consultation with a UDP electrician, had even begun to produce them for mail order.) Though etiquette did not dictate that refreshment necessarily be offered, a visitor always knew that if she happened to stop by when the inhabitants were eating or drinking, her hosts would invite her to partake. Hel missed all of this—the predictability, the ritualized coziness. Here she stood, fully clothed by the edge of the pool, which echoed with the shouts of the children's swim class going on in the shallow end, the splashing of the lane swimmers, the lifeguards' talk, all of it overlooked, through a layer of glass, by exercisers stretching their limbs on torturous-looking machines in the next room, and she felt as terribly exposed as she ever had.

Oliveira snagged a white towel from the set of bleachers where he'd left it folded and draped it around his shoulders like a cape. "What can I do for you, my dear?"

"Do you know Ayanna Donaldson personally?"

"Not really, no. Why do you ask?"

Could she trust him? She'd tried the hotel, the one on top of the footprint of Palast Park, where the fundraiser had been held. A deferential front desk clerk put her on hold to check the lost and found and then connected her: first to the Events Manager and then to the Head of Hotel Security and then finally to the member of the janitorial staff who'd led cleanup that night.

No one remembered her book.

"Carlos, tell me something. Why do you think I should go back to work? As a doctor, I mean. Because work is good for people generally? Or are you thinking of me in particular? Or is it because of the kind of work I'm trained for? Like, I owe it to humanity to use my medical skills to heal others?"

Or was it, she wondered, because *surgeon* reflected better on UDPs as a group than *bum*?

"I'm not going to scold you today."

"Good," she said. "You shouldn't."

"I often consider the fact that as UDPs, each of us has been rent from our social fabric. It's not just our world that is gone but our individual parents, our children . . ." He looked at her keenly. "Also our mentors and friends. Everyone we might once have wanted to impress. Anyone we might try especially hard not to disappoint."

"I'm not your daughter."

He sat on the aluminum bleachers. He reached for a kickboard, setting it across his bony knees. He smoothed his arms across its surface. "No. You're not. Tell me how I can help you."

"Ayanna Donaldson stole something from me. I don't know how to get it back. I confronted her, but she denies it."

"What was it that she took?"

The Pyronauts.

If she spoke the title aloud, how precious his recognition would be to her. Yet a part of her didn't want him to know the specifics. "An important cultural artifact," she said instead, watching his expression. Where did his loyalty lie? Would he believe her at all? "I showed it to Donaldson at that party, and she took it from me—took it from my hands, goddamn it— and acted like she wanted to be involved, but now she won't answer my calls. And she says she doesn't have it, and I have no proof of any of it." She couldn't keep the words, her frustration, from spilling out.

"You feel she's deceiving you."

"Yes."

"And yet no one knows what the item is. Its very rareness prevents widespread recognition of its value. This isn't the Rosetta Stone. It's not the Elgin Marbles."

"Right," Hel said. "That's it—the problem—exactly."

"Well, what do you think I can do about it?"

"I don't know. I don't know what to do. That's why I came—"

"No, I'm really asking: What do you want me to do? Shall I accuse her? Expose her? Even if I believed you, do you think I have any real power in this world? To the extent that I have accrued a sort of capital, why would I spend it on this? You must look at it the way everyone else is going to. Disgruntled, unemployed trauma victim, missing some property that may never have existed at all."

"You're saying you don't believe me?"

"On the contrary, my dear. Museums steal from the vulnerable. They always have. You're Greece in this situation. You're Egypt."

His warm brown eyes, nested in kindly wrinkles.

"You do believe me. But you won't do anything for me."

"I'm not your father. Even if I were. I have to behave myself."

She remembered her first trip on a commercial airship, years ago, when she was a medical resident. She'd sat in the back row, just in front of the vending machines, crowded next to an elderly couple who looked far too elegant for third class. Midflight, somewhere over the Great Plains, turbulence took hold of the ship, shook it like a toy in the sticky grip of a child. Though the captain kept his voice soothingly routine over the communications system as he reminded passengers to return to their assigned seats and put on their harnesses, Hel felt herself becoming upset. Her sister had warned her, half joking, to do her own Truth reading before the trip to see if transcontinental travel was auspicious, and Hel had refused and now here she was, unprotected, without forewarning of her own demise.

This metal tube is going to crash, she'd said to herself. It is going to break in half.

The airship had bucked, shuddered. The aisle lights dimmed. She became possessed of the conviction, all at once, that she was seeing herself and her seatmates from the outside, looking down at them the way an outsider would observe them, God or an alien or the person dealing out the cards.

Below her, she saw the girl with the dark hair in the aisle seat, noticed how she curled her fingers around the buckle of her harness over her heart. Overwatched, too, the silvery lady in the window seat, how she slid down the shade and closed her eyes. Those paper-thin lids, that fragile skin dusted with powder. Those fretful shallow breaths, quicker now, distractingly audible. She saw the man, the lady's husband, seated in between, reach for his wife's hand. He took it in both of his.

She saw that the girl noticed this gesture of comfort and that she was touched by it.

Then, gripping his wife's hand tightly, the man turned her wrist. He rotated it, angling her watch so that he could read its face. Gentle movements. Checking the time.

There was no mercy, she realized, floating outside herself. There could be no kindness for its own sake.

Hel found she had that same floating sensation now. She saw the pool, big and square and reeking, strangers laboring in their separate lanes. She saw the old man get up from the aluminum bleachers with his kickboard and walk five steps to the edge of the tile. She saw him lower himself awkwardly to his knees, and then swing one leg and then the other around, careful not to put too much weight on the ends of his poor, shortened arms. There he sat on the lip of the pool, his feet dangling. She saw the woman—herself—alone on the bleachers now, saw her disordered hair, the bruised, stupid look on her face. Saw herself take the damp towel in her hands and wring it.

Without turning around, the man spoke. "I have to behave myself," he said, "behave the way they expect me to. I have to be unfailingly polite, dignified—maintain that image. I can be angry only at specially chosen times, and only in response to egregious injustices against my people. I have to, or I'll give it all away."

Hel saw the woman drop the towel and follow him to the pool. She saw that woman place a booted foot between the man's shoulder blades and shove, pushing him right over the edge and into the water with a messy splash.

She saw the young lifeguard sit up in his high chair, suddenly alert.

She didn't care. How fearless of consequences she'd become. How shameless. Who did that? What kind of a person did that to a cripple?

She nudged Oliveira's kickboard into the pool after him. "You fucking gootch. You traitor."

○

The interloper came over the ashy ridge one day while Asyl and John Gund patrolled. When they spotted the figure in the distance, they stopped walking to watch his approach; a man, moving easily, unencumbered by a protective suit—he wore a cloth mask tied over his nose and mouth and a ragged jacket and pants the color of the wasteland around them, and shoes, and that was all. To the pyronauts, it was inconceivable that he had not been sickened by the fumes from burned stubble and dying plants all around them, but he did not seem to exhibit any of the typical respiratory symptoms of those few stubborn folk they'd encountered in the past who insisted on living outside the safety of the bunkers. Still, they hailed the stranger at twenty paces to demand that he stop, and stop he did, once he saw John Gund's sidearm leveled at him. He stopped and laughed at them.

He told them his name was Aitch. (Vikram said that he had once written and attempted to publish an entire scholarly paper on the possibility that John Gund had misunderstood the stranger, that he was actually going by an initial, H. What, then, might the H have stood for? Heaven—or hell? Hiram, the name of Sleight's uncle, who'd succumbed to the dreaded battle flu? The slang term for heroin, a vice in which certain biographers believed Sleight occasionally to have indulged? The H train that rumbled on its elevated tracks down New Lots Avenue two blocks from the cottage in Brownsville where he wrote the book?)

Aitch lingered, conversing with the pyronauts. He was a strongly built young man with a ruddy, untroubled countenance and broad shoulders. Asyl, a member of a postapocalyptic Christian sect whose adherents believed that they had each been personally pulled from the pit by the hands of God, maintained perpetual celibacy as penance. But surely, John Gund thought to himself, she must notice how handsome the stranger was.

John Gund ordered Aitch to find shelter; he was in violation of the quarantine laws and anyway, no man could last long out in the Neverlands. Aitch disagreed. He'd been born in the Never, he said, and there were plenty of others like him who survived off the bounty of these abandoned lands and had never been sick a day in their lives. Still, when the stranger looked at Asyl, taking in her features through the smeared crystal of the faceplate of her suit, he agreed to come with them to the nearest settlement.

The three of them walked all day together through the ashy fields of former farmland, and Aitch explained about the quick-developing shoots and roots his mother had taught him to find and harvest out in the wastes before the periodic patrols arrived to test and burn. At first, it seemed to John Gund that Aitch was watching Asyl too attentively as he spoke, directing all of his remarks to Asyl in a disconcerting manner. It made him feel itchy. Yet as soon as John Gund developed this opinion, Aitch abruptly turned his attention.

He began asking pointed questions of John Gund instead, questions about his past before the aliens' advent. These, John Gund found even more uncomfortable. Asyl was well attuned to those topics he preferred not to discuss, but this stranger lacked her sensitivity. Though John Gund remained convinced of the necessity of his protective gear out in the poisonous open of the wastes, he felt foolish addressing this man whose only barriers against it were fragile cloth and skin.

They walked together as the shadows lengthened, as the silhouette of the skyline of the abandoned city in the distance blurred and grew indistinguishable. When they reached the outskirts, it was time to set up camp. Asyl argued that it would be cruel to leave Aitch at the mercy of the wind. At her insistence, the stranger joined them in their tent. As usual, once the seal was set, Asyl removed her suit, and John Gund did not like the way that the stranger watched her then in her modest but clinging undergarments. She touched the man's face mask, and he showed her how it was constructed, how he'd cut a salvaged pillowcase into a shape that would cover the lower part of his face, fitting over his short beard. "It's not one of those fancy filters, like what you've got," Aitch said with a grin, "but it's lighter to wear and it keeps the dust out well enough."

John Gund himself elected to sleep in full protective gear that night, and he kept his flame pistol close to hand.

In order to fit into the two-man tent, they arranged themselves head to foot to head, like the rationed sardines in tins back in the stores of some of the more frugal communities the pyronauts had visited. John Gund couldn't sleep for a long time. He watched, over the lump Asyl's upward-pointing toes made in the blanket, the other man's face—eyes scrunched up and lips unselfconsciously parted, baby-like in sleep. Finally, John Gund's vigilance and worry slipped away as he drifted off.

In the morning, Aitch was gone.

INTERVIEW TRANSCRIPT:
MICAH LEE, AGE 24, BROOKLYN

When I was called, I wasn't supposed to answer. Keepers don't participate in any kind of gambling, no matter what the stakes, because the Commentaries prohibit the casting of lots. So when my number got called in the evac lottery, that was the final break. Other members of my church felt they had nothing to fear from the plant meltdowns and missile strikes. They were counting on a continued life in heaven, so they said no. I said yes.

In my world, the Keepers of the Covenant was the fastest-growing Christian denomination on the planet. Now, I'm the last Keeper there is, if you can still call me one, after my heresy.

I was already lost to them, way before the evac. I remember it to the day. I just didn't want to admit it.

Here's how it happened. I was about to finalize my engagement to marry this girl. And when I say girl, I mean it. She was fourteen years old. The official date of our union was two years away still, so that she would be legal in the state of New York by our wedding night, but she was set aside for me and I had paid the bride price agreed on by our parents. I knew her name was Hannah, but I hadn't even seen a picture.

My uncle and I took a velocab to meet her at the Keeper Hall in Midwood where her family were congregants. Having fixed the match, my uncle was extremely pleased with himself. He kept leaning back to make conversation with the driver. I scrambled out of the velocab as soon as we arrived and stood on the stone steps of the hall—an old one that used to be a Methodist church. I'm trying to remember how I felt then. Excited, I think.

After a minute, my uncle took my arm and led me inside, where Hannah's oldest sister was waiting to bring us to the classroom next to the sacristy, where Hannah waited. On Tuesdays after school, she volunteered in the child-care center there.

Though I tried not to look at Hannah's sister's body, I couldn't help noticing that her bottom was round and shapely. Was it a family trait? Her attractiveness filled me with nervous anticipation. It seemed to take a decade to walk down that corridor with the music of the service leaking right through the floor, the faithful singing at their worship, and as we drew closer, I could hear kids calling out too, shrill voices laughing.

The sister indicated the classroom door. I stepped near. A narrow window allowed me to see inside. There was a group of lower-form children sitting on the rug, and kneeling in the middle was Hannah. My uncle, crowded next to me, drew in an approving breath.

The first thing I noticed about her was how serene she appeared. Her eyes were almost shut; her lips moved faintly as she talked to her charges. She had very black hair, like her sister, and though it was twisted up into a knot at the nape of her neck, I could see how heavy and full it was. I imagined it unpinned, spilling over shoulders and breasts in the conjugal moment the two of us would someday share.

Yes, she was beautiful.

I looked more closely down at Hannah's hands. Small and delicate. In each one, she held a figurine shaped like a giraffe, one just a little taller than the other. She made the two giraffes waltz up a ramp built of plastic blocks toward a cardboard box meant to represent, no doubt, the Ark. Her students also clutched toys. Animals from Africa, mostly—elephants and antelopes and lions—all part of the same cast-resin set as the giraffes. I also saw two mismatched toy bears, a stuffed rabbit, and a wooly dog. The kids copied Hannah, marching their own animals up the drawbridge as she smiled at them with delight.

And then it hit me. She wasn't teaching these children. She was playing with them.

I go to Reintegration Education. I go to Adjustment Counseling. I go to therapy. I have a profile on a nondenominational Christian dating website, and though I've enjoyed messaging back and forth with some women on there, I don't go on dates. When I see a Bible Numericist on a street corner, preaching about how UDPs are God's chosen, I cross to the other side.

Hannah's probably dead now, wherever she is. There would have been riots and food shortages after we left. Experts predict that everyone in the tri-state area would have been sickened by the radiation. There may have been more bombs, too, after the plants. So Hannah's dead, with the rest of our people.

"Knock," the sister urged me, that day in the hall, but I didn't need to. Hannah saw us through the window. She stood up to greet me, smoothing her skirt and smiling. A smile for her future husband; not the same smile from a minute before. An expression she'd learned to make.

You could see it as God's will. But that only would make sense if I'd turned away. If I'd told our families I wouldn't. I didn't do that. I just went along. Like she did.

I think of the animals. Two of a kind, two by two, or one at a time like the toy rabbit, the dog. It doesn't matter. I tell myself it's all right that I'm not sad all the time. No one can be sad all the time.

No one on the Ark had regrets.

CHAPTER NINE

Wes and Dwayne, who'd come to some kind of a financial understanding in the past week, had excavated enough junk from in front of the kitchen door in the cottage that it could be opened for the first time in a decade. The three men stood on the rotten boards of the back porch and looked out over a three-foot drop onto a rubble-strewn patch of dirt seeded with fragments of broken glass that sparkled in the midmorning light. "Pretty ugly back here," Dwayne said.

Vikram handed him one of the sandwiches he'd brought from the deli around the corner. "I don't know how long I can stay today." His sleep hadn't been good since the encounter with Cristaudo in the warehouse, and he had priorities he ought to keep in mind that were more important to him than Dwayne's cleanup efforts. Like keeping his job. Like maintaining his relationship—not that Hel seemed to care much when he told her how he spent his days.

Wes jumped down into the yard. "Hey, it's a lot of space for New York, though, right? It's not so bad. You could get a little picnic table or something, if you wanted. Or grow stuff back here. You know, basil, tomato plants . . ."

"Yeah," Dwayne said, "I think my grandma's mama had a garden here, back in the day. World War II. Dig for victory."

"How long has this house been in your family, anyway?" Vikram had never before considered the question of how Sleight came to live on this particular street in Brownsville. Was some long-ago Sealy this white man's landlord? Had Sleight bought it from some alternate-world progenitor of Dwayne's? He couldn't figure it out.

Dwayne shrugged off the question. "Got to look into that."

"I like how much meat they put on," said Wes. "They're serious about this. It's two inches thick."

"It is good," Vikram agreed, looking down at the sliced turkey piled on the roll he held in his hand. He squeezed gently and extra mayonnaise and shredded lettuce splattered between his shoes.

"Other than my fiancé's friends, I mostly just hang out with other UDPs," Wes said. "It's been cool to see what you guys keep in your houses."

Dwayne raised his hands, palms out. "Please, don't judge us all by my grandma."

"No, I didn't mean—I was only trying to say, the gadgets, the brand names, the variety. Going through it, I don't know. It's like a whole separate twentieth century."

"That is literally what it is," Vikram said, staring across the gap between the cottage and the building next door. The first-floor apartment had old curtains made from a fabric with a repeating pattern of Barack Obama's head—he recognized Obama from their Recent History unit in Reintegration Education—and the words *President of the USA*.

"It seems ordinary to you, but it's fun for us," Wes said.

"Guess it must be pretty crazy," Dwayne said. "I never thought about all the, like, microscopic shit that's different. But I guess I know what you mean, because to me, anything you tell me about your lives is mad interesting. Y'all got interesting stories."

"Everyone has an interesting story," Vikram said. The blue parts of the fabric had faded quicker than the red, so the stripes behind the little Obamas had lasted better than the vanishing stars. So specific, that pattern, and, in its way, beautiful, and Dwayne's dead grandmother had probably stared at it every day for the last ten years. He thought about all the things he knew about, all the minutiae he would take to his grave.

Dwayne went back inside. "Tell me a UDP thing," he called from the kitchen. "Something all y'all know that none of us do."

Wes nudged Vikram. "I'm going to tell him about Dop Peters."

He couldn't help but play along. "You can't tell Dwayne about that. It's a secret."

"Did you hear that, Dwayne? I'm revealing our alien secrets. Dop Peters. He's this middle-aged pop musician, OK, with one self-released album out and some very homemade-looking videos online. But those videos have thirty, forty thousand views each. Kind of weird, right?"

"I've never heard of him," Dwayne said.

"Yeah. That's because he's a UDP and other UDPs are responsible for every single hit. Every view and every share. It's all us."

"I've made my contribution," Vikram said. "A couple hundred times." He brought his crumpled sandwich paper inside and tossed it toward the corner where they'd been piling the most irredeemable of Dwayne's grandmother's junk.

Dwayne was on all fours now, scrubbing at the grubby linoleum with a brush. "I don't get it. What's the joke?"

"All the so-called originals he plays were actually massive hits," Vikram told him. "Back in the '60s, in our world. They were written and performed by this huge band, Baccarat. It's like if someone here tried to pass off a Beatles song as their own."

"And," said Wes, joining them inside, "I guarantee that every single UDP who has ever heard him play knows it. But old Dop there takes credit for writing the songs himself. I even heard him on a podcast bragging about his golden voice and his creative process, how the words to the songs just come to him. Believe me, it's hilarious."

Dwayne sat back on his heels. "You know what this reminds me of? That famous time-travel paradox. You're a huge Beethoven fan—"

"A Beethoven fan? Really?"

"Yeah, Wes. Why not? Go with it. You're this huge Beethoven fan so you invent a time machine and you go back to Vienna in the 1700s, right? You want to find the big man himself and get his autograph, so you take all of his CDs with you. What do you all call CDs?"

"We didn't have CDs," Vikram said. "We went directly from reels to sixers."

"Fine. Whatever. So you've got his sixers, then—something physical, so he can sign them. But when you get there,

Beethoven didn't write those symphonies yet. You play the music for him on your portable sixer player or whatever it's called"—here, Dwayne held up his hand to stave off possible interruption—"I don't care; it's useless knowledge. Anyway, you play the music for Beethoven, hoping to jog his memory, and he's like, 'Whoa, this some pretty good stuff. I've gotta jot this down,' and he takes notes and he writes the symphony later and he publishes it and the orchestra performs it and it gets famous and goes down in history."

"OK," Wes said slowly. "And?"

"So who wrote the symphony? If Beethoven couldn't—not until he heard someone else playing it—who is the author?"

"Easy," Vikram answered. "Dop Peters."

Wes gave him a high five.

Dwayne picked up his brush again. "I guess I just don't get it. How come no one exposes him? Y'all are letting him get away with that? Why?"

"I downloaded all his stuff," Vikram said. "Legally. I paid for it, so Dop would get his cut. I love Baccarat. Better that joker's versions than nothing. And if he does another album, I'll buy that one too, right on the day it comes out." That word, the one Hel had shown him in a newspaper article: *Ostalgie*.

Wes took his time responding. He stood in the doorway, looking out the back door at the barren, gardenless yard, the tenements ranged around it on every side. "I don't have a golden voice," he said, at last. "I don't have a plan, I don't have a game. Why would I shit on someone else's?"

After that, subdued, all three of them went back to work. Wes and Dwayne hauled the final loads out of the kitchen while Vikram took on the cramped downstairs half bath alone. By now, the variety and incongruity of the items stored in the rooms no longer surprised him. This was where Dwayne's grandmother, Gloria Washington Defoe, had seen fit to keep her financial papers and junk mail. The pink porcelain bathroom furnishings swam knee-deep in outdated documents, some filed haphazardly in cardboard boxes bursting at the corners, some simply scattered in a heavy thatch of loose paper. The late addressee had apparently removed every piece of mail, examined it, then refolded and inserted it back into its neatly slit envelope. After Vikram had hauled out six black trash bags for Dwayne to sort through or shred—fifteen years of utility bills and bank statements and credit card offers, yellowed with age—the muscles in his back felt pleasantly sore and the grimy hexagonal tiles of the floor showed at last.

The sight made him feel a way that was hard to categorize. As tired as he was from his night shift, from the shock of the encounter with the old woman, from having to deal with a version of Hel who would barely speak to him, he found the rediscovery invigorating. Sleight's tiles, perfect puzzle pieces. One out of every seven black, like specks of pepper floating in milk, like flea shit on a white dog, like the dark pistils of strange, pale-petaled flowers. He remembered them now, a passive memory he'd have never been able to unearth without renewing his acquaintance with the house.

A detail lost and found: the fact that years ago, he, Vikram, had planted his feet wide on this floor, unzipped his trousers, and pissed in this very bathroom.

And years before that, Sleight had.

Vikram donned gloves. He sprinkled powdered cleanser—
its smell and color as familiar to him as its brand name was
strange—in the sink and found an ancient plastic brush hidden
behind the toilet to scrub out the bowl. He sprayed down the
mirror with vinegar and used a wad of newspaper taken from
one of the stacks dating from the mid-'70s that almost blocked
the stairs to scour its surface.

As he pressed against the glass, a compartment opened up.
A medicine cabinet, spring-loaded and hidden for years. So
well concealed that old Mrs. Defoe seemed to have forgotten
to clutter it.

He touched the items inside. A bottle of iodine. A bottle of
rubbing alcohol. A rusty pair of scissors and a roll of gauze. A
cardboard book of matches from somewhere called the Califone Hotel. A tortoiseshell comb set. A few loose safety pins. A
bottle of aspirin. Everything belonged; everything looked old.
He had to remind himself that these were not relics. They were
just things everyone who'd ever lived here had forgotten about.

Old. Old enough, but not his. Not Sleight's. An alternate
history of sickness and hurts.

○

Hel learned how to follow on foot from the internet. In half
an hour of research, she picked up useful tips about everything
from the optimal distance to maintain to the correct way to
use windows, car mirrors, and other reflective surfaces. She in-
formed herself about the possible legal penalties for recording
video and audio in various states without a subject's permission.

It wasn't wise to hang around the Domino Sugar complex anymore; the employees at MoMT and at the apartment leasing office all knew her by sight. Besides, everything about the place—the half-preserved buildings, the intangible lingering memory-smell of molasses—reminded her of her failures, her humiliation. Pinch-faced Klay, all 110 pounds of her, the world's smallest enforcer. Klay, who would never understand, daring to show her sympathy.

One of the articles she read specifically recommended against black clothing for surveillance missions, suggesting that the best way to blend in with a crowd was to wear neutrals. That morning, she'd chosen a large gray sweatshirt that belonged to Vikram for her disguise, tied her hair back under a navy-blue beanie, and donned the largest pair of shades she could find. Now she lurked among a mixed group of tourists, Upper East Siders, and students with sketch pads on the sidewalk in front of the patch of Central Park directly opposite the Guggenheim, waiting for Donaldson to emerge from a board meeting she might or might not be attending. To pass the time, Hel counted the number of people nearby wearing all black. Twelve. Obviously, the author of the surveillance article had never been to New York.

This was her only option now. Direct confrontation had failed. Powerful intervention through Oliveira—and who else did Hel know?—had failed. This was all that was left to her.

Neither Ayanna Donaldson nor her wife, Angelene Silva, made their home address publicly visible on the social networking sites they used, but after some searching, Hel had located an online list of public arts charities and museum boards.

Some of these posted the dates and locations of their events, not that Hel could know if or how faithfully Donaldson attended any particular gathering. So when Donaldson emerged after a scheduled meeting of the African American Artists' Coalition into the bright sunlight of Fifth Avenue (wearing all black, of course) and turned onto East Eighty-Eighth, away from the park, Hel felt her heartbeat speed, the way it used to when she was a resident prepping for surgery. She sprinted to the other side of the avenue and fell in behind, pulling her cap lower and shrugging her shoulders tight. This was it.

Aboveground, keeping Donaldson in sight was easier than she'd anticipated. They walked east, crossing Madison and Park, and then turned downtown at Lexington. At first, Hel's insides lurched every time Donaldson's steps faltered, every time the other woman turned her head to look at a window display or paused to fish her phone out of her purse and answer a text. Each time, Hel convinced herself she was about to be found out, confronted, arrested. What she was doing could certainly be interpreted as stalking or harassment, and she didn't need Oliveira to tell her with whom the law would side. However, as she continued to observe the tall figure in black from ten paces back, Hel became aware of her quarry's distraction, her obliviousness to everything going on around her, and she became bolder. Donaldson stopped at a bakery. Hel waited outside, half-crouched behind a free-newspaper box, pretending to tie her shoe and controlling her breathing, until Donaldson reappeared, hand already reaching dreamily into her paper bag for the pastry she'd purchased. It was almost endearing, the way she munched as she walked with her head tilted back, as if taking in for the first time the gargoyles and drainpipes and balconies they passed. That and the Manhattan lunchtime crowd made it easy for Hel to stay within a few paces without being observed.

When Jonas was young, they'd played hide-and-seek inside the Park Slope apartment. Raym always pretended not to see him, no matter how obvious the hiding spot he'd chosen. Hel went to him right away. Jonas's expression of concentration: brow furrowed, nose wrinkled, lips pressed together. The subtle differences between that look and the one he got right before he was going to cry: brow furrowed, bottom lip protruding. She wouldn't allow her son to think it was that easy. If you closed your eyes, the world stayed right where it was. Looking back at you. Searching you out.

At Eighty-Sixth Street, Donaldson checked her phone one more time and descended the steps for the green line. Adjusting her sunglasses, Hel followed to the downtown platform. She kept to the opposite side of a pillar. When the train arrived and Donaldson stepped on, Hel felt herself gripped with a momentary fit of indecision. Should she get in the same car and hope not to be seen? Should she get on the car behind and look out the door at each stop, trying to catch a glimpse of Donaldson disembarking? The doors slid shut before she could step on. She watched the train leave without her.

Hel checked her phone for the time. Though it felt as if an eternity had passed, she'd stayed with Donaldson for only twelve minutes.

Next time, she'd do better.

○

Vikram saw the yellow light streaming out from under the door while he stood in the hallway, fumbling for his keys. As he worked the two sticky locks, he caught himself expecting it to blink out, the way Cristaudo's signal had, in Jamaica. What if he'd never waited for the old woman, what if he'd left her alone to her signals? He'd walked back into this trap, the trap of feeling his loss again and again. He should have known it wasn't over.

Inside the door of their apartment: the old brass floor lamp with the watermarked shade, the upholstered armchair he'd assembled from a flattened kit bought at IKEA in Red Hook. He'd never before seen anything like the mock apartments there. If only the whole world could be more like IKEA, cool and faultless, artfully decorated, with hidden drawers where mess could be stowed away. Then he'd never turn around and forget where he was. Yet he'd become habituated to the shabby objects and furnishings of this apartment, even to the armchair. The books he'd brought, lined up on their shelf, looked much like the books he'd bought here. And seated cross-legged, an open volume in her lap, Hel, whom he'd known for less than two years. Home. Seven thirty in the morning and she'd pulled the shades and blackout curtains, shutting out the day.

"What are you reading?"

She started, as if surprised to see him. "Nothing." She displayed the cover; he recognized the not-quite-lost love poetry of Nakamura Hideki. One day last week, she'd come home late; she said she'd been at a place called Staples, making digital scans of every page of every one of their books.

He crossed the room to her now, pushing pillows out of the way to make room on the couch. Automatically, she scooted away, and Vikram thought of the words from Nakamura's best-known poem, the one that had been widely read at weddings in their world alongside "Sonnet 116" and the Song of Songs. Nakamura's speaker described cutting into a wrinkled passion fruit to expose its vivid innards, about the hard black seeds between his teeth, the tang and the crunch and how that complemented the sweetness of the flesh. The speaker said he would take his own insides out to demonstrate his devotion.

He could recite those words to Hel and she would rebuff him. Or would she? Today, he didn't want to find out for sure.

Hope, that little hardness at the center. Hope and its consequences.

Hel's eyes were shadowed. It was easy to see she was up late, not up early. "Can't sleep?" he asked.

"Won't sleep."

"*How do you know you won't like it if you've never even tried it?*" He heard the singsong pattern of his own words and wondered at it, then realized he was quoting an old commercial for boxed potatoes from his and Hel's childhood. "God, sorry."

She smiled weakly, recognizing the reference.

"No one else thinks I'm funny," he said. "Not even a little bit. No one in my life. Not even before I passed through."

"And no one else ever will." She shut the book, but kept her finger in her place. "Isn't that romantic?"

He bent to untie his boots. "Shall I read you a bedtime story?"

"No, thanks. That's all right."

"Come on. You can pick."

"I don't feel like it," she said. "I've heard them all before."

"There are 155,998 other people out there who might re-member Easy-Mash. But there's no one else in the world like you."

"Come on. You know that's a wildly irresponsible overesti-mate. How many memorial services have we been to in the last year? Our survival rate isn't that good."

He snagged the cord of the blind, pulling it up. "You're in a fun mood tonight. This morning," he amended, as daylight stretched its way across the carpet to meet the bookcase on the other side of the room. All this time, he'd thought he'd ac-cepted his loss. Now he had to pretend, and she wouldn't even make an attempt. "I think you should get a job."

"I'm sorry, what?"

"Ask for a reevaluation and apply for a work placement. Something to do would, you know, get you out of the house more. Even a dumb job can be pretty satisfying." She was wasting her life, hidden away like this; she was squandering her talents, and although her government check almost matched his pay, she was, in a sense, subordinate to him. The old Hel in the old world—that proud woman he'd never met—wouldn't have stood for it. But he couldn't bring that up. It was a topic as forbidden to him as her son. "Maybe you could meet some people—"

She barked a laugh. "Right. You have your one non-alien friend now, and you think that's what I need, too. Thanks for the assimilation advice, but no thanks. That's not my goal in life."

Vikram was an expert in sadness, for he felt it himself, but her anger always blindsided him. It ran deep, to self-righteous rage. It was the loss of her place in the top caste that had done this to her, Vikram thought. She was a doctor. She was a white woman. She thought that if you followed all the rules, you'd eventually win the game.

She'd never been despised before.

"I'm not trying to assimilate you, Hel." Helplessly, he scanned the spines of the volumes on the top shelf, his own private Museum of Vanished Culture. "What would make you feel better? That's all I want." He'd arranged the books not by author or title but by color. He looked for the robin's egg blue of *The Pyronauts*. He didn't see it. "Hey, where's the Sleight book?" Hel ignored him, paging restlessly through the poetry volume. "Did you bring it into the bedroom or something?"

Hel found her way to the list of first lines in Nakamura's appendix. "I loaned *The Pyronauts* to a friend."

"Wait—you did what?" He'd never been particularly protective of his own property; as a student and later, as a teacher, he'd been happy to loan and borrow. He even shared his hand warmers with that mooch Kabir. What had come over him? "Sorry for snapping. You lent it to Oliveira?" They'd never met, but the sociologist's public persona certainly indicated that he was conscientious. The book would be safe with Oliveira. Maybe Sleight could even be useful to his work in some small way.

"Oliveira's *not* my friend," Hel said with surprising vehemence. "I wouldn't let him touch your book."

"The museum woman, then? I didn't think you liked her much."

"No." She slammed the Nakamura shut. "Not her. Her assistant. This young woman—Teresa Klay—she's been very helpful. With my project. I thought she'd like to see it, OK? And when I showed her, she was interested. She wanted to read it. So I said she could take it home, as long as she was careful. I'm sorry—if it's a problem for you, I can ask her to bring it tomorrow, when we meet. I mean, she might think it's a bit weird, but I'm sure she'd understand. Do you want me to?"

"Do you trust her?"

Hel looked him in the eyes. "Don't you trust me?"

"Yes."

"Then don't worry about it. Let's go to bed."

CHAPTER TEN

The initial decision, the justification—that was the hard part. The act of following was simple. Hel picked up Angelene's trail at the Jacob K. Javits Convention Center in Hell's Kitchen, where a two-day exposition featuring suppliers to the chemical process industry was underway. Assiduous internet searching over the last week had revealed that Donaldson's wife would be speaking at a session entitled "Real-Time Monitoring of Four-Component Liquids for Material Characterization and Purity Assurance" at 16:00. Hel couldn't afford the entrance fee, so she spent most of the afternoon on the nearby stretch of the High Line at Thirty-Fourth Street. The vast, glass-sided cube of the conference center looked odd to her, but the elevated view of the Hudson from the park reminded her of riding trains at home. While she waited, Hel caught up on the Micallef case in a series of old *New York Daily News* issues. At last, she spotted an attendee throwing away his conference badge and lanyard. Once the man and his friends were out of sight, she retrieved the badge from the trash can, wiped the droplets of coffee from its laminated surface, and thumped down the stairs to the street.

She'd dressed herself in dark neutrals—a pantsuit from the Salvation Army this time, to blend in with the professional crowd. She entered the massive building from one of the Eleventh Avenue entrances and proceeded to a basement-level ladies' room to wait for the session to end. In the last stall, she sat on the toilet with her legs tucked up so her feet wouldn't be visible, and popped the tab of a Rockstar. An element of risk could not be eliminated, but Hel felt that this might be her day. They had an affinity, she and Angelene, as two scientists. Two rational people.

At 16:55, she pushed her crushed can into the tampon receptacle and left the bathroom. With the help of a map, she found the room on level one where Angelene and the rest of the panel had just finished speaking and stationed herself ten meters down the hallway, where she could scan the stream of attendees leaving the room. She hadn't actually seen Angelene since the night at the fundraiser when the book went missing, but she remembered her round, affable face and blocky body. Men and women in business casual—probably four men for every woman—poured out of the room, heading for the next session or the exhibition hall or the long twin escalators. Hel checked each of the groups lingering in conversation by the doors, wishing she'd kept the newspaper. Something to read would shield her face in an inconspicuous way.

There, out of the corner of her eye—Angelene Silva, looking as dapper as Hel remembered in a plaid button-down and a bow tie. As Hel watched, Angelene joked with the tall white man beside her, a coworker, no doubt. He handed over a sheaf of papers. Angelene opened her yellow leather briefcase and put the papers inside, and the two of them walked off together toward the food court farther down the corridor on this level. Hel followed at a distance, trying to look small and ordinary.

In the food court, Angelene headed to Mendy's Glatt Kosher Deli while her companion opted for Grazie Italiano. Hel wasn't sure whether this separation was a good thing for her surveillance mission or not; Angelene would be easier to follow on her own, but might be more observant of her environment without the distraction of a conversation. Hel pretended to use the ATM nearby and monitored the fast-moving line at Mendy's. Angelene picked up her food and walked to the seating area.

As she stood behind a column, watching her quarry devour two hot dogs with the works, Hel realized how hungry she herself was. It was dinnertime, and the conference exhibit hall would be open for another two hours. She might be stuck here till 19:00, ducking behind booths as Angelene toured the exhibits floor, dodging industrial chemists and the people with whom they did business, watching from afar as deals were made. She jumped with alarm when her phone buzzed. Two missed calls from Vikram. Normally, he'd be getting ready for work now—why would he call her? She ducked back behind her column to tap out a quick text—*What do you want?*—hit send, then looked up.

The table stood empty except for a mustard packet and some scattered chopped onions. Hel whirled around, scanning the large space. She breathed again when she caught sight of the yellow briefcase resting on the floor between Angelene's feet as she swept trash into the bin and stacked her tray.

Hel tracked her out of the food court, back to the bank of escalators at the center of the building. There, she had to wait; Angelene chose to ride backward, bouncing on the balls of her feet and looking out at the crowd. Did she know she was being followed? Impossible. Hel decided it was simply her nature: observant, restless, interested in the world around her. Much more of a challenge than Hel had prepared for.

Twenty paces apart, they pushed through the registration crowd in the main lobby. Hel saw Angelene pulling out her own phone, and she quickened her pace to close the distance between them. Angelene answered, speaking into the phone inaudibly. Hel drew as near as she dared. Nothing would shield her now, if Angelene turned.

"Yeah, babe." Pause. "Yeah." Pause. "Yeah, OK. I promised I would." Pause. "OK. I'm headed home."

Immediately, Hel dropped into a crouch, pretending to tie a shoe—this had become her favorite move. She was just in time; Angelene glanced over her shoulder before striding through the automatic door.

Outside. Fading daylight. They proceeded south on Eleventh Avenue, Hel trying her best not to be seen and hoping they were headed toward the Thirty-Fourth Street stop for the 7 train, not to one of the parking garages. The walk took no more than three minutes but the challenge posed by Angelene's constant attention, her birdlike responsiveness to her surroundings, made it seem like three weeks. Unlike her wife, the sleepwalking Sword Queen, Angelene looked around her at the people she passed. Hel gave her extra space, glad they'd talked only briefly, the one time they met, glad Angelene had been drinking that night.

Girl, they really did a number on you.

Hel swiped her MetroCard without faltering, passing through the turnstile as Angelene stepped from the platform onto a Flushing-bound train that had just pulled in. The same dilemma as before: Was it wisest to get on another car and potentially miss seeing Angelene's exit? Be bold, she told herself. She chose a seat at the opposite end of the same car and let her head hang low. The doors closed and the train began to move.

At Times Square, the train filled up. Hel watched Angelene give up her seat to a hugely pregnant woman, saying something to her that made the expectant mother laugh. Hel stayed seated, blocked from view by a thirtysomething man with a skateboard who hung on to the bar over her head—a marvel; at home, skateboards were toys, used by children only—and by a fat woman in scrubs printed with unfamiliar characters. Hel peeped at Angelene over the fat woman's shoulder.

Grand Central, the last station in Manhattan. Angelene remained standing, still engaged in conversation with the pregnant woman. Glimpses of the dark tunnel walls flashed by outside the windows across the way, punctuated by those niches for workers that Jonas had always marveled at.

The train pulled into Vernon-Jackson, the first Queens stop. Hel checked for Angelene, and there she was, pushing her way off the crowded car and into the station. Keeping her distance once again, Hel followed.

They emerged on Fiftieth Avenue in Hunters Point or Long Island City—she wasn't really sure where the neighborhood borders were, here—and turned onto Jackson Avenue, moderately busy at this time of day. Hel felt insubstantial, but not in the powerful way she had when she'd followed Donald-son through Manhattan like an all-seeing ghost. Now, Hel's legs were floppy and weak. Gusts of wind threatened to blow her away and normal city sounds—a car alarm, a whining child, music leaking out from a passerby's headphones—carried inor-dinately. Up ahead, Angelene walked with a bounce in her step, swinging her marigold-yellow briefcase almost too innocently.

Left on another street. A blind corner. Hel counted to twenty before rounding it, imagining an ambush. But when she turned onto the street, she saw an empty block. A Citgo gas station on one side of the street, town houses on the other. Angelene was mounting a set of red-painted stairs. The stairs led to a three-story redbrick apartment house sandwiched be-tween two others. Hel took in the crisp middle-class awning. The wrought-iron security bars of recent gentrification on the first-floor windows, painted a neat white. The unmistakable shape of a blazer—a scooter, they were called scooters or mo-torcycles here—shrouded under the canvas of a fitted cover in the tiny courtyard next to the trash cans and the recycling bin and the stairs that led down to the basement. It all looked so ordinary. Angelene unlocked the door and stepped inside.

This was it.

Hel had done it. She'd found it. Their home.

She was still standing on the sidewalk congratulating her-self when Donaldson came sailing around the corner.

For a fleeting second, she hoped the other woman—dreamy, distracted Donaldson, with white earbuds showing in her ears—wouldn't notice her, but Donaldson was already say-ing her name. "Helen?"

The familiar weight of the knife in her pocket. Not that she would use it. That was not an option.

She turned and ran.

○

By the time she got across Queens to Jamaica, it was 20:00; Vikram's shift had started an hour ago, and the big empty bottle of wine clattered around at the bottom of the brown paper bag with the much smaller plastic bottles of vodka she'd bought at the bodega to steady her nerves. Cobalt-blue bottles, the color of the cough syrup she'd taken as a child. She'd never bothered to call Vikram back and he hadn't replied when she'd texted that she was headed to his work.

She walked the eight blocks from the subway, hyperaware but with her reaction time diminished, flinching at shadows too long after they'd spooked her. She traveled brightly lit streets. She was thankful for the trucks that rumbled past carrying their nighttime loads, how they made her feel part of a well-ordered world where goods and services were transferred with efficiency, where each person had his or her own role, where everyone was a part of the same machine.

She'd almost forgotten what it was to have the satisfaction of a worthy job to do.

When she arrived at the warehouse, she followed the fence around two corners to the guard shack. There, she gripped the chain-link in both hands and shook. "Vikram! Let me in!"

Above her, the blinded brick warehouse loomed. Above that, the sky, the light from one or two stars breaking through the city fug. No Vikram. No one breathing out here but her. She sidestepped along the fence, moving closer to the nearest streetlight while maintaining her palms' contact with the looped galvanized steel wire of the fence. "VIKRAM!"

"Jesus, Hel." Dear and dependable in his pressed pants and jacket, his cap securely on his head, her lover crunched toward her across the gravel, the flashlight in his hand not turned on, as if he'd trained himself to see in the dark. She marveled at how the sight of his familiar shape, the way he carried himself, calmed her. Allowed her to focus. "You scared me," he said.

"Yeah, well, I'm sorry. Let me in. Where's the gate?"

"I can't let you in. There are cameras."

She couldn't see his face; she could discern the general outline of his nose, distinguish the contour of his cheekbone in three-quarters profile, but she wanted his eyes. "Shine your light up. Shine your light at your face."

He turned the flashlight over in his hands, as if he were just discovering it, then clicked it on and pointed it in her direction instead. "What are you doing here?"

She blinked in the sudden brightness. "You called me, remember? You called my phone. Come on. No one looks at the security footage. You let Kabir stay here all the time when he's not supposed to be."

"That's different. Kabir's responsible for himself."

"And I'm not?"

"You're drunk."

"Yes," Hel said. "I guess I am. Talk to me through the fence, Viki. Stay here and talk to me through the fence. I'm frightened."

176

"I don't believe you." He spoke the words calmly, as if the proposition were impossible, as if she were not capable of being frightened. She found this touching and ridiculous. "Why are you here?" he asked. "What do you want?"

"You can stop pointing that at me. It's hurting my eyes. You called me. Why?"

For a moment, he hesitated. "I don't know," he said at last. "I just miss you. I mean, where have you been recently? What do you even do during the days?"

The old scars from the knife across the meat of four of her fingers suddenly stinging, her heart beating that hard, purposeful beat, that rhythm she knew from the moments before the first incision, when the patient lay before her, anesthetized face blank and trusting. She was feeling that for the first time since she'd stepped out into the wrong Calvary, and Vikram dared ask her this. What she was—what she still *was* inside—was more important than what she did. "What do *you* do during the days?"

"I told you. I'm at the cottage."

"Every day? Working with that guy—helping him clean out that junk heap? He thinks you're an alien." She laughed, and as she laughed, she was aware that she was acting inappropriately and she laughed louder.

Vikram didn't seem to notice. "I guess," he said. "Me and Wes too, from my Reintegration Education group—he definitely thinks we're weird. But we're all getting pretty used to each other. I've been thinking maybe you're right. Maybe individual stories could help people here relate to the UDP experience a little better."

"That's sweet," she said. "But I was wrong. Nobody gives a shit."

INTERVIEW TRANSCRIPT:
HELEN NASH, AGE 40, THE BRONX

The two little boys were big enough to walk ahead. Stairstep brothers, or maybe fraternal twins, neither older than five. The mother carried the baby in its sleeper, slung over her shoulder like a bag of flour, and she pushed the baby's empty stroller with her free hand. The man who was with them tried to help, but she wouldn't let him wrench the stroller from her grip.

No one told me this story. I saw it all myself.

At Calvary, the Homeland Defense Force had removed some of the larger monuments and tombstones and tipped over other ones so that they lay flush with the ground. People stepped on them. You remember that. We all walked over them like paving stones, forgetting that this was a cemetery at all, or too shocked to care. Desperate times. A big group of onlookers already stood beyond the roped-off area, and that was really making me nervous, but no one acted violently. There was just this sense of potential, like a crowd always has. Military staff scanned the codes of those who'd been chosen and conducted them forward, shielding them from the jealous crowd.

The little boys, of course, had no codes, but the authorities let them through when the woman showed hers. Because of operational regulations, family members weren't supposed to be let into the restricted area, but no one had the heart to enforce that, not on the first day of evac. They were still figuring out their procedures, what worked and what didn't.

I heard that later, they built a fence topped with razor wire. I heard that later, the officers guarding the area wore masks. Not like the anti-rad masks lots of people were wearing. Balaclavas, just so no one could see their faces when they ripped mothers from their children. But it wasn't like that on the first day.

A sort of staging area was roped off from the actual breach site. Two checkpoints. They let the little boys into the staging area, and the woman and her baby—though they made her leave the stroller outside. They even let in the man who followed her, two paces behind. The family had ten minutes to say good-bye before she would need to hand the baby over to the man and enter the line, where I waited with the other soon-to-be-UDPs—lucky, terrified—waited for the hole in the sky to open up again and swallow us.

"Who is in charge here?" the woman asked. She was from some other country—I can't even guess where—she wore a long skirt and a head wrap. She had an accent from somewhere. But she was a citizen now. Everyone knew it must be so, because of the code associated with her ID when they scanned her card. The baby, in its yellow sleeper, had woken, but it didn't fuss. The mother turned it around and held its body against her, its fist-sized face outward, so it could see. With one hand she supported its bottom, under the bulge of the diaper, and she pressed her other hand against its small chest. It blinked at us, its expression stoic.

When the mother asked that—*who is in charge here*—they should have known she was going to make a scene. But the attacks were so recent, so shocking, the implications so unclear. They'd only been evacuating people for six hours. Not knowing what it meant, I hadn't even called my son to tell him goodbye. The process wasn't smooth, the stakes not quite evident. Not to the soldiers manning the checkpoint and providing perimeter support. Not to the unchosen people outside the ropes on the graves. Not to us—strangers waiting in a line beyond the second checkpoint, knowing that in a minute the buzzer would buzz to signify that we must be ready to move, the scientists would power up their machines, the mirage we'd been warned about but which none of us could quite imagine yet would hang in the air, and the tone would buzz a second time indicating that we must step forward, all together.

None of us anticipated trouble from the mother. We wondered which end of the line she would join, who would take her hand and how her palm would feel—soft or callused, damp or papery dry. We wondered who would watch her boys as she left, who would help the man with her baby. One of the guards, we decided. Perhaps one of the young women in the green canvas deployment uniform would put aside her automated-fire gun.

Then, the mother called him forward, that man who'd followed her. "This is my husband," she said in a resonant voice that carried. "This is my love. But *I* am the mother of his children—they came from me and only I know how to look after them. They cannot do without me. Let him go in my place. Let me stay."

You were supposed to decline before you got to the cemetery, so they could pick someone else.

An officer stepped forward, a sub-commander, not the highest guy there. "Come with me," he said. "We'll talk about it outside." And instead of ushering her through the second checkpoint—that propitious checkpoint for which the lottery authorized her—the sub-commander walked her back the wrong way, through the first checkpoint.

That was her death, right there. But she didn't know it yet.

She looked around at the crowd, and the baby looked around at the crowd too. We let out a sigh. "I'm sorry," the sub-commander said to her. "You've had it explained to you already. It's nontransferable."

"The lottery wasn't done fairly," the mother said. "He never had a chance!" By the fence, her husband lowered his head, as if he were embarrassed. He rubbed his hand against the close-cut head of one of his sons.

"I'm sorry," the sub-commander said again. He gave a signal, and two of the younger guards left their posts and came to stand behind him. "Rules are rules, ma'am."

"What does it matter to you?" she asked. "You need one hundred. Why does it matter who?"

I've talked to other UDPs from later lots. The crowds grew until they sealed off Calvary, all 365 acres of it, permitting no one to watch anymore. But this family—this man and woman, these boys and baby—they all stayed. They watched us depart.

Once the Gate achieved full power, I couldn't see them anymore. I only had eyes for the gap, the blue hole. I couldn't see them when I stepped into it, into pearlescent haze like an oil slick suspended in the air, when I stepped from one snowy day and into another. But I knew they were in the crowd, watching the ninety-nine of us leave them behind.

CHAPTER ELEVEN

Hel woke the next day thinking she was all right, but as soon as she sat up, her headache came pouring out of some hiding place like a python dropping coil after exploratory coil from a tree. The clock by the side of the bed said 13:00, which meant it was really noon—she'd forgotten to adjust it for daylight savings time a week or so ago.

Next to her in bed, Vikram slept, his face relaxed with mouth slightly open, his hands folded together and tucked under his cheek in praying position. He looked peaceful. She forced herself to sit. A sweating glass of water sat on the windowsill next to three capsules of acetaminophen. She vaguely remembered filling the glass the night before and counting out the medicine. Now, she thanked her drunk self as she downed the water and pills in one gulp.

If you can't trust yourself, who can you trust?

The bedroom door creaked behind her. She set about making coffee and finding something she could stand to eat without

vomming. She jammed two slices of bread into the weird verti-
cal slots on the toaster, got the coffee machine going, and sat
down on the high chair at the small table in the kitchen–living
room area of the apartment to wait. Through the pain of the
headache, she felt herself filled with an uncommon sense of
direction, an unfamiliar purposefulness.

She was finally in charge now—no one else. She had to
take action to keep it that way.

First, she'd need the two playing cards, which she'd left in
her pants pocket. She snuck back to the bedroom as quietly as
she could and found the right pair of jeans crumpled on the
floor of the closet. As she eased the door closed again, Vikram
murmured something, moving his hands and burrowing his face
into the pillow, but he didn't wake. What he said was incompre-
hensible to her, words in Bengali—his first language, but one
she rarely heard him speak. Perhaps, if things were different, she
would have had to wait through mystifying Saturday evening
phone calls home, guessing by the expressiveness of his tone
what he was saying. Perhaps he would have taken Hel home
to New Jersey and his mother or sisters would have said disapproving things about her in Bengali and Vikram would have answered back—sharply, perhaps, or gently—and Hel would have
sat there, fuming at her inability to understand what was going
on, never knowing how good they had it.

Back in the kitchen, the toaster snapped up, sending one
piece of toast skidding across the counter and onto the un-
swept floor. She scooped it into the trash and crammed the
other piece into her mouth, then took out an aluminum mix-
ing bowl and placed both found playing cards inside. She felt

she'd dreamed it all up, that queen, but there she was, looking straight at her with her black eyes, impolitely direct in a way no Truth deck figure ever dared. Hel lit two matches, tossed them into the bowl.

There.

While the cards smoldered, she sat back down, chewing her toast, feeling not particularly mystical. It was more like cleaning house. She never spent much time missing her sister, but for the first time in years, she thought that if she could link to Seff right now, talk to her on the screen, she'd do it. Oh well. To the bowl, she added more lit matches and a crumpled page from an old takeout menu. The stench of burning plastic filled the room, but it took a few more menus to get the cards to really catch, the edges finally curling, the face of the queen and the eight little hearts turning brown and then black, leaving behind indistinguishable ashes. This was good. It felt good, healthy. Like fertilizing a field by plowing under a cover crop.

The question: how to proceed with Donaldson. How would the other woman interpret Hel's appearance outside her home? Should Hel ask Donaldson again for what she wanted, or should she attempt to take it by force? What was the best way to approach her now?

Truth. She knew, of course, that cartomancy was just storytelling, not real magic, that it all came from her. The Rider-Waite look-alike Tarot Vikram gave her as a gift a year ago felt almost right—the exact expressions of the figures and the details were unfamiliar, but their postures and positions and actions were still those of old friends. But she'd never tried to use it to foretell.

She found that knockoff deck in the jumbled kitchen junk drawer and took it back to the living room. She did not lay out cards for a proper reading. She wasn't ready yet. Instead, she reclined on the couch with the deck in its still new-looking box resting on her chest, hands crossed over it, and concentrated on her question. As she did so, she remembered her last hours with her personal ordinator, when she knew there was nothing she could do to keep it from dying.

Initially, they'd confiscated all UDP possessions in the cemetery, but a week or so into Debrief, her shoulder bag reappeared in the dorms along with most of her lotmates' things, its contents searched through but unmolested. After that, she kept the ordinator always powered off and hidden under the pillow in her bunk, but she knew that wouldn't preserve it. No matter what she did, the energy cell would eventually lose its charge and fade, and once it was gone, her files would be lost, like treasures locked in a safe with no combination. One day, in a last-ditch attempt to preserve what was most important to her, she borrowed a phone equipped with a camera from the shift commander. Other UDPs left her alone, watching TV on the opposite end of the common room while she sat cross-legged on a folding chair, ordinator on the table before her. She slid the display and the command unit out of their case for what she knew would probably be the last time, and fit them together.

She worked as methodically, as desperately, as a diver swimming for the surface with a limited tank of air; panic would not help her cause. One by one, she accessed the images she'd stored on the device over the years, photographing the screen whenever she came upon one she hoped to save. There were too many. Fleeting moments rolled past, and Hel pressed the camera-phone button over and over again to preserve each digital simulacrum digitally. She did not stop to think about what she was doing: taking pictures of pictures, imposing one new remove, an additional step away from the sensory experience. The files on the ordinator presented themselves chronologically, earliest first, but as she moved through worthless memories of her post–Alt Service travels and early years of medical training, she stopped, skipped ahead—years ahead—to the birth of her son. Agitated but unsentimental, Hel revisited Jonas's infancy, toddlerhood, and young childhood. (Now, she had printouts of some of those secondhand pictures—that face she loved at various ages and in various places, always framed by the edge of the ordinator's screen. She kept these pictures in an album she couldn't bear to look at. How apt that *dying* was also the word used to describe what happened to a manmade device that could no longer be powered.)

Breathe, she'd told herself, that day in the dorm. She was a diver, swimming. She was saving her own life. No. Breathe deeper—from the diaphragm. Blood, stop racing. Heart, stop throbbing so. Clinically, she'd known what a panic attack was, but had never experienced one. Breathe.

That feeling. Why was it back now?

She lay on the couch and remembered, years earlier, lying on another couch on some quiet afternoon with her arms around her son—this was when he was three or four, when she and Raym were still together—how warm and heavy Jonas had felt in her arms and how vehemently, how distinctly his heart had beaten.

The heart is a very strong muscle; it cannot burst.

It was in the early days of subway riding that Vikram handed her this deck, still in a paper bag from the New Age gift shop where he bought it, and asked her how, in the light of all that had happened, she could bring herself to believe in preordained purpose.

She'd turned her mind from her lost son. She'd taken Vikram's hand, large and clammy. "We're here. How can we not?"

Now, she withdrew the deck from the box and let the cards move in her hands, pips, faces, and trumps arranging themselves in the order they wanted to rest. On the coffee table, she laid one card before her. In the voice of that long-ago girl at the party: *This card is you.*

Then, the other cards, the words in their order, an incantation. *This is your disguise. This is your past; this, your future. This card is above you. This is below you. Your house. Your lover.* She turned the cards over quickly, one after another, their symbolic possibilities registering only at the subconscious level she'd developed through long practice.

Your riddle. Here, she paused. Strength, a trump card depicting a woman prying open the jaws of a lion. (It was a tiger, Hel recalled, in the Truth deck.) What did that mean? Courage, patience, resolve, control. In her case, a failure of these things. A failure, so far, to get what she wanted through peaceful means.

She laid out the last card, *your answer.*

The Three of Pentacles. Pentacles were the same as Loaves, the suit that represented the earth element. In the Three, a young apprentice in an apron stood on a bench with tools upraised, reaching high to work on the design—three circles— in a cathedral cornice. Older architects crowded around with rolled-up plans. There to advise him, but also praising his work. Assistance, collaboration, teamwork.

Teresa Klay.

○

"Wes should be out of the shower in just a second," Ari said. "I just heard him turn the fan off. That means he's probably standing in there in the steam, drying his beard and admiring himself."

Vikram sat on a stool in the living room part of the grimy Lower East Side studio while, three feet away, Ari tidied the kitchen. Almost three years of Reintegration Education with Wes, and he'd never seen the man's apartment or met his fiancé.

"Can't I help or something?"

"No!" Ari began to toss clean dishes from the drainer into their places in the cabinet. "Seriously, that's OK."

Wes came in, still pulling on a shirt. Vikram took in the other tattoos and cutting marks that snaked across his upper body. Wes tugged down the hem, concealing an uncensored lucky swastika just above his hip. "Hey, man. What's up?" Wes grabbed a handful of mixed silverware from a can next to the sink and began sorting it into a drawer, forks with forks and knives with knives.

"I got some news from Dwayne and wanted to ask your opinion. Maybe we could take a walk, when you're done with that?" The apartment felt as crowded as his own head today—concern for Hel vying with Dwayne's proposal.

"Sure thing." Wes dropped a kiss on Ari's cheek. Then he and Vikram descended the narrow stairs to the street. The day was unseasonably warm for November, the late afternoon sun shining right into their eyes as they walked toward the avenue. "So, what do you want?"

"Dwayne says he wants to let me use the house."

You and your girl. For your museum. That was how Dwayne put it, on the phone. Then, as if trying to undercut his own generosity as much as possible: *No one's trying to buy in this neighborhood, anyway. I've had it on the market for weeks and haven't even gotten other calls.*

"He wants to draw up a legal document giving me the lease for some token amount every month. All I'd need to do is help finish the renovation and cover the property taxes."

"He told you?" Wes asked. "That's terrific, man!"

"Wait, you knew he was thinking about this?"

"Yeah. But that's great news, right? This means you can pull together the exhibit thing!"

"Yeah, well, it's going to take a lot of money, though, won't it? The living room ceiling looks like it's about to cave in, plus there's all those scary water stains on the back of the house. And the upstairs has still got old Mrs. Defoe stuff packed in to the rafters—"

"Whoa! Calm down! We just have to finish cleaning the place up and then we'll figure out a way to pay for incidentals. We can try one of those—what do they call them? Crowdsourcing, crowdfunding? Have you heard of that? Get online, ask our friends and family to throw in ten bucks, and we'll be in business in no time."

"None of us UDPs have any friends or family," Vikram pointed out. "They're all dead." He saw the look on Wes's face. "Sorry—sorry."

"Even so, we can take care of a lot ourselves, don't you think? I can do basic electrician work—I'm not a guild member or whatever you need to be in this world, but no one's going to check, right?—and Ari's sister is really handy. Dwayne probably knows some other people who can help."

"He obviously doesn't. He's been relying on two aliens with nothing better to do to help him under the table, remember."

"OK, fine. But we'll ask around. And anything we can't figure out ourselves, we can probably watch videos of on the internet. We can learn how to hang drywall together; it'll be fun. And the best part is, we don't have to worry about preserving anything! You know what I mean? No need to bend over backward to save the original woodwork or whatever. Face it—Sleight never touched it, anyway."

The thought depressed Vikram, though he had to acknowledge its truth.

The world could still end. This one, this world, his miraculous backup. Carbon dioxide pollution was worse here and every year warmer than the last. It was possible that Vikram and the others had avoided dying in a nuclear conflict only to be drowned by a rising sea.

He'd seen a picture exhibit of identical twins adopted out as children to separate families. In some cases, the pairs were unrecognizable as siblings. One twin might be wrinkled and stooped from decades of fieldwork, while his brother had soft hands and expensive clothes. One sister healthy, the other with H-scarred arms and a thousand-yard stare. Was this the right analogy for his world and this one, starting the same and hurtling off to two wholly different fates?

But it wasn't all choice. They shared their genes.

Two million years ago, a lava field under Yosemite eighty kilometers long and twenty wide caused an eruption that brought on an ice age and winnowed the human population down to perhaps thousands. Vikram had read that the groundwork was laid already for another such explosion. If—when—it happened, he would know that a mirror-image disaster was happening across the impenetrable universal divide. The same plates and chemicals, the same gases and particles. The same eruption wreaking similar havoc on an already ruined, unreachable world. Or a meteor could hit Earth, a meteor on a path determined through all of cosmic time. The two universes like estranged brothers crumpling in tandem, each man clutching at his chest, felled by a shared tendency. It could happen that way to the whole world.

Sequelae beyond the sphere of individual endeavor. A guilty, secret part of him was comforted by this thought.

From the right distance, all movement looked like fate. And if major world-shaking events were predetermined, why not minor? Why not the small births and deaths of all the people Vikram had loved, and those of the people he hadn't? Cristaudo's friends, the scientists, running around in the graveyard like deckhands on a floundering ship. The millions uncalled by the lottery. Jonas, whom Vikram would never know. Were all these losses as incontrovertible as the melting of the rock under their feet, the movement of celestial bodies far above their heads?

No. He believed in the human scale, too. Decisions. Hope and consequences.

"Look, I've got an idea," Wes said. "Anything for the house that we can't do ourselves, we need to convince strangers to pay for it. People with money—not UDPs. So what we need is bait."

"Bait?"

"Something to draw their interest." Wes punched him lightly in the chest. "Dwayne was into the Dop Peters thing, right? We'll find more stuff like that. We could even interview people from our world about their lives. Go high profile, you know? What about that sociologist from the news who's a UDP—maybe we should see if we can get in touch with him. Who can explain us to the world better than him? What's his name?"

Vikram knew it. The man was—or had been, until recently—Hel's only friend. "Dr. Carlos Oliveira. I think I can get his number."

○

"I can't believe you came back here. They're supposed to be watching out for you." Klay sounded more amused than disapproving. "What did you tell Bernardo at the front desk?"

"Well, presumably he called you down to deal with me," Hel said. "So he did his job. I was hoping we could speak frankly to one another."

They stood together in the toy section of the gift shop at the Museum of Modern Thought, just inside the entrance. The shelves were crammed with board games and puzzles, art supplies and construction sets—brightly colored blocks and interlocking metal pieces that could be snapped together or connected with magnets.

"You realize that I can't let you in to see Ayanna—it's worth more than my job. You're lucky she didn't call the cops on you last night."

"Why would she have done that?"

"Hel. Come on. She knows that was you, sneaking around."

"I don't know what you're talking about." Hel found a bin filled with plastic models of spacecraft, cheap versions of the ones she'd seen Donaldson handling earlier. "I'm not here to see Donaldson. I came to talk to you. You were there with me, at the lake. Someone died there once because there was no one around to help him."

After her outburst, after she saw the place where the painting did not hang and lost control, Klay had led her outside and made her sit on the lawn that sloped down to meet the artificial shoreline. There, they'd glimpsed the lake through the trees, its surface as flat and dull as a dirty penny, and around them, fallen leaves from the grand, spreading beech trees dotted the grass, burnt umber and copper—those colors, too, like a sepia print. Hel had pictured how, more than a century before, the older students at the boarding school might have lolled in this spot in their school uniforms on spread plaid picnic blankets, boys crunching on apples or passing back and forth an illicit flask. She imagined races to the dock, young men fighting for a spot in the rowboats, splashing at each other with their paddles.

A boat that capsized, little Ezra in the water. Were his friends there? Did they laugh, perhaps, as he beat futilely at the water with his hands, mistaking it for a joke? Or was he alone? Was it nighttime, early morning, lesson hours, out of bounds? By himself?

Did he kick his feet? Did he yell and thrash, or did he hold still and drift down into the silt like a waterlogged stick, the sun or the bright moon winking good-bye to him through the obverse side of the rippled surface?

Breathe, Klay had said, as Hel sobbed by the shore.

"You helped me once."

"I remember that," Klay said. "Let me give you some unsolicited advice. You should watch out. Ayanna said she's going to take out a restraining order. Do you know what that means for someone in your position? If you step too far out of line, they'll revoke your Resettlement Permission."

Hel crossed to the rack of postcards. "If you care so much, just tell her not to. I know you have influence on her."

"That's flattering, but I really don't."

Hel had never actually seen MoMT's collection. The postcards highlighted its best-known works, abstract paintings in primary colors. Sculptures fabricated from glass, from metal, from felted-wool tubes. A reproduction of a black-and-white photograph of grocery store ham wrapped tightly in barbed wire. Another reproduction of an oil-pastel drawing of the Twin Towers—a realistic depiction, unexpectedly sentimental in this context. The buildings' outline was familiar to Hel only through memorial postage stamps and the credit sequences from midnight TV reruns.

"Can you just ask her to give me the Sleight book back? That's what I want—the only thing I want. It doesn't mean as much to her as it does to me. It can't possibly."

"But she says she doesn't have it. She's a professional. She's my boss. I believe her."

Hel remembered the upstairs workroom where she'd once met with the director. Metal cabinets lined the walls there. A museum typically displayed five percent of its assets or fewer. Catalogued objects in storage, accruing value, waiting for the right exhibit. Or forgotten. Locked drawers and shelves, housing art no one could access. Donaldson in her blue gloves, reverently handling the spacecraft models. She was a collector, just like the old woman who'd cluttered up Sleight's cottage. A professional at acquisitions. Was Hel just supposed to take her word?

Klay wrenched the postcard rack from Hel's grip and twisted it one half turn. "I'm not trying to be rude, but have you considered the possibility that it could be you? That you're misremembering where you left the book? That would be understandable, with all you've been through."

"You have no idea what we've been through. You don't care about people getting hurt. You pretend to care, but it's just an academic interest, isn't it. I remember how you asked me about nearly dying. Do you remember that? After I told you I was assaulted in Park Slope one time, you asked me what it was like."

"So? Maybe I was curious. Isn't that what you want—to tell people about your world? Maybe I was trying to be that person for you."

"Why would you do that?"

"I don't understand why you're so angry, when I was only trying to be kind."

"Don't patronize me," Hel said. The Three of Loaves, reversed. Stagnation, obstruction, lack of progress. "I thought you could help. I was wrong. All I need is for you to stay out of my way."

CHAPTER TWELVE

There was a locksmith named Fenny in Hel's entry group, an easy-tempered guy in his midtwenties. When they played the game, the What Did You Take Through game, he told them he'd filled his suitcase with sixers and with the blanket he'd slept with as a baby. No sixer player, he said, but he'd heard someone from Lot Fifty had one. Upon release from Debrief, Fenny immediately found work at a True Value store, cutting keys and ringing up cans of paint for the contractors and home-improvers of the South Bronx. He used to bring Hel little presents, things from work she'd never seen before. A package of no-damage adhesive picture-hanging strips, a glitter-embellished self-retracting measuring tape, upholstery spray that smelled like chemical lilacs. Once, he asked her to go out with him for coffee after Reintegration Education. She said no.

Still, he was happy enough to explain to her about thieves' tools, when she inquired. What she ought to find, he said, was a thing that housebreakers in their world called a jumper—a skinny key used to knock the tumblers of a lock out of the way, one by one. "It's the neatest way," he told her. "People might come home and not even know someone's been in and out till they see something missing days later."

"Where do I get one?"

"Not from me. I don't cut those. Not anymore."

"Do you know someone who would?"

Fenny shrugged. "The weakest point in a house that isn't your own is a window. Lots of ways to get one open. Glass cutters. Special tape. Or you wrap up your fist. That's the very easiest. Just don't get seen by no cameras. And don't get cut."

Hel imagined the paperback waiting for her on a bedside table in Donaldson's apartment with a bookmark saving a spot, and she could barely resist heading off to Hunters Point to rescue it right away. But of course, *The Pyronauts* could be any number of other places. Stored in Angelene's lab for safekeeping on a shelf of gleaming glassware. Slid into the long metal sleeve of a bank's safe-deposit box. Thrown heedlessly down a garbage chute. Resting at the bottom of Donaldson's purse, right this minute. She cycled through the possibilities. All of them seemed equally plausible.

That night, she trailed Donaldson on foot from MoMT to a Duane Reade on Bedford Avenue. She could no longer afford to risk being recognized, so she'd taken steps, arranging a paisley-printed shawl over her hair, tying it the way she'd learned in yet another internet tutorial. She'd also bought a pair of dollar-store reading glasses. The magnification gave her a headache, but they improved the cheap disguise. She hid herself in the condom-and-diaper aisle and watched Donaldson up at the checkout, buying an all-natural brand of deodorant, a bottle of iced tea, and—at the last minute—a copy of *Us Weekly* with Joslan Micallef on the cover.

Outside, Donaldson pulled up the hood of her raincoat and checked her phone. Hel feared she was using an app to call a car, but after a minute, she began to walk down North Third, high heels ringing out hollowly against the sidewalk. Hel waited until the other woman had passed the wine bar on the corner and then began to follow her, staying a full block behind. It was simple, like the subway game she'd played with Vikram. The only rule was not to get caught.

She did not worry about the movement of her blood or the cadence of her noisy breaths the way she had the first time she followed Donaldson. Her footsteps fell silently. The coordinated movements of her arms and legs felt hyper-natural, smooth and powerful, and the rhythm of pursuit filled Hel with clearheaded joy. The goal of a surgeon is to remove all the cancer, taking as little healthy tissue as possible while leaving a clean margin of resection. Even with years of theoretical and practical experience, intuition had guided Hel's scalpel, once. That feeling of mastery she'd lost. It had returned to her at last.

A greedy wind pulled at Donaldson's coat and rattled her plastic drugstore bag, and she ducked into a storefront—a bookstore. Did Donaldson have *The Pyronauts* with her at this very moment? Was she having it appraised?

The shop looked pretty small, so Hel waited under an overhang across the street, barely able to contain herself. She felt invisible, intangible, as if she'd finally come to the end of a tiresome process. No one would give her anything and no one could see her. At long last she'd vanished from this world completely.

A group of young women passed by, clad in the long dark robes and veils that some Muslims wore in this world. They glanced at Hel's makeshift hijab, taking her in without interest, and then returned to their own animated conversation, of which she could understand no English words but "body wax" and "spatula."

Dusk fell and it began to mist faintly. Hel wrapped her sweater-coat tighter around her, pulling up the knitted collar. What was keeping Donaldson's attention for so long? Should Hel risk going inside? At last, able to wait no longer, she crossed the street. The windows glowed, showing one deep room lined with shelves. About thirty folding chairs had been set up in rows, as though an event were about to start. A few people had staked out spots, but Donaldson wasn't one of them. But in the back, Hel saw the curly hair of someone else she recognized. Teresa Klay.

Have you considered the possibility that it could be you?

She shrunk back reflexively before remembering how well-lit the bookstore was. All Klay would see from the inside was reflection. It was safe to look around for Donaldson. No sign of her through the glass, though—just books and books and more books, all the way up the walls. Shelves of print, forests of paper. Pre-1910 titles from Before that she would recognize if she went inside, and scores of After volumes she'd never heard of and didn't want to read. Pop history, psychology, medicine—the kinds of books she'd pick up to pass the time during airship travel or flip through when clinic hours were slow. How could she just dismiss a century of collected knowledge, how could she be so incurious, so internal and contained? She hadn't always been like this. What happened to the person she used to be?

Mist continued to fall, gathering in beads on Hel's sweater and dampening her shawl, but at least it wasn't really raining. She blinked droplets out of her eyes. Staring so intently through the unneeded glasses made her head ache. She took them off to clean the lenses. When she glanced up again, Donaldson was seated in a chair in the last row, her dark head bent toward Klay's. Their backs were to the door. In front of the assembled crowd, a white man in a denim shirt buttoned all the way up shuffled through a stack of papers, getting ready to read or speak.

Just then, the door swung open with a jingle of bells as a customer exited. Before the door could close again, before she could think twice, Hel was darting into the store.

Klay and Donaldson had their backs to her, their attention focused on a bookstore employee introducing the denim-shirt man, a journalist, apparently. He had reported from war zones all over the world. Polite applause. Under Donaldson's chair, her black leather clutch—just large enough to contain a paperback—lay next to the Duane Reade bag, unattended. Could she snatch it and make it out to the street in time? Or was she simply courting disaster? Can't stop. Won't stop.

Hel moved closer, keeping a wall of books between her and the other women. "You definitely made the right call," Klay was saying. "You've got to keep yourself safe."

"She hasn't actually done anything, you know. I feel kind of guilty."

"Don't. She's acting crazy."

Was this conversation about her? Hel had assumed Klay's honesty and believed that she really didn't know Donaldson had stolen *The Pyronauts*. But something about their easy intimacy now made her wonder if the two of them were in this together, laughing at her.

At the front of the room, the journalist cleared his throat. "I'm going to start out with a piece I wrote while I was investigating conditions in the infamous Jungle refugee camp," he said. "If you remember, this tent city near Calais was home to thousands of asylum seekers who'd paid all their savings to traffickers to escape their countries of origin . . ."

Hel sidled around the corner, along the other side of the Philosophy and World Religion shelf. She was fully exposed now; she kept her face averted, stealing peeks over her shoulder. The women seemed to be listening intently. Hel ducked low and looked under Donaldson's chair as the reporter droned on about the Iraqi and Yemeni teens he'd met at the camp who were teaching themselves the English language. The zipper of the clutch gaped open. She could see a cell phone inside, a pair of sunglasses, a small bottle—maybe lotion? No book. No room for a book. Hel hurried back into safety, out of sight.

Donaldson dropped her voice. "This whole thing is making me reconsider her. Look at them, floundering around. Why aren't UDPs like other refugees, trying to make a place here? They've lost too much. That would completely fracture your assumptions about how life is meant to be. It's certainly an interesting perspective."

"It doesn't excuse stalking you," said Klay. The traitor.

Hel pushed through the door, not caring whether heads turned when the bells on the door rang out. Last she'd heard, Fenny was dating a non-UDP woman. He'd adopted the woman's child and they were expecting a second together. He still worked at True Value, that chain with the hopeful name. Not all UDPs were alike; he was different from Hel. They saw each other at the required weekly meetings, but Fenny never followed her out into the street with hardware anymore. After soliciting his advice about housebreaking, she'd tried to start a conversation. She asked if he ever tracked down the sixer player from Lot Fifty. He told her he'd thrown away the discs. She'd have to use her fist, just like he said.

○

Vikram didn't want to ask Hel about Oliveira, not if he could help it. Instead, he called the man at his office number, listed on the website of the Department of Sociology at CUNY. Oliveira had recorded his own oddly formal voicemail message: "You've reached the office of Carlos Oliveira. If you care to leave a recording, you will have an opportunity after the tone. Or, if you'd prefer to speak to a human, press zero and a secretary will gladly take a message." Vikram left a voicemail first, giving his name, mentioning Hel's, explaining the project briefly and requesting a phone interview. No response.

"Keep trying," Wes said.

Dwayne agreed with this advice; he liked the idea of celebrity attention. "Blow the man up," he said, then noticed the two UDPs' expressions. "It's just a saying. It means calling somebody over and over. He's busy, but he can't be that busy. You leave enough messages, fancy-pants won't be able to forget about you."

So Vikram tried the secretary next; she was polite but discouraging, informing him that since Dr. Oliveira was a professor emeritus, he was rarely in his office at predictable times; she couldn't hazard a guess as to when he might hear back.

After two more days, Vikram finally brought it up with Hel. "What happened between you and Oliveira?" he asked over their evening meal—dinner for her, breakfast for him. "Do you know how cool that is, to make friends with someone like him? You liked each other, right? Then, when I asked you about him the other night, suddenly he's Attila the Hun or a KomSo commandant or something."

"We had a disagreement about something."

"Yeah, I figured that. I just meant, what was it this time?"

She twirled some linguine around her fork. "This time? What's that supposed to mean?"

"You have these . . . these *things* with people all the time. These fallings-out. Secret offense taken or insult given, cold shoulder, whatever. Your entry group, your old housemates, people from Reintegration—you don't see them anymore." Though her mood for days now had been an unusually sunny one, he knew how quickly dark clouds could blow in. But he was tired of being careful around her all the time. "Sometimes it seems like when you decide unilaterally that you're disappointed in somebody—that he isn't worth your time anymore, that he should get a cancer and die—you make the call and don't even bother to tell him. So is it one of those types of situations, whatever it is that happened with Oliveira? Do *you* even know why?"

"I don't know what you're talking about."

Was it, then, unconscious? Vikram knew one thing for sure: he was waiting for the day when she would do it to him, too. "You push people away. You and I both know why. You haven't dealt with losing your son."

She leaned over and kissed him, her mouth tasting sour with garlic and capers. "Don't worry about it, OK? I don't need Oliveira."

"Are you ignoring me? I'm talking about Jonas." There. He'd said it.

"You told me you're working on my project," she said, her face impassive. "You're interviewing UDPs. If you reach out to Oliveira, do yourself a favor and don't mention you know me. It won't do you any good."

"Stop trying to derail me, Hel! I'm saying his name! Jonas!"

"I kicked Oliveira into a swimming pool when he wasn't expecting it."

"What?"

Hel stood up, took her plate over to the counter, and dumped her uneaten food into the trash. She put her plate in the sink. She extracted a plastic storage container out of the cupboard and scraped all of the leftover pasta from the pot into the container. "You heard me. That's exactly what I did. I wish he'd drowned, but I'm sure if he had, it would have been in the *Times*."

"Hel, please."

"I'm sick of you feeling sorry for me. I make my own decisions. I make terrible decisions!" She dug in the cupboard for the lid that matched the container. "Listen to this one." She turned her face to him, devoid of all expression. "I lied to you about your book. It's lost."

Vikram watched, trying not to understand, as she took two similar lids out from the cupboard. The first was too big for the container. The second snapped into place. "What book?" But he knew.

The Pyronauts.

"I lost it. I'm not joking. It's gone. I've looked everywhere. I don't know if I will find it. But, hey. Who cares, right? It's just some memento to you. Or a paperweight, like your dissertation. Fucking two hundred thousand words, who knows how many hours that took you. You act like you don't give a shit, you with your big flashlight and your uniform, but I know what it must mean. Somewhere inside you, you buried the bodies, right? Where are they? How did you shut it all off?"

He didn't speak.

"Teach me your secret. Teach me your secret!"

He sat in the hard chair, his hands flat on the table's surface. He knew the chair as well as he knew anything he'd inherited in this new world. Its quirks were as familiar to him as Hel's. One leg's slightly shorter length set it off balance; if he didn't hold his body completely still, he would rock a little in the uneven seat. That leg would thump against the floor, a *knock knock knock* for a tenant who'd long ago moved away.

Throughout his childhood, Vikram had observed his parents' quarrels. At a certain point in every one of their frequent disagreements, his mother would lock herself in the bathroom. Vikram would watch his father in the hallway, shouting through the keyhole. He would reason with his wife. He would attempt to see things her way. He would cry. But Vikram's mother did not respond to any of it, and she wouldn't come out until she was good and ready. She could sleep in there. She would curl up in the bathtub, piles of clean towels for her pillows and blankets.

Thus Vikram didn't believe in walking away from a fight. He'd seen what it did to the other person. Hours of ugliness and recriminations on both sides were, to him, preferable to the cowardice, the ignobility of withdrawal.

His chair rocked. The leg knocked. Hel bent to slot the storage container full of pasta into the crowded bottom shelf of their cold box. Her face in profile. Her lips pressed tight, the familiar mole by the flange of her nose.

She turned her body, but she wouldn't meet his eyes. "I'm sorry," she said.

The next thing he knew, he was out of the kitchen. Not just out of the room, not just out of the apartment, but down the hall, down the stairs, through the lobby. He was on the street outside, looking up at his own bright windows.

How had that happened?

But he was not alone. No one is ever alone in the most populous city in America.

Leaves rustled at his feet and cars hushed past on pavement still wet from rain that had fallen and stopped. Two middle-aged women came out of the payday advance store and halted on the corner under the streetlight, talking softly and seriously. A small child across the way shrieked as her father lifted her up to carry her on his shoulders. The building super of a complex nearby hauled his bulging trash bags, tossing them into their bins. Ordinary people, like the ones he'd left behind. The hair on Vikram's arms stood up.

He imagined seeing Hel's shadow passing from left to right, her elongated shape dark against the glowing yellow curtains, watching for him. But he didn't look up to see it.

○

When Sleight was a little older than Hel was today, he'd lived in the cottage in Brownsville across the street from the synagogue. She spoke aloud the titles of the books he'd written there like a recited prayer: *What to Do with the Night. The Poorhouse. Chinese Whispers. The Pain Ray. The Pyronauts.*

He'd lived alone with his cat, Catamount, bereft of all human companionship aside from that of his fiancée of half a decade, Ada Green, who had by this time given up on Sleight ever marrying her, but who still came by occasionally, bringing gifts of food to supplement what scanty produce grew among the weeds in his wild garden. This was the '50s and war with America Unida was on, again. Every night, city wardens announced on the airwaves blackouts still in effect across the five boroughs: the city darkened to foil the small Abeja and Avispa bombers piloted by El Mero Mero's Mexican allies on their stinging missions up the coast. In addition to the opaque fabric curtains most people used, Sleight taped sheets of butcher paper over every single pane of glass in the house; no lamplight could get out during the nights and no sunlight could get in during the days. Day and night became interchangeable while he composed *The Pyronauts* on the old typewriter at the scarred kitchen table.

Vikram was the one who'd relayed these facts to her. She found the picture they painted very satisfying.

A month ago, she'd paced the floors of Sleight's house, inspecting the haphazard piles of possessions that crowded the space where that historic table might once have stood. Young Dwayne Sealy didn't offer to take her to the upstairs room where Sleight once slept under the eaves, and she did not insist on being shown. She preferred the picture in her head, a room as empty as a monk's cell. An iron bedframe, paint flaking off. A narrow mattress piled high with quilts. A shelf for the old-fashioned pitcher and bowl he used to wash his face, the great tangled beard she remembered from the back cover of the book; if Hel could have grown such a beard in memoriam, she would have. A second shelf for a console radio with a lighted dial. And on the slanted papered walls, notes for his novel written in pencil, outlines and maps overlapping each other, plot points and lists of names.

Aliens.

Visitors from fathomless space.

A wiser power who turned out, of course, not to be so wise.

The upstairs room of the cottage. Had Vikram seen it? Surely, he would have mentioned it to her when he talked about his work there. He talked about the otherworldly junk instead, talked about the present and all of the worthless possessions that got in the way. Or he talked about the people he worked alongside, their stories. Their reactions to his.

She felt as if she had somehow donned the protective equipment John Gund wore, as if she were carrying his eighteen kilograms of gear—the compact dustproof tent, the nutritional paste and water ration he and Asyl needed to survive in the Neverlands, the heavy tank of chemicals that powered the flame pistol, the testing supplies. And she wanted to take off the pack and leave it behind. She was tired of squinting through the fogged faceplate of a protective suit. She wished to walk through the world naked, like Aitch.

Vikram was the one who should be so attached, so entangled. Not her. She had taken his book, but he, he had taken her purpose.

Upstairs in the house, under the sharp-angled roof, the rain and its audible echo. Each of the Novembers Sleight lived there, it would have come down on him, but she thought specifically about the year that he wrote *The Pyronauts*, a year of attacks from above. It came down on Sleight while he lay still and listened and worked out the plot. That's where fear came from: the sky. Just as she had lain in her son's tiny bed that night in Park Slope after the attack, knowing then what it was like to grab a knife by the blade. She heard the rain scream at her on the fire escape outside, and she was certain for the first time that she could not protect him. She'd never be able to protect him again, no matter what she did.

She'd been right about that.

She didn't want this connection. Maybe, if she got the book back for Vikram, they could switch.

INTERVIEW TRANSCRIPT:
STORMIE URDANETA, AGE 31,
STATEN ISLAND

The first time was with one of the receptionists at the optometrist's office where I'm a tech. Trinh, her name is. She beckoned me over to her desk to ask me under her breath if I had a tampon. I told her no, sorry, and she looked offended like I'd broken some cardinal rule of sorority, so I explained that where I'm from, most women have a reusable menses catcher instead, like a soft silicon cup.

Where I'm from being, you know, the least awkward way to refer to my status.

And it's true, about the catcher. Though they're not exactly mainstream here, they do exist, a design similar enough to what I was used to, and I didn't see anything weird about it. Not until that conversation, when I noticed Trinh's reaction. This look of mild disgust crossed her face. But she didn't come right out and express her discomfort. Instead, she said something fake like oh, how wonderful that is. How ecological.

"It is," I said to Trinh. "It's very ecological. And healthy. Because where I'm from, what women do is we drink the captured menstrual blood out of the catcher. We find it fortifying."

That knocked her out of her pretend open-mindedness.

"Your *own*?" she asked, her voice quavering.

"Or our mothers' or sisters'," I told Trinh. "You know how women synch up? We think that's why."

After the first lie, I knew I would do it again. That night, I made a list of all the things I couldn't remember how to say in my polite and rusty childhood Spanish. Stuff about bodily functions. Suicide. Sexual mores. Bereavement rituals. If I'd lost the vocabulary—or never had it in the first place—that indicated a topic that wasn't discussed in public. I would lie about all of them.

Who would know? Who would I shame, now?

My parents fled El Mero Mero in the '80s. I was born here and I'm as American as anyone else, but the kids in elementary school who called me comrade didn't know that, or care. My father told me I was always going to stick out. From an early age, he trained me to believe it was essential that I behave unimpeachably. Under no circumstances was I to draw negative attention to myself, because by so doing, I'd be drawing negative attention to my entire community. If an ignorant person made rude assumptions, I was supposed to remember my dignity as a Venezuelan anti-communist as well as the dignity of every *mestizo* and *pardo* around the world when I responded.

"But Papa," I told him, "I just want to be like everybody else."

"Too bad," he said. "You're not."

While my landlord repaired my dripping sink, I told him
that in my world, people only have sex standing up and prefer-
ably in the shower because the man's ability to defecate just
after the woman attains orgasm is prized as erotic. I told my
roommates that we encourage young children to smoke cigarettes when they have the common cold to loosen the throat.
I told my server at a Lebanese restaurant in Bay Terrace that,
where I'm from, people with bipolar disorder are permitted to
carry their pet cats with them everywhere because cats are believed to absorb bad mental-health energy and, furthermore, I
planned to return the following week with my own cat. I told
the flamboyant guy who works at the bodega down the block
that at UDP funerals, all attendees line up to gently slap the
cheeks of the corpse in its coffin, one by one, to assure themselves that their loved one is really dead.

In deference to my father's memory, I made certain to mention that this tradition wasn't a Venezuelan thing. I told him
that, in my world, Swedes and Finns from the upper Midwest
had been especially zealous about the ritual slapping.

At first, it felt really good to say all this. Maybe I've always
wanted to tell lies and I just didn't know how to do it. I've always been a good girl. An obedient daughter.

There are thousands of us UDPs and no one really knows
us—not intimately. When I told people these things, they almost always nodded, outwardly accepting. They didn't question
me. They told me our traditions were interesting.

Last week, I was feeling under the weather. I was in the
kitchen, pouring myself a glass of tomato juice, and my room-
mate Amina came in. She had a pack of Parliament Lights

with the cellophane still on and a book of matches, and she pushed them across the counter to me.

"Here, Stormie," she said. "Maybe this might help?"

Even though I've never smoked—I've never even tried sniff—I know how much those things cost in this New York City, what with the taxes. I felt moved by her gesture, just a little. But I quashed that impulse down. It was pathetic. I said to her: "I mean, thanks for the thought. But I told you, that's for children."

It was depressing, is what it was. Knowing she was so gullible. Knowing that she and all the others were willing—eager, even—to believe any outrageous nonsense I could make up about me and my people.

My people. I can't believe I just said that.

Look at me, fitting in, now that it's too late.

I'm going to have to think of some worse lies to tell.

CHAPTER THIRTEEN

Vikram stood in the gloom at the foot of the stairs, picking at a long tear in the wood of the banister. He tried to imagine how the damage might have been done. Some previous tenant moving furniture up the narrow steps, the half landing, the tight turn. Scuffs marred the pale wallpaper and one rip exposed an older pattern just below the surface. Wear and tear. A palimpsest of lives, moving things in, moving things out.

Stand still enough, for long enough, and he might see them. A parade of previous residents, shadows on top of each other, moving through one another unperturbed and going about their various businesses, cast onto the walls of this house, of every old house, like the pictures projected from a magic lantern. Vikram waited to watch them dance.

"Incoming!" Dwayne tossed a full garbage bag into the front hall, barely missing Vikram's head. "Shit, man. Look alive down there. Stop moping. I've got a better idea for you, anyway."

Ever since Vikram mentioned his failure to reach Oliveira, Dwayne had made valiant efforts to cheer him up. But Dwayne didn't know it was impossible; he didn't know about the book. "Give it a rest, OK?" Vikram said.

"No, listen. Are you ready for this? My high school friend works for the city now, investigating police misconduct claims. People make complaints about the police, he looks into them. And guess who's got an open case?"

"You might want to not throw those around." Vikram stooped to examine a split in the trash bag that had just fallen from on high. "You bought the cheap kind, didn't you? The plastic can't take that kind of punishment." He poked the contents—children's clothing, still with tags on—back in through the hole in the bag, and tossed the whole thing into the corner of the now decluttered living room reserved for items to be donated to charity.

"Guess who?" Dwayne insisted.

"No one we've heard of, probably." Wes's voice filtered out, muffled, from one of the upstairs bedrooms.

"Wrong! Joslan Micallef. She made a complaint about discriminatory anti-UDP language being used against her after her arrest."

"Her arrest for murdering an eighty-year-old?" Vikram said. They were talking about giving up on the most respected UDP and settling instead for the most reviled. "Are you kidding me?"

"No, I am not. She made a complaint, and an investigator interviewed her. It's perfect. Incoming!"

Vikram ducked as another bag of clothes sailed down the stairs. He kicked it over to a clear spot next to the first, careful not to let it snag on the loose nail protruding from the threshold. "I'm not interested." *The Pyronauts*. All he had of it now was a memory as transparent as his feeble imaginings.

"Here's what I'm picturing," Dwayne continued, ignoring him. "Joslan's in Rikers now, right? In the women's facility. Max security. No one's getting in to talk to her again. But the interview she already did—it's all recorded. What if my friend could get you a copy? Put *that* in your museum."

Wes came around the corner to the landing, a big box in his arms. "I see a couple of problems here. Why would Vikram want an interview with Joslan Micallef?" He sidled past Dwayne. "The whole point of this is sympathy, right? To get people to see us as people too."

"Use your head, man. Notoriety. She's notorious. You don't want sympathy—you want attention. Anybody would like to know what's going on in that woman's head, right? She's all over the tabloids. And you've got her talking about herself. It's great! Hey, are you even listening down there?"

Emptied out, the living room where Vikram stood appeared much larger than it had the first time he was in the junk-filled house. Daylight sifted in through the two windows that gave onto the front porch and the one on the north wall, all three of them shrouded with the disintegrating lace curtains that predated Mrs. Defoe's tenancy. Gold linoleum covered the floor, curled up in the corners. They'd scrubbed at that linoleum for hours on their knees, but the stains persisted. Someday, Dwayne said, it could be stripped to expose the hardwood floorboards beneath, but Vikram thought that what the place really needed was some rugs or carpeting or something to

219

muffle the echoes and make it feel more inhabited. Less like a tomb.

"Vikram?"

"Yeah," he said. "I'm listening. How is your friend going to give me a recording to use without getting himself in trouble?"

"This is the best part. You do a FOIA request for the file, once the case is closed."

"Foil?"

"FOIA. It's the Freedom of Information Act! Government agencies have to give you the information you want. It's for transparency."

Vikram was skeptical. "How long is that going to take?"

"Hold on," Dwayne called down after a minute. "I'm Googling it."

Wes came clomping down the rest of the stairs in his boots. He dropped the box—collectible china figurines, it looked like—in the hall. "Wanna take a smoke break?"

"You don't even smoke." Still, Vikram followed him out through the cleared kitchen and jumped down after him onto the soft ground of the bare yard. Over by a fence post, Dwayne had placed a flowerpot containing an ossified African violet discovered on the top shelf of his grandmother's linen closet. It sat in the dirt, half full of cigarette ends now. Vikram pulled a new one out of his pack and lit it. "You want?"

"Nah." Wes pulled out a tin and pinched a pea-sized amount of whatever was inside onto the webbing between his outstretched thumb and forefinger. He inhaled sharply, a practiced gesture very familiar to Vikram.

"Hold on! What's that?"

"Calm down. It's just snuff, not sniff. I assume you've tried it."

Vikram sighed, disgusted by his own momentary hope. "Snuff? Yeah. I tried it when I first got here."

"Nasty, right? Not the same at all."

"Sometimes, I wish I'd thought to fill up my whole bag with cans of sniff when I crossed. Just think what I could sell that for."

"Are you joking? You would have used it all by now."

"Right." Vikram laughed mirthlessly. "I'd be sitting here regretting that, on top of, you know, everything else in my life."

"Look, dude, don't take it so hard. There's plenty of other UDPs out there besides Oliveira. What about trying someone else? There's that guy who was on reality TV—"

"No. I don't care anymore." He flicked his cigarette. "I'm sorry, but I just don't."

"You don't have to apologize."

Vikram looked at Wes's neck, at the scar like a face in a photograph clumsily scratched out. Once again, like a man probing an unhealed wound, he considered the missing book. He knew the concept of a museum wasn't about Sleight, but about every vanished individual Sleight stood for.

He'd tried so hard to convince Hel that the very premise of her obsession was faulty, that Sleight's death couldn't possibly have been the catalyst for the changes to the world. But did he believe that she was wrong? Without knowing it, he too had started to believe.

Such a little thing, 328 pages, paper and ink, pocket-sized. Pulp from trees that never grew. Different trees had grown in their place and were cut down in their stead to have different words printed on them. For Vikram, the museum idea was rooted in this house. The house was Sleight and Sleight was Jonas. Jonas their collective loss. Without the book, none of it made sense.

○

As far as the pyronauts could determine, their erstwhile visitor had left camp without taking a thing that did not belong to him. This discovery came as a pleasant surprise to John Gund, but Asyl had an opposite reaction. She insisted that they go after Aitch. A lone man wandering the wastes would surely die, unsupplied and unprotected. John Gund pointed out that Aitch was no victim of fortune. He'd left them voluntarily and in the same condition in which he'd arrived, and he seemed to have been getting along just fine without them for most of his life. She wouldn't listen to reason. She insisted.

Sometimes, John Gund couldn't help but feel pity for Asyl, native to such a blighted world. Her childhood, spent in a bunker. Her youth, dominated by the warnings of the aliens and the protective rules of the community elders. The reproachful stories men like him told her. In choosing the life of a ranger, she'd taken the most adventurous option that chance had offered her, but there was so much she hadn't seen. Even the danger of the microbes became monotonous in its unrelenting consistency. What could she know about risk? About a man who walked through the world without a helmet and liked it that way?

John Gund's own youth was a bygone era and though he did not mourn its passage as much as he pretended to, he wouldn't have traded away the experience. For better or worse, it had formed him. The women, free in a way that Asyl was not. The drink. The weight of dice in his hands. Cards facedown on the felt, the thrill of that. A ball bouncing from slot to slot and the wind in his hair as he rode through the night in an open pod.

This man Asyl wanted to follow was as young as she, born After the fall of the world, but Aitch lived closer to the way John Gund once had, back when he was a youth himself. Gund forced himself to admit it—Aitch would have understood about the wind. Outlaws always do.

Every stupid risk and misstep, he thought to himself. Even every weakness forms us.

So John Gund did not protest. He sorted through their unmolested gear in anticipation of their departure, distributing it between their two packs. Fuel and heater in his, compressed tent in Asyl's, water bags in his, nested pots and food packets in hers—he always did his best to take the slightly heavier items without skewing the division so obviously that she would notice. Meanwhile, having won the argument, Asyl set about determining which way they should go to overtake the stranger.

First, she unpacked the spyglass and scanned the surrounding hills in all directions, hoping for a glimpse of Aitch's departing figure. Other teams before them here, assiduous in their burning, made sure that no trees stood to obstruct Asyl's view. The regrowth of foliage on even the farthest hills was insufficiently developed to hide a fleeing man. She should have been able to spot him if he were anywhere around. John Gund pointed out that this meant the man must have quite a lead on them.

Undeterred, Asyl paced the perimeter of the area where they'd spent the night, searching for traces in the dust. He knew her to be an expert tracker. When she chose a direction, he didn't try to argue. They turned their backs on the coordinates they'd been assigned to test and clear and walked in the opposite direction.

○

Hel adjusted the focus on her binoculars. A waste of money, as it turned out, since Donaldson and Angelene kept the blinds in their third-floor apartment shut at all times. When Hel twisted the knob, she could make slats come into clear relief, but magnification couldn't give her the power to see through. Both women were inside now; she'd seen them come home an hour ago. Would they stay in place, or would this be the night they both went out together, giving her a chance? If so, she'd be ready.

Only two stars visible tonight and in commemoration of her mission, she'd named them Gund and Asyl. The bright one after Asyl, of course, the one that she could always find, every night—the one to steer by. Refuge. The North Star. John Gund's lesser star hovered above the horizon. Maybe it was not a star at all but a satellite or a planet. Venus.

In order to maintain a sight line from the building across the way while staying low enough not to be seen from the street, Hel had to lie on her belly. She'd brought Vikram's ski parka and a scratchy plaid wool picnic blanket, misshapen from an accidental machine drying, but her elbows were sore from leaning on them and her arched back ached. If she'd taken a moment with the binoculars, she would have been able to look at all the other rooftops around, where residents hunched with secret cigarettes in the short winter evenings or spread their towels to tan in the summer sun. The sky-high cocktail bars Hel's city had been known for were beginning to be popular in this New York, too. With their finite dimensions and age-old geographical peculiarities, these five boroughs were destined to be crowded with a population strangling itself. For space and light and freedom, people went up. No matter what the differences, there would never be anywhere else to go.

But Hel didn't have time to look around. She kept her binoculars trained on one particular building, on the left-hand side of the top floor. Two evenings in a row, as the dark came on, she'd watched the yellow rectangles light up. A switch being flicked, lamps going on in those secret rooms.

Please let them leave. Please.

As far as she could tell, Vikram hadn't been home to the apartment in the Bronx since their fight. Yet it occurred to her that their lives were running more tightly in parallel than ever. They were both nocturnal now. She spent the daylight hours in his bed while he slept somewhere else—at Kabir's house or with his new friends—and when the late fall sun lowered in a sky the color of a healthy tongue, they each commuted to Queens. Him, far east to Jamaica for his security job. Her, here, to Long Island City. On her mission. Potential consequences to her actions, the risks she was running—once, these might have troubled Hel, but now, they didn't seem to register. Yet she didn't feel empty, as she had in the long days of depression. Her fascination with the recovery of the book animated her in the same way the idea for the museum once had.

Today, she'd skipped her Reintegration Education meeting. No excuse, which meant an automatic write-up.

Then, there was the breaking and entering.

This building where she watched and waited had SPACE FOR RENT signs posted, and the camera mounted in the corner looked fake. It wasn't hard to clamber up on top of the angled piece of corrugated steel that shielded the external stairs. The metal had rumbled noisily under her feet like stagecraft thunder. It should have scared her, the thought that it might give way, but instead it made Hel feel brave, like a comic book hero—the Peregrine Falcon from her childhood—as she boosted herself onto the roof. The 7 didn't emerge from its tunnel until it reached Hunters Point Avenue, one stop deeper into Queens. Without elevated trains, it was quieter up here than she was used to. But really, the roof around her looked like the roof of every building she'd ever seen, her whole life. Tar was tar, after all, and air was air.

She rubbed at her eyelids with gloved fingertips. Under her blanket, she hunkered down, like a squirrel, high up in the branches of its winter drey. All the leaves that hid her from view in the warm summer months had fallen—dead—but her nest remained, a tangle of messy branches. The hidden illusion of the world ripped away and everything underneath exposed.

People would steal. They would work to cross you in any way they could. They didn't need a reason to do those things. They were driven by forces beyond understanding.

This card is below you. The thing you must overcome.

Motion across the way. The green door of Donaldson's redbrick building swung open and a figure stepped out. Without shifting position, Hel raised the binoculars. Angelene stood on the stoop, reaching behind her to pull the hood of a sweat-shirt out of a hastily thrown-on Yankees jacket. Hel had been a Dodgers fan at home, but the Dodgers were across the country here; she'd come to like the Yankees simply because of the geographical and historical continuity. Angelene looked both ways and crossed the street, walking briskly in the direction of the subway a few blocks away.

Where was Donaldson? Not with her wife. She must still be inside. One down and one to go.

Angelene's shape had passed entirely out of sight now. "Please," Hel said—under her breath, but aloud. "Please." She thought of Vikram, how he'd risen from the table, face obscured like a moon in a polluted sky. She remembered the pause as he stood there, the long moment in which anything from him had seemed possible. How he'd bumped his shoulder against the doorframe in his hurry to get away.

Might she have stopped him, if she'd followed?

But she'd had nothing to say to him. No excuse. This was the only way.

Lost in rumination, she almost missed Donaldson's exit. It was the lights going out—the abrupt vanishment of those yellow rectangles—that attracted her attention. Biting her lip to shock herself back into her body, Hel pointed the binoculars to the door downstairs in time to see it open.

Ayanna Donaldson wore sweatpants, but they were the nice kind—the kind that was seemingly acceptable outside the home in this world—and a tailored leather jacket. Braids hung down to the collar, making her look girlish. She did not linger on the doorstep. Without hesitation, she pounded down to the street and took off in the opposite direction from Angelene in a loping half run.

Now. The apartment was empty. Now. And Donaldson was alone.

She could break into the house, or she could follow. Where was the book more likely to be? Hel froze with indecision, knowing that if she wanted to follow, she'd need to get moving.

As she watched Donaldson's silhouette below, its progress down the block abruptly halted. She stood just beyond the bright circle cast by a streetlight, and seemed to be conversing with someone else, a short man with broad shoulders. A friend she was meeting? Where had he come from? The two faced each other in front of a shuttered shoe repair store, its pull-down grate splashed with graffiti. The man leaning into Donaldson's space as if he were whispering in her ear. The intimacy of their body language deceived Hel so completely that she was shocked when Donaldson flinched back, alarmed when the man roughly grabbed her arm.

She seemed to say something to the man and snapped open her clutch purse, rummaging inside. Hel watched as, with a short and economical movement, the man knocked it from her hands, the contents spilling at her feet. Donaldson dropped to her knees, but the man hauled her upright by the arm he was still holding. He was speaking, his mouth moving.

The man didn't seem to have a weapon. But Hel did. She always did. She felt the knife's weight by her side and reached down to touch it.

A rushing in her ears that whispered *go!*

CHAPTER FOURTEEN

The man who slipped Hel off had grabbed her on a stretch of sidewalk just beyond the trolley line terminus, brandishing a large clasp knife with a fake mother-of-pearl handle. He'd backed her up against a low wall at the edge of Prospect Park, the rough bricks snagging at her stockings, and he'd breathed in her air as he told her what he wanted from her, nice and easy, nice and easy.

Somehow, the attacker had mistaken her for a woman headed home alone. He didn't realize Jonas was with her. Her son was young then—five and a half—and forever running up ahead, eager to be the one who got somewhere first. The thought of him had played urgently in her mind while the man threatened her. Where was Jonas? Would he stop, realizing his mother wasn't following? Would he come back to her, putting himself in danger too?

As the stranger displayed his weapon in front of her eyes, too close for Hel to focus on as he held her pinned, he told her in a surprisingly soft voice how he would start by carving up her face and finish with her gootch. He made the knife dance in front of her, pricking her bottom lip with the tip, and when she reached out to stop it with her right hand—not a plan, by any means, but a terrified reaction—the blade bit into all four of her fingers, bit deep, and she'd yelled, both in pain and surprise. He'd thrown her to the ground, where she caught herself with her hands—her good hand and her bad hand, hot blood and cold, damp leaves—and regretted the noise she'd made. Where was Jonas? How desperately she'd hoped that if he was watching, he would be terrified into speechlessness. Stay still, Jonas. Stay quiet. Do nothing to attract the bad man's attention.

Later, in the back of the police van, the start of that haunting, piacular feeling in her chest, she'd hugged Jonas tight and told him how proud she was. How brave and smart he'd been, to run and get a trolley guard to help.

And after that, she'd carried her own knife—always.

○

"Here you go," said Dwayne, handing Vikram a bundle of translucent plastic that looked something like an enormous folded shower curtain. "I've got blankets downstairs. Let me find the pump." He thrust the plastic, heavier than it seemed it should be, into Vikram's arms. "Unfold it," Dwayne said, shooting him a look of frustration modulated somewhat by pity. "You never seen an air mattress? Don't answer that."

An assortment of boxes and storage bins still filled the master bedroom all the way up to the eaves. On the other side of the stairs, a cold-water washroom and a second bedroom took up the other half of the floor space. It was here, in this half-cleared smaller room, that Vikram was to sleep. He knelt on the bare boards just inside the door and unfolded the vinyl into a square.

Though Wes and Ari had been nothing but hospitable, Vikram could tell he was underfoot in the flat, getting ready for work when the others were coming home and cooking dinner. His back complained from two days on a couch too short for his full height. In the middle of the afternoon yesterday, he'd woken from a fitful sleep to the sound of someone in the apartment directly above, running water. He'd stayed there in his fetal curl, listening to the water in the pipes, and remembered his mother and her bathtub martyrdom. But he couldn't go back to his own apartment, no matter that he paid the rent, no matter that he knew he was in the right, no matter that he longed to hold Hel in his arms.

The irony that he now sought refuge from her here, when he'd spent restless days in this house hoping to make her happy. Even if the museum wouldn't work out, maybe he would just hole up in the cottage like a hermit. Tape up the windows.

Dwayne came back in with the camping lantern and a heavy black battery-powered device that seemed to be the pump. "It fits in the valve like this, see?" Slowly, the mattress began to inflate. "You think you're going to be warm enough?"

"Sure. I'm actually really excited to sleep here," Vikram said, trying to convince himself. "After all, a genius slept here. Sort of."

"In this room?"

"In the big room, I think. But still."

"That was my grandma's room." The mattress made little popping noises as the air forced apart layers of plastic that had been stuck together. "Me and my brother Shawn slept over all the time when we were kids. She already had some strange collections—that I remember. Meat grinders. Thimbles. I used to like the souvenir glasses she had best, all painted with flowers or animals. I would make him take them out of their box and unwrap the newspaper, every time we were here. Our mom would drop us off and leave us, usually just for the weekend. One time, though, it was more like a month. My grandma was still working then—she was in her fifties, probably. She did bookkeeping for a construction company. I remember she took the first Monday and Tuesday off to stay with us, but when my mom didn't show up after that, she just gave Shawn the key and told him to keep an eye on me. Told me to keep an eye on him and call 911 if his breathing got bad. I could tell she was feeling guilty, like it was a really irresponsible thing for her to do, her leaving us alone. Guess she didn't know our mom had been leaving us in charge of each other since Shawn was in grade school."

"How much older was your brother?"

"Two years. He was twenty-three when he died, and that was three years ago. That means I'm older than he ever got to be. Much as I try not to, I've been thinking about him a lot recently. It's funny—with an old person, you can see why they get called home. But Shawn. Guess it still don't make sense to me."

"Yeah," Vikram said.

"I should go see his grave. Tomorrow, I'll do it." Dwayne got to his feet, leaving the pump connected to the still-expanding mattress, and walked to the door, peering out into the hall, the other bedroom. His back to Vikram, he continued to talk. "We weren't supposed to go in that big bedroom when my grandmother wasn't home, but of course that's what we liked to do. She had the stuff she said was valuable back there. All these dolls she'd ordered out of ads in the *TV Guide* that she kept in special clear plastic cases."

Vikram thought of the sentient heads in jars from Sleight's early novel, *The Pain Ray*. "Weird."

"Yeah. They scared us, like Snow White at the end of the Disney movie, that dead lady lying there in her glass coffin, waiting for the prince to kiss her. Wait. You wouldn't have seen that."

"We had our own Snow Whites. Half a dozen, probably—cartoon, live-action, versions from Indian cinema—just not the one you're talking about. I don't remember a glass coffin in any of them."

"That shit was pretty dark for kids. But me, I always wanted to look at the dolls, and at that painting Grandma had. Took up the whole wall, almost, from floor to ceiling. Shawn made up a game. One of the rules was you couldn't step any closer to it than the edge of the carpet by the bed. So I couldn't see whatever the little people on the edge were up to. Still, that iceberg and that ship gave me a chill."

"Iceberg?"

"It was a big old thing."

"Iceberg," Vikram repeated dumbly. He remembered sitting in the abandoned mental hospital in the children's ward while the sticks ran from room to room below. His breaths, shallow in the pitch dark, his extreme sensitivity to the input of his four remaining senses. The feeling that he was in the presence of a ghost. He felt that now: every inch of skin alive and his heart a dead, frozen block.

"The big waves and the storm clouds and the ice. I'll tell you, it made me not even want to go in the paddleboats you could rent at Marine Park in the summer." The Coleman lantern lit Dwayne's face from below, shadowing his forehead and cheeks, illuminating his eye sockets, nose, and jaw like a skull in reverse. A parody of someone telling a scary story around a campfire.

Of course Vikram had seen reproductions of the painting, color plates in library books. He'd read Sleight's own childish description from his collected schoolboy letters, *tho they cast out to the drowning man he can't ever seem to find their ropes, papa, and the blue sea-ice shews the water to be killing cold*, not to mention technical monographs written by experts. Still, he said, "Tell me. What did it look like?"

"The sky was on fire. Sunset, big ocean, big sky. Blueish-white icebergs and the top of a drowning ship. That's what it was. And the frame—big and heavy, gold-painted wood. Looked like something that belonged in—well, a museum."

○

"Hey!" Her own voice sounded shaky and jarringly loud; there were no cars around, for once, no one outside but her. "Hey, you!" She ran toward the two figures—Ayanna Donaldson and the stranger. Over her shoulder rode her stars. She felt them there, faint and weak but asserting themselves nevertheless through the smog and light pollution. Following her.

At the sound of her voice, the man jerked his head. Behind him, Donaldson looked up too, her eyes dark like pits, but she didn't appear scared. Hel pictured that first card she'd found on the ground at Kent Avenue and its Truth deck analogue, the Sword Queen. In Smith's design, that queen was the one who appeared to sleep sitting up, while all the eyes carved on her throne stared impassively outward, watching out for her.

If Jonas had come to Hel that night in Prospect Park when she yelled, if he'd run to her arms instead of seeking outside help—she'd never said this to Jonas, but of course he must have known it, must have learned this lesson more indelibly than it could have been taught any other way—if her son had stayed with her, she wouldn't have been able to protect him.

But this time it would be different.

"Back up, or I'll call the sticks! The cops!" Donaldson's face, frozen like wood. "I've got my phone ready. I'm going to take a picture of you, and when they find you, she's going to press charges." The weight of the knife dragged down the pocket of Vikram's yellow-and-black ski parka, the coat that kept her warm while she surveilled. She thought of Vikram at the storage warehouse, how she used to worry about him patrolling alone inside the cyclone fence. But he was fine. He'd shown her how he would protect himself. He'd demonstrated clubbing someone, in the safe domesticity of their apartment, with that standard-issue flashlight. Indeed, an improvised weapon could be much better than a blade. A blade could always be turned against you.

She kept her hand on it, inside her pocket. Safer not to show that she had it, but if the man didn't obey her, she would stab him right in the eye.

The would-be thief dropped his hand from Donaldson's arm. "Go," Hel ordered. "Get the fuck out of here." Swords, the suit associated with action and danger. Hel stood firm, like the youth in the five of that suit, a figure who treads upon the weapons of his enemies, smiling cruelly as they flee him. A card signifying conflict and tension. Loss.

Without a backward glance, Donaldson's attacker jogged away from them—heading toward the river, turning right when he reached the corner—and then they couldn't see him anymore. Hel was surprised to feel regret. She'd wanted more. In the Ten of Swords, a man lies on the shore, ten swords growing out of his body, pinning him to the sand. "Do you want me to call 911?" she asked.

"No." Donaldson moved as if to crouch, to pick up the spilled contents of her purse, but then half fell. Catching herself, she sat ungracefully on the sidewalk. "God. Actually. I guess we should."

Hel punched in the numbers and then handed over the phone so Donaldson could give the address. Then she helped Donaldson to a nearby stoop, the baby-soft feel of the sleeve of the leather jacket reminding Hel that this wasn't a dream.

Her job had been both destruction and reconstruction. She would take a bone plate using a craniotome and drill, shape it to fit the defect, the area that had been excised. She would harvest strips from the scalp and suture it all in place. Right away, while the patient was still anesthetized, she'd be able to tell how well he or she had tolerated the procedure. She had an instinct for that. Donaldson's scared eyes were somehow harder to read. "Are you all right?"

"I'm—yes," Donaldson said. "I think so. Thank you. Thank you. That was really—are *you* all right?"

"Did you know him? That man?"

"No." Donaldson looked off in the direction he'd run. Hel noted the positions of the lit bridges, the shapes of the Midtown buildings, familiar and unfamiliar. "You can see the Chrysler Building," Donaldson said. The contents of the purse were still strewn across the sidewalk. She took a lipstick tube in her hands, uncapping and recapping it. "From the roof of our building. Our realtor told us that. He called this neighborhood 'up-and-coming,' but I know an MTA employee got murdered inside the Hunters Point station, the year we moved here. The killer—whoever it was—got away with it."

It was the job of the patient-care team to test for neurological defect, afterward. Hel would make herself scarce for this, when she could. She didn't want to be thanked. She didn't want to be asked about future prognosis. After she left the operating theater trance, her own hands would sometimes shake, as they were shaking now. That series of little snaps as Donaldson played with the lipstick cap. They bothered her. "You should really carry a weapon." Hel said, "A gun or whatever, to protect yourself. They're easier to get here, aren't they?"

"You seem to have these two beliefs that are in fundamental conflict. That everything is worse here than it was where you came from. And that everything's easier for us—that we're all soft and we don't know about danger. Which is it?"

"No matter what I answer, you'll tell me I'm wrong."

"People are the same, that's what I think. People are people. Good and bad, safe and dangerous. People are always the same." In the distance, a siren approached. Donaldson heard it too. "I guess you should go," she said. "We took out a restraining order against you. I'd hate for you to get into trouble. You know how cops are, with that UDP murder case in the news."

"I'm not going anywhere until you've given me back my book. You owe me now."

Donaldson laughed, a little hysterically, but Hel wasn't joking.

"Where is the book?"

Donaldson put the cap of the lipstick down on the step next to her. With both hands, she twisted the base of the tube. A waxy nub grew in the dark. "I handed it back to you, Helen. I never saw it after that night, the party."

"Why should I believe you?"

Donaldson shrugged. She tossed the open lipstick to the ground. "I'm never going to wear this again, am I?"

"I guess not."

Now, the unmarked police car turned off the avenue, lights flashing on the dash. "Go," Donaldson urged.

"Yeah, I'm going." Hel began to walk toward the Citgo, then turned to call over her shoulder. "Hey. Next time, don't stay quiet, at least. You need to yell for help. Take it from me."

She was all the way to Jackson Avenue when the cops pulled up alongside.

INTERVIEW TRANSCRIPT:
ORSON YOUNG, AGE 54, QUEENS

In 1905, railroad men calculated out the perfect spot in the desert for refueling the trains of the San Pedro, Los Angeles, and Salt Lake Railroad, and those moneymen plotted out my hometown, drawing the streets clean, with rulers. For a hundred years, it kept that same spirit: a place for supplying practical demands. They never built no dams to light up the desert, and gambling wasn't tolerated. Bone-dry town in a dusty state. That's where I grew up.

I guess they call it Sin City here.

But the Las Vegas of my childhood was neighborhoods of four-block apartments built in the '70s to house a population of two hundred thousand, the built-up ruler streets lined with dwarf palms. Everyone who wasn't military worked for one of the two big visor games development companies in town. Missile defense and missile sims, those were our industries. Seemed dull to me at fifteen, sixteen. I dreamed of sky-tall neon buildings and cold, cold ocean. Couldn't wait for my call-up, hoped to be stationed far away, see another slice of the world, somewhere else.

Then I went somewhere *else.*

I went rats. I guess they call that bats here. Or bugs.

You know—crazy.

Dementia praecox was my diagnosis. Schizophrenia. It started out I heard things. Not voices. Ill spits, battle taps. I always liked music, but this was entirely else. Unseen enemies, insulting me in rhyme, and I spit right back to them. Then I started seeing things too. I remember snags of time out on the back streets and in the desert, before my moms got me sectioned and locked up tight. For my own good.

After some stretch, seemed like the volume got turned down so it was bearable, and I found I was on a new drug. Was staying at a Supervised Home out on Alameda Boulevard by the remains of the Old Mormon Fort. I'd lived there for years, they told me. I'd missed my chance for Alt Service. I'd missed everything. My counselor wasn't hopeful for me, neither. He said, "The biggest obstacle with prescribing this treatment tends to be a poor rate of compliance."

But I was scared of the older guys I saw in the halls, who'd led rat lives for even longer. What curses echoed in their ears? I didn't want to know. So I complied.

First I learned to manage the chores on the chore list. When I stayed with that, they got me a job doing supervised janitor work in the public housing buildings. The routine of it helped, the patterns. And the little orange tablets. After a year, I moved out of the Home and applied for Guild training as a coolant tech. For years, I worked that job, inspecting ductwork all over

Vegas. I was happy enough, and I knew I couldn't risk a change. Even when my moms died and I got her pension, I did nothing.

The day I turned fifty, I heard a voice—but it was my own, this time. I said to myself, they got them pills anywhere. You always wanted to leave. This is when. New York is where. So I bought a one-way airship ticket. I told myself, what have you got to lose now? Nothing.

Turns out I was wrong about almost all of that.

When I saw my personal number on the ordinator screen, when I reported to Calvary and they scanned me through the barriers, I was more terrified than anyone else in the entry. Why me, I thought, and not others who were healthy? On the other side, I told anyone who would listen that I needed help, that there was something wrong with me. The Debrief officers got me evaluated and the doctor put me on something right away, and I knew it wouldn't work. I'd been on my medication at home for two and a half decades, but I didn't know the chemical composition. The look of these new white pills almost made me cry—not my friendly orange moons. I took the first dose and waited.

UDPs. Other people say we *all* bats. I look at the aimless and angry folks in my Reintegration Education group, and I know what they mean. But that's not bats. That's just standard UFO shit. Alien is how anybody sane would feel, in the face of a life that's so unfair.

As for me, seems like the drugs they got in this world work for me as good as the other. A miracle.

I don't really like spending time with UDPs. Instead, I go and sit with my man down the block. His name is Ralph. Guy about my same age, same diagnosis. He lives open-roof. They call that sleeping rough here. He ain't from my world, Ralph. He fought in a war I don't know nothing about. He's my brother, all the same. A rat is a rat. Or a bat. Or a bug.

I got things I think about at Reintegration Education, when Officer Dunn asks us to share. About the way I'm rushing to learn a whole language, because my native tongue of slang and nuance is suddenly rare. About what it feels like hearing gootches talk *aliens* right to my face when they don't know I got the wrong ID in my pocket. Worst, about the shape of the mountains. I think about how the same mountains still float above Vegas, waiting for my visit, but I can't go there knowing the city itself is gone. How I miss that empty, nothing place, my home. And that feeling after I left it all through the blue, that long backward glance.

I can't say these things out loud. I been taken apart before and I don't want to be taken apart no further. But I sit with Ralph sometimes, and I whisper it to him.

CHAPTER FIFTEEN

"Can I use a telephone directory?" she asked the officer who'd accompanied her to the wall telephone.

"Nope." The officer scrutinized Hel with a level of interest that suggested she was new on the job. Either that, or she'd never seen a UDP before.

If Hel hadn't been following Donaldson last night, no one would have stopped that man from attacking her. Maybe the man would have taken Donaldson's money, her rings. Or maybe he would have beaten her, raped her. Maybe Donaldson would have struggled and maybe he would have killed her.

Donaldson had told the truth. She was a curator, after all. She understood the value of artifacts.

The only phone numbers Hel knew by heart were Vikram's and Carlos Oliveira's, and Vikram never picked up calls from numbers he didn't recognize. He hadn't even figured out how to set up his voicemail, yet. What she wanted was a lawyer.

"Can you possibly look something up for me on the internet?"

"No. You want to make a call or not?"

"Fine." Hel punched in Oliveira's office number.

Unlikely that he would be in this late.

Six rings and then Oliveira's recorded voice. The tone.

She wasn't supposed to feel disappointed.

"Uh, this is Helen Nash," she told the machine. "I've been arrested. I know you don't care, but maybe you could text Vikram Bhatnagar and let him know what happened? I can't reach him because—well, never mind. Anyway, please tell him I'm being held at the . . ." Here, she turned to her babysitter, who stood five feet away with her arms crossed over her uniformed chest, listening in.

"One-hundred-fourteenth Precinct station house," the officer provided.

"At the 114th Precinct. In Queens. Thank you." What could it hurt to be polite, at this point? She hung up the receiver.

"You can make another call if you want," the officer told her. "Most people don't know this, but you can actually make three."

"No thanks," Hel said and the officer, shrugging, led her back to the holding cell.

Only one other person inside, an older woman in heeled boots, tight jeans, and a sweater patterned with snowflakes, who lay down with her head to the cinder-block wall, taking up the entire bench. Her face showed all the signs of a serious dross smoker. Or whatever it was desperate people smoked here instead.

The door clanged shut, locking Hel in. Without opening her eyes, the other woman drew her knees up to make room. Hel sat down in the space she'd vacated. "Thank you."

She could see the drosshead's chest rise in a sudden breath, could see her eyes flick beneath her lashes, but the woman didn't speak.

If Donaldson were dead, she wouldn't do all the things she was meant to do, whatever those things were. Her absence would change the course of the world—in some unknowable way, small and insignificant or large and far-reaching—change this world to which Hel had now reluctantly and accidentally committed herself. Here, they called that the butterfly effect.

The butterfly effect. Beautiful.

But where was *The Pyronauts*?

○

Vikram listened to the ring, waiting for Hel to pick up. The stubborn part of him that resented being the first to back down from their standoff had been fully overpowered by the part of him that was very, very excited. He knew she would be, too. He had to share that feeling.

He knelt on the floor of the big bedroom in front of it. *The Shipwreck*.

Together, he and Dwayne had dragged boxes, parcels, bags, and loose items into the upstairs hallway, tunneling through the hoarded junk to reach the wall where Dwayne guessed the painting had once hung. The camping lantern illuminated the stuff in their way. Piles of paperbacks. Folded quilts and blankets and a musty, sweat-stained pillow. A massive stack of plastic containers printed with the logos of different brands of yogurt, sour cream, and margarine, all ten years old, Dwayne said, all washed out and nested inside one another as if ready to be reused. Then, more framed art: a map of the London subway system, a midcentury depiction of a Native warrior slumped on a horse with an arrow protruding from his back. A framed cork bulletin board.

Finally, a glint of gold—the edge of the frame Dwayne had described—and the few leftmost inches of dusty canvas. Sea and sky. The broad brushstrokes with which Lowery had rendered the matte, bluish-white prismatic surfaces of the iceberg, sheaves of dirty ice.

The thrill of dread Vikram felt when he pulled the final things away made him think of what it might be like to be called into the office of the medical examiner to identify the damaged corpse of a long-lost loved one. Even if you couldn't see the face, you could tell. You could tell just from the tiniest details. The shape of a kneecap or the faint hairs on the knuckles. A scar from an old burn. The bitten-down fingernails.

Yes. This was it.

"OK. It's confirmed," Vikram told Dwayne. "I can dig it out the rest of the way in the morning, when it's brighter in here."

"You working tonight, man?"

"No, I've got two days off. I'm just going to hang out here. Look through some of these *National Geographic*s. You should get home to Eden, I guess."

"I feel kind of bad for you," Dwayne said, as he put on his coat. "This the city that never sleeps, you know. You should go catch a movie or something. Go to a club."

"Nah, I'll be fine here."

But once Vikram was alone, he felt lonesome. From his place on the air mattress, he watched the hours turn on his watch to bad luck time and beyond, too keyed up to concentrate on the photo essay about the Padaung women of Burma. He found himself back in the room with the painting. He crouched, worshipful.

He thought he'd lost the capacity to feel this way.

He was no art historian—anybody looking closely would see what he saw, that this was no reproduction. He could make out the texture of the surface, how the artist had worked up layers of pigment to produce the luminescent clouds. It didn't take an expert to note the lamentable damage inflicted by neglect, the fine cracks in the paint.

Vikram thought back to that morning fifteen years ago in the Sleight Museum with his vanished friends. The rival, the flatmate, the tour guide, the woman: all of them out of reach now. But being here and seeing the painting brought them back.

He'd climbed to the second floor with the woman he'd loved, watching her movements. Vikram remembered what she'd been wearing, the wide-legged trousers cut from a draping fabric, wet below the knees where the cloth had wicked up water as they walked in the rain. She climbed the stairs, and he followed. Down below, the others left behind in the kitchen exclaimed audibly over an empty tin, long stored in one of the cabinets and produced with a flourish by their guide. "This was Sleight's favorite brand of tea." And he'd trailed the young woman down the hallway to the big bedroom—to this very room—and there kissed her in secret. She'd kissed him back.

Had the painting hung behind them, then? No. Vikram knew for a fact that *The Shipwreck* was accounted for in the other world, on display in a Canadian museum's collection. It had never been missing. Still, to check, he put a floor underneath his young self and his companion, erected sloping walls around them, papered them with shabby wallpaper. His mind's eye had to invent the detail of the pattern.

What else, what else had been in the room? Try as he might, he couldn't see anything but the down of a soft cheek, out of focus, a tendril of hair that touched him.

A skill, not remembering, one he'd cultivated. After all, holding on taxes you. You do it for a while, but eventually, you choose to stop working so hard. Drowning—drowning that part of you—begins to seem preferable to fighting.

He had no idea what might have hung on the wall in Sleight's bedroom.

Not this painting though.

He couldn't explain how it got here. And Hel wasn't picking up to have the miracle revealed to her. The tone echoed in Vikram's ear. Impatient, he ended the call and dialed again.

On his visit in the other world, this had been a place of preservation, a place one went to see things that had been deemed worthy of study and protection. A sturdy gate placed in the doorway of this room, like others in the cottage, kept visitors from entering Sleight's boudoir with their grabbing hands and dirty shoes, and so he'd bent the girl back over the barrier, bracing one hand on the sloping wall—a touch more forbidden than the way he touched her body—and they'd kissed breathlessly. He'd smelled her perfume, a pungent and musky scent, reminiscent of dead leaves. It had seemed to him then like a scent an older woman might wear, a dowager, rich and worldly. A smell from across a boundary.

He remembered the perfume, the trousers, the spring in her step, and the coil of hair, but not her name. It was lost at sea. And it didn't matter.

Hel still wasn't answering. Vikram put down his phone and used both hands to clear away more of the junk. Shoe boxes heavy with unknown contents. A lamp, its cast-resin base shaped like a shepherd girl, the shade badly dented. A cardboard box with a bird's nest inside. Dishes wrapped in yellowing newsprint. A small dusty cabinet of dark wood—some piece of music-playing equipment, a speaker or amplifier. He pushed them all away from the painting or picked them up and moved them behind him, careful not to touch the surface of the canvas, careful not to cause a collapse. He was blocking himself in, he realized, sealing the tunnel he'd created earlier and burying himself with *The Shipwreck*.

To whom did the painting belong?

Dwayne didn't know which of his people had first inhabited this house, but he'd mentioned his great-grandmother, his mother's mother's mother. Allowing twenty-five years per generation, that put them close to the beginning of the twentieth century, a decade or two into After. How much further back did they go? And how had the painting gotten here from Sleight's school? Who was its legal owner?

"What do you want me to do?" Vikram asked Dwayne, when they uncovered the first corner of the canvas, enough to confirm his suspicions. "This has been in your family—"

"Does me no good hidden away up here," Dwayne said. "People ought to be looking at it, if you think it's that important."

Figure it out. He wanted to. He pulled away one last overstuffed garbage bag.

Now, he'd fully exposed it, every square inch. He backed up—as much as he could in the maze he'd created—to take in the most important element of the composition. At the bottom center of the canvas, just below the foundering ship, grasped the white arm and hand Sleight wrote about, the sailor who had so terrified Sleight and Dwayne as boys, reaching up blindly from the water for a coil of rope he would never find.

The color plate Vikram pored over in an old book, the image translated to pixels on the screen of an ordinator—neither did justice to the experience of being right here with the painting. He stretched out his own hand, extending his forefinger, but he didn't touch, knowing the oils of his skin might damage the fragile surface.

The arm was painted small, really—an inch and a half long, perhaps—and Lowery had chosen a ghastly blue overlay for the flesh, only a few shades lighter than the roiling waves. The foreground of that vast ocean nearly swallowed up the sailor's signal for help, an arrangement that emphasized the unseen man's centrality and his insignificance at the same time.

It would be cold in that water.

With his phone, Vikram snapped a picture and texted it to Hel. Surely, she would call him now. She would tell him what to do about this.

Close to dawn, too overwhelmed to dig himself out, he slept in the sea of Mrs. Defoe's collections, his head pillowed on a stuffed toy, an orange bear someone—he imagined Shawn Sealy—might have won for her at Coney Island, if the carnival park were still there. Vikram was not used to sleeping at night and his dreams were uneasy ones, obsessive in their repetition.

He was walking on a dark beach, making for a point of land that never seemed to get any closer, his calves aching, his feet sinking into the sand. Sometimes a stranger pursued him and other times he was the one in pursuit, following a dim figure he could make out ahead only intermittently. When he woke with a crick in his neck and a sore hip, he found the solidity of the bare floorboards to be a relief. He reached for his phone.

Midafternoon already. How had that happened?

Still no missed calls, no texts. He tried Hel's number yet again. No answer. The call went straight to voicemail, as if she hadn't charged her phone. That wasn't like her. They had no home phone at the Bronx apartment. What else?

He called Oliveira. No answer there either.

The assistant at the museum who'd been helping Hel. He remembered the name, Teresa something. Vikram didn't have her number, but he knew where she worked. Maybe Dwayne would give him a ride over to MoMT on his way to Williamsburg.

He went downstairs, walked around the echoing rooms of the cottage. Normally, Dwayne came to clean in the mornings, but there was no sign of him today. Had he gone in for an early shift? Maybe he could get Wes to run him over. Then he remembered that it was Wednesday. Wes would be at Reintegration Education now, where he should be.

He was late.

○

After a few hours in the brightly lit cell, Hel drifted off. She slumped on the very edge of the metal bench, Vikram's parka pulled tight around her. At some point, she heard the cell door open to admit a third arrestee—an impossibly young-looking prostitute with a tear-streaked face—but Hel had run out of sympathy, and did not stir or speak to the new arrival or give up her spot. Some time later, officers loaded the three women and all the men from the holding cell down the hall into a van, which would bring them to Queens Central Booking for arraignment. Hel followed her arresting officer out the station house door, shuffling so as not to lose a shoe. They'd taken away her laces. The sky outside: still black.

The drosshead in the snowflake sweater cupped her hands around her eyes and looked through the grille and out the windshield of the van—as if trying to keep track of the route the speeding van was taking. "Ya estoy," she whispered softly to herself. "Otra vez."

They had her now. Hel rotated her wrists inside the cuffs, which were not uncomfortably tight, but certainly tight enough to hold her. They had her now; it had just taken them longer than she'd expected.

After the mother with the baby and the small boys left the site at Calvary, the entry group consisted of Hel and ninety-eight strangers. None of them talked as they stood where they'd been placed by the evac personnel, watching the small team of technicians in rubber jumpsuits working to expand the dormant Gate for passage. They weren't the first group; they knew that by now, whatever waited on the other side must be expecting them. Hel had looked into the shimmer and prepared for two very obvious possibilities, which no one in charge of the evacuation effort had spoken aloud. First: that this other world might be damaged worse than the one they were leaving. Second: that if it wasn't, its inhabitants might be ready to defend it from encroachment with whatever weapons they had.

Hel prepared herself for gas, for lasers, for bullets, for electric charge.

It was common sense. It was human nature.

She and the others weren't required to hold hands, but as soon as the countdown started, someone grabbed Hel's and she squeezed back hard—half comfort and half punishment—and a thought came to her, as they all stepped forward together: *This could be the last person I touch before I die.*

That blaze of lights that blinded them, in the other Calvary, her first memory of a new world. Floodlights, and the sudden noise of a crowd. A beating thump that she learned later was the sound of helicopter rotors up above. The odd uniforms of the police and military units all around them, the news cameras rolling, a hectic welcoming committee.

But no chemical cloud, no machine-gun fire. No hoods, no handcuffs, not then, not yet. Just a voice, amplified by some mysterious means. "Drop your bags and step to the side," the voice told them. "Please step to the side. Hands on your heads, folks. Each of you will be patted down. Hands on your heads. Welcome to New York."

Nearly three years had passed. Two years and eight months. She'd stopped counting the days. And they'd been keeping an eye on her ever since.

Inside the court building in Queens, there was more paperwork, more waiting, though it seemed that whenever a new officer saw the UDP mark in her file, a restrained sort of hurry, a subdued excitement, ensued. After they moved her for the third time to a third bench, Hel found herself sandwiched between the baby prostitute from the holding cell at the 114th Precinct and a tall woman with thick black hair who confided to Hel that she'd recently undergone gender reassignment surgery in Thailand—"the whole shebang"—but that her ID still classified her as a man. She'd been held in lockup with male prisoners. "I mean, luckily, all those guys in there were real gentlemen about it," she said. "Luckily! God, I can't believe I was so dumb! My ex told me to get my license changed, but I was like, why bother—it's not like I even drive in this city."

A rumpled but handsome young man called Hel's name, and she came to attention. Standing before her, he sorted through a stack of folders. Her public defender. That meant Vikram either still hadn't heard about her arrest or didn't care. "How are you going to plead?" he asked, leading her to a booth just outside the holding area.

She'd already decided not to speak, no matter what, so she shrugged mutely.

"Look, my job is to defend you, but I need you to help me out. It looks like you violated a restraining order, that's a charge of Criminal Contempt in the first degree. A class-E felony. And as you know, they took a four-inch gravity knife off of you. They'll probably go for Stalking in the second degree, plus Criminal Possession of a Weapon in the fourth."

"But I wasn't—" she said, startled out of her resolution. "That's for protection! I always carry it."

Around the corner, out of sight but still in earshot, the whole-shebang woman whistled. "Damn, mamí!"

"You're gonna want to plead to Stalking in the third, if I can swing it with the ADA. Get you one year in jail, with post-release supervision. Not a bad deal, for someone like you."

"What? No! I'm not guilty. I didn't do anything wrong."

The lawyer shrugged. "All right, then. Your funeral. Come on, they're calling your docket number."

Inside the small courtroom, dim and stifling with dry radiator heat, a judge, a clerk, some kind of stick—a bailiff, maybe—and a second suit sat waiting for them. The prosecuting attorney. Hel listened numbly as her lawyer waived the formal reading of the charges against her. She listened as the prosecutor argued that her lack of employment and lack of ties to the community made her a flight risk despite her previously clean record. He mentioned the antisocial tendencies typical of UDPs, stopping just short of referring to Joslan Micallef by name. Hel's attorney attempted to argue that since Hel reliably presented herself at Reintegration Education classes and since she was prohibited by law from changing her residence without approval anyway, she'd have nowhere to flee, but the judge set bail.

Her attorney bargained the initial figure down to some slightly lower amount, which she still couldn't pay, and it was all over.

They left the courtroom. Hel felt exhausted. Did any of her associates have that kind of money? the attorney wanted to know. Did she know anyone who owned property? She didn't answer him, and after a minute, he left her in peace, taking her folder along with him.

An officer returned her to the bench to wait some more; no doubt additional paperwork would need to be filled out before they sent her to wherever they were going to hold her until trial. Her friend the whole shebang was gone by now, but the young cherry was still there. Hel looked at the girl's thin legs, clad in sheer tights. She felt in her pocket, searching for something to give her, but all that was in there was her carbon of her property voucher. "Are you all right?" she asked.

The cherry sniffled. "What you fuckin' think, bitch. Fuck off." But there was no hostility in her voice. Their shoulders were an inch apart. Hel felt that inch like a touch. It was a comfort to her and a scourge, just as the hand-holding in Calvary had been. She resented the proximity but wouldn't have moved over if she could.

After a minute, the sound of heels signaled that someone else approached them, a woman dressed in a nice skirt and a silk blouse. Surely another lawyer—the cherry's. "Good luck," Hel told her sincerely.

"Are you Helen Nash?" the lawyer asked.

The prostitute rolled her eyes. "No."

"I am," Hel said.

"Come with me."

No one looked twice at them as they walked down the hallway. The lawyer woman held the stairwell door open.

"What's happening? Did someone pay my bail?" Vikram, she thought, hopeful despite herself.

The woman shrugged. "Dr. Oliveira says to pull yourself together."

○

Vikram thumped down the stairs to the basement and sprinted to the end of the hallway, out of breath. He was only twenty minutes late for Reintegration Education and he'd never missed a session before. He peeked into the room through the wire-embedded window set in the door. There was the group, sitting in a circle. Wes picked at his cuticles. Agnew, the new addition, worked out some kind of equation on the back of an envelope. Catalina Calderón appeared to be sound asleep.

Vikram opened the door. "Mr. Bhatnagar! We were worried you were sick, or that you'd gotten into an accident." Sato reached behind her for the tablet she used to take attendance, tapping on its screen. Would he be written up, or was she letting him off the hook? He'd find out later, he supposed.

The metal chair squealed as he dragged it into position. "No. I'm not sick. The train was stopped." Old Catalina scoffed at him under her breath. "I guess somebody was on the tracks killing himself," Vikram said. "Trying to touch the third rail." He hoped this was plausible. He'd never been sure exactly how that worked.

"I have days like that," Catalina said.

The comment was loud enough that Sato had to address it. "Mrs. Calderón, it's not your turn to talk. Mr. Pikarski was about to check in. Please continue, Mr. Pikarski."

"Yeah, so this was a really good week," Pikarski said. "I had no idea that my cousin's son made it out. He's been living here—in Kansas City, Missouri—since he passed through. I never would have known, but I was searching for names on the internet the other night. You know."

Yes, they knew. They'd done it themselves, fishing blindly in the ether.

"He was in his local paper. He came in third in a 5K, can you believe it? And I'm like, there can't be that many Andre Pikarskis out there. And there was a picture. I knew in a minute—would have known him anywhere."

"This kind of thing wouldn't happen," Poornima Anthikkad said, "if they'd just publish the damn directory." Certain members of the group groaned or shifted position restlessly; this was an old topic of debate and most of them were tired of hearing it hashed and rehashed.

"Are you crazy?" Agnew asked. "Sure, a directory might be convenient, but can you imagine what it would be like if anyone and everyone could find out who we are? If they put all our names in one place, publicly accessible? Thank God someone filed a cease and desist on that."

"They put the mark already on our IDs," Catalina said. "If the government wants names, look, they already have! Look at us all, here, under their thumb. They can round us up anytime they want."

"I'm not even talking about that," Agnew said. "I'm just talking about all the sad shitfoots out there who resent us. Who call us aliens and say we're taking their jobs and whatnot. You want to find trash burning on your doorstep?"

"But think of the human cost," Anthikkad said. "Think of poor Ed, the years he could have been spending with his cousin. What if that was you? Wouldn't you want to know?"

Vikram tried to make eye contact with Wes as the UDP registry argument, now predictably reignited, raged around them in the basement, but Wes's eyes were shut, as if he were in pain. Vikram, too, stopped listening.

Pikarski's cousin.

Any of them could know someone who had made it out. One hundred fifty-six thousand was around 2 percent of the population of Greater New York. A small fraction, yet significant. Every UDP had heard anecdotal evidence of someone who'd said good-bye forever to a sister, a husband, or a mother and stepped through the Gate alone, only to be reunited hours or days later when the loved one's number was chosen. That was how the authorities kept the system going during those desperate days. Don't despair; maybe you'll meet again on the other side. That kind of platitude. Didn't mean it couldn't happen.

If Vikram widened the reckoning of his acquaintance to everyone he'd ever known, every coffee vendor and loan officer, every fencing instructor and fellow Emergency Clinic patient, well. It was hard not to see connections everywhere. Proper names—the list Agnew talked about—wouldn't have helped here; ferreting out connections so tenuous required a conversation. It became a game they all played, one less serious and intimate than What Did You Take Through, but just as common: *Yes, we used to live on that block, but not since the '90s—was the Youth Home still on the corner when you moved in? I was at that very baseball game, and I remember the score. Yes, that was my favorite place to get my eyebrows threaded! I used to ride the same trolley route to work every day; surely we hung on the same strap, did we ever sit next to each other?*

Vikram grabbed Wes's arm when the session ended. "Have you talked to Dwayne?" He remembered Dwayne had said he had to do something today but, in his excitement about the painting, couldn't remember what it was.

Wes shrugged. "He texted me earlier that he might not be around, but said that I could get some hours in finishing up, if I wanted. I'm about to head over there to get started on that big bedroom. Want to come?"

He didn't know about *The Shipwreck* yet. "I've actually got an errand to run. I need to get to Williamsburg, fast. Do you think you can take me?"

He held two fistfuls of Wes's jacket as they zigzagged up to Eastern Parkway, where they cruised in the far right lane. The top speed Wes's scooter could muster, according to the dial, was forty-five miles per hour. Vikram struggled to convert that to kilometers per hour and gave up. Compared to subway travel, it seemed fast. He felt he was riding on the wind's back.

No way to talk over the roar of speed and traffic, and no face shield on the spare helmet. Vikram kept his eyes closed, aware only of the movement of traffic around them. Big cars and big trucks, but no vacuum trailers or rigs—in this world, the cross-borough highways all ran north and west of here. Instead, over Vikram's shoulder, morning foot traffic and the parade of Crown Heights businesses—hair braiding, Caribbean bread, MoneyGram, fresh fruit, furniture on installment plans—all the innumerable things of this world. Vikram knew where he was. He knew. Still, he was filled with the nonsensical conviction that if he opened his eyes, he would be riding on a blazer in another New Jersey.

He peeked. There, inches from his eyes on the flesh of Wes's neck: the horrible scar. A world erased.

Just before they hit Prospect Park, Wes steered them onto Bedford Avenue. They coasted past alternating one-ways, a poor neighborhood on their right and a gentrifying one on the left. Why? It was unknowable. At the red light at Wallabout Street, Wes flicked on his turn signal and they zoomed under the BQE toward the water.

When they got to the Domino Sugar complex, Vikram climbed off the scooter and headed straight for the museum entrance without looking back. He'd head over to Brownsville to meet Wes later. As he approached the front door, he felt his phone buzz in his pocket. The display read DWAYNE S. Vikram reversed course, walking over to one of the granite seats between the buildings as he picked up the call.

"What's up," Dwayne asked, his voice uncharacteristically hoarse. "I saw you been trying to reach me. Something important?"

"I'm about to talk to someone Hel's been working with—she's an art history person, works at a museum, has a lot of connections." He lit a cigarette. "I've never met her, but she seems like a good bet for figuring out the provenance of the painting."

"Oh."

"The reason I was really calling was to ask if you'd try reaching Hel from your phone. She's not picking up for my number and I'm getting a little concerned. I'll text you her number."

"Mmm. Yeah, I guess." He sounded extremely unenthusiastic at the prospect.

"Hey, am I interrupting something? Are you at the bowling alley?"

"No. Just taking a day off from everything today."

That was when it came back to him—Dwayne's brother's grave. "Look, man. I'm sorry to have bothered you. Forget about what I asked." He dragged on his smoke, fighting an intense feeling of foolishness.

Dwayne had lost one person. Vikram had lost everyone. Almost certainly.

The year he left Boston for New York, he went to Union Square with coworkers to see the Halloween bonfires lit. They'd all taken pictures of themselves—him with his now-dead co-workers—the thronging crowd behind, and yes, many of those out-of-focus faces would have been tourists, dead now too, back home in another Nashville or another San Jose. And yes, many of them would have been New Yorkers who didn't make it through, dead now too in another Morningside Heights or Battery Park. But surely at least one of those strangers had been displaced, too.

What if that was you? Anthikkad had asked. *Wouldn't you want to know?*

Cristaudo in the storage unit with her machine, signaling and signaling and never a response.

Knowing for sure would be unbearable.

"I'm really sorry," he said again.

"It's OK," Dwayne said and ended the call.

His phone was still out. To cheer himself, Vikram called up the pictures he'd taken of the painting. Ill lit and blurry but unmistakable.

He crushed the butt under his shoe. Time to go.

CHAPTER SIXTEEN

Oliveira's lawyer furnished Hel with cab fare sufficient to get her back to the precinct station house. There, she could recover her vouchered property: her phone and her wallet. The gravity knife, the lawyer warned her, she would never see again. As soon as the courthouse building was out of sight, Hel told the cabdriver to bring her to Old Calvary instead.

They traveled via the Long Island Expressway, the pavement slick and wet, though no rain was in evidence now. Traffic moved fluidly. She shut off the TV screen mounted on the back of the seat in front of her, watching for the approach through the smeared windshield as the driver bobbed his head to the music playing on the radio. A song Hel recognized came on; she hummed the chorus as she tried to place it. Was it one of those awful Dop Peters covers? No, it was just an ordinary top 40 song that had become popular recently, within the time she'd lived here. She'd heard it a million times, no fewer than anyone else.

Now, the newer part of the cemetery spread out below them, extending in every direction, the grave markers indistinct in the mist. Today seemed to her very unlike the day of the evac when she and the others in her entry group walked from one world to another, an intangible seam somewhere in the space between one snowflake and the next. But the grayness was the same, the shrouded sun. Down below, the grass spread like a duvet and the squares of white were Truth cards, the engraved letters and motifs on the face of each one showing the fate of the person lying beneath.

The taxi took the Laurel Hill Boulevard exit. The driver stopped right by the tall wrought-iron gate and Hel handed over all of her money without looking at the meter. She intended to come as a supplicant, pockets and hands empty.

She chose a winding path, always turning toward the place she remembered, though she hadn't been here since that night. The anniversary—the third anniversary—approached, just a few months away. Would any UDPs come here then? Bouquets lay scattered across the walkways, blown like tumbleweeds by the strong autumn wind. She picked one up. Plastic poinsettias. A winter flower.

The mist played tricks with distance, making the Manhattan skyscrapers look no bigger than the skylines of memorial stones presenting themselves on every side. The breach created by the Gate setup had been somewhere in this section of the cemetery. With no map, she had only fallible memory by which to steer, and all of her recollections of this place originated from the frenzied journey to the evac site in her world. She retained nothing but vague impressions from the hour following her crossing: the blinding lights, the crackle of the emergency blanket someone had put around her shoulders. Still, as Hel walked deeper into the cemetery, the occasional marker looked familiar, the ones old enough to have persisted unchanged. She tried not to read the names of the dead.

At last, a stone angel she might know. She stopped, staring up at the statue, formed to resemble a young woman standing with one hand hidden in the folds of her robe. The angel's hair waved, motion frozen in stone. Wings extended above her shoulders, folded in, and she held her chin up, head unbowed. Sightless eyes pointed out at the world, dark streaks of sediment staining the stone cheeks like tears, the scars of decades of acid rain.

Hel had always been good with faces. If this wasn't the place, she would never find it.

This is it, she thought. This is where the tide will reverse. Where time can flow backward.

○

Teresa Klay suggested that she and Vikram talk at the cafe that occupied part of the ground floor of one of the old Domino Sugar buildings. Over a plate of delicate cookies, he showed her the picture on his phone. "There." He'd framed the image so as to cut out everything but the magnificent painting itself, but a tennis racket and the spines of some Harlequin romances were visible near the bottom of the image, and in the corner, part of the London subway map poster overlapped the gilt frame. "It's just sitting in someone's house. Don't you think this should be part of the exhibit?"

"The exhibit," she repeated. "Right. About Ezra Sleight and the lost treasures of the UDPs." There was something tentative about the way she spoke that gave him pause, until he realized that it was possible that she didn't grasp the connection.

"It's the one mentioned in the introduction to *The Pyronauts*. Did you get a chance to look at it?"

Across the little table, Klay nodded. "Iceberg. Ship. Hand. Yeah, got all that." Her features were delicate, her pale face overpowered by the frames of her glasses and a halo of fuzzy dark hair. If Vikram had to guess, he would put her at twenty-eight or twenty-nine, but she had the calm self-possession of an old woman.

"Did you know the painting's been missing for more than a century? The artist, George Lowery, exhibited it in Paris in 1828 after he finished it, and a private collector bid for it and brought it to America. After the collector died, ownership of his house and most of its furnishings, including his art collection, passed to his niece, who was what they called an old maid back then. She started a private school, the one that Ezra Sleight later attended. All this is Before, you understand, so it applies to my history and yours as well. Then the divergences started. In my world, the school folded in the '30s and *The Shipwreck* ended up in a museum in Vancouver. But here, sometime right around 1910, it disappeared."

A bearded server brought the green tea Klay had ordered in heavy ceramic cups. Klay stirred in a packet of sugar, then turned her attention back to Vikram. "Just out of curiosity, how do you know what happened to it in this world?"

"Wikipedia."

"Excellent." Her tone reminded him of the one Officer Sato always used when congratulating them for attempting some basic skill that two-year-olds born at the same time the Hundred Fifty-Six Thousand entered this world had long since mastered. "I checked out Lowery's page too, actually," Klay said. "Back when Dr. Nash first showed me the book. I hadn't heard of him, so I looked him up. Moderately famous guy in his day. Painted mostly allegorical scenes, right? The Christ child in the jungle, stuff like that? But he's pretty much unknown here now."

Vikram felt affronted. "I understand why the man's work might not be to your taste, but this is a famous painting in its own right, and its documented connection to Sleight seems to me to be of interest—"

"No, absolutely. I agree." Klay leaned forward. Her eyes were a changeable hazel, subtly lovely. "You've made an important discovery, Dr. Bhatnagar."

"Vikram, please. Anyway, I never finished my PhD." He slid his own cup around on the table's surface, mollified despite himself.

"Sure. Vikram. No matter Lowery's current reputation, *The Shipwreck* is obviously a fascinating painting, and it will be essential to the UDP exhibit. Where did you say you found it?" He saw she'd taken out her phone. "I think it would be a good idea for a professional to take a look first. Being stored haphazardly with no temperature control really isn't good for an oil. And we should consider the possibility—forgive me—that it's not even genuine."

"I've seen it in person. I'm pretty sure it is."

"And I'm sure you're right. But what could it hurt to have it authenticated? We can arrange a time for you and I to meet with a conservationist. Just to look it over, before we go any further."

That sounded reasonable. "All right. It's at the old Sleight house."

"That old school? All the way upstate?"

"No," Vikram said. "The house. Where he wrote his books. You know."

Klay looked surprised, much more surprised than she had when she'd seen the pristine iceberg on the screen of his phone.

"In Brownsville," Vikram clarified. "It's still standing. It's a dump, but it's still standing."

How strange, he thought, watching her note the address in her phone, that Hel had never thought to mention this fact to her.

○

Asyl tracked Aitch due west, following the curve of the valley. She picked out a trail invisible to John Gund. When it grew too dark to see the ash beneath their feet, they camped outside an abandoned filling station. John Gund set up the tent on the cracked concrete apron where the pumps had been and warmed up rations for them both while Asyl climbed up on top of a twisted metal cabinet that had mostly survived the first burn. John Gund recognized what its purpose was—holding bags of ice offered for sale in the long-ago Before—and knew that Asyl didn't know, that she didn't care. She crouched on her haunches, staring out into the darkness.

"He could be getting away," she muttered. "He can travel at night and we can't follow."

"He has no food, and hardly any water," John Gund reminded her. "He won't get far." Between the helmet and the encroaching night, it was impossible to make out her expression, but he could tell from the way her shoulders slumped that she was not comforted by this truth. "I think he must be headed for Vic City."

Twenty years ago, survivors had dug beneath the hills, creating a network of tunnels that began just half a day's journey in the direction they were walking already. "He wouldn't," Asyl said. "Never." Victory City was her own birthplace.

"Why not?"

Without answering, she jumped to the ground, unfastened the door of the tent, and went inside. The walls glowed, and he could see her shadow. He knew she was removing her protective gear. "Because that would be a compromise," she said from inside, her voice slightly muffled.

"And outlaws never compromise?"

"If they do, what's the point of being an outlaw?"

Silence from inside the tent for a moment, and then he heard her begin her nightly prayers, thanking out loud the God who had pulled her from the pit and set her in a place where she could not burn.

To give her privacy, John Gund walked away from the tent, away from the filling station. He felt a vestigial urge for a campfire, and wondered at it. These days, flames meant something else to him. They were not special. All day, every day, he burned things.

A cement-block structure stood twenty feet away, its fire-marked walls uncollapsed. He walked through the gaping doorframe into what he imagined had been a small cafe. Long ago, traveling salesmen would have sat before cups of coffee, slices of pie, chicken-fried steaks, and boxed mash. Checkered oilcloth on the tables. A radio. Now, there was nothing but piles of charred rubble. At the back of the space, the door to the old kitchen stood open, miraculously preserved but hanging askew on damaged hinges; he knew from experience that the room back there would be a dark husk or, if not, that anything of value would have been cleared out by a scavenging party. He stuck his head in and saw, to his surprise, that most of the back wall looked relatively undamaged. There was a stove and some empty shelves and even two kitchen chairs, whole. Looking around, he saw rubbish in the corner, ration packages and empty cans.

People had stayed here. Not pyronauts, but certainly people who'd traded with pyronauts.

Someone had dragged in the chairs—why, only Asyl's God could tell them.

John Gund pulled the nearest chair away from the stove and brought his booted foot down savagely on one of the wooden legs, breaking it off with a splintering crack. Yes, this would catch easily. He carried the legs outside, made them into a pile. Asyl had fallen quiet—praying silently, perhaps.

He didn't use his flame pistol. Instead, he struck one of the matches he kept in a tin with a photo of his mother and her sister, arm in arm in front of a house he could almost remember growing up in.

"I'm going to Vic," Asyl announced. "As far as the watch-tower, at least." She said the words through the tent wall, knowing he could hear her outside. "Tomorrow."

○

Ten cards would have told her.

This is you.

This is your disguise.

This is your past.

This is your future.

This is what is above you.

This is what is below you.

This is your house.

This is your lover.

This is your riddle.

This is your answer.

How Hel wished the deck were with her. She knelt on the ground between two graves, orienting herself by the angel over her shoulder. The wet grass froze her; her fingers itched. She wanted her knife back, but more than that, she wanted answers.

For Truth to work, the reader must first be sure of what she is asking.

Where was the book?

But it wasn't so simple. Other questions clouded Hel's mind, confusing the mantic properties of the cards that she did not hold. Questions layered like sodden leaves beneath the surface of a placid lake, questions she'd already asked over and over. Where was *The Shipwreck*? Why had Sleight died? Why had Hel's number come up? Why had she found Vikram and then driven him away? Why must she suffer this world, so familiar at every turn, yet so alien?

Where was Jonas?

You never heard any answers if you asked a dozen at once like that. You had to think small. You had to settle. Settle in.

She didn't recognize the man as he approached, though maybe she should have known him by his bouncy walk, his skeleton frame. Her first deluded, hopeful idea was that new voyagers were passing through the old barrier. But no, he was just one person, wearing jeans and an army-style coat with the collar turned up, the hood of a sweatshirt worn underneath protruding, pulled up. No one at home wore a hood. Sweatshirts didn't have hoods. If he came from her world, he'd be wearing a hat. Always, these little details oriented her. The ground under her feet remained solid, the sky gray, mundane, and devoid of the blue-lightning trace of the Gate.

Never for a moment did she think he might be a ghost. She didn't believe in ghosts.

The man coming toward her was Dwayne Sealy.

"What are you doing here?" she asked. Weeks had passed since their only meeting, but she knew him now, and he clearly knew her too.

He shrugged, shoulder to shoulder with the angel. "Saw you get out of a cab on the boulevard just now. Followed you from there."

"Did Vikram send you?"

"No. I had no idea you'd be here."

"I don't believe you." The more she thought about it the angrier it made her; the idea of Vikram declining to help her when she needed it, sending a stooge to keep tabs on her only after the crisis subsided. "Fuck him! In fact, you and Viki can fuck each other! Get a cancer and fuck each other to death!" She felt foolish yelling like this, from her knees in the dirt. She struggled to her feet, eye level with Dwayne, who looked unimpressed by her outburst.

Actually, now that she thought about it, she remembered how she'd declined to try Vikram's phone number in the station house. How could he have known she needed his help? And besides that, what could he have done? Her chest throbbed, not with anger but with faint stirrings of guilt.

Dwayne backed away. "Have some respect," he said. He gestured with an out-thrown arm. "Look around you. I'm here to see my brother's grave."

"Really?"

"You UDPs. Think everything's about you, all the time. Even Vikram. I like the man, but come on. There's a whole world of pain and suffering and shit." He started to walk back down the path in the direction from which he'd come. "You don't have a monopoly on it."

"Where are you going?" Hel asked.

"I said already. My brother. He's in New Calvary."

Suddenly, she did not want to be left alone. "Hold on," she said to his retreating back. "Wait. I'm coming with you."

"What if I told you I needed some peace and quiet?"

"Oh." Now she felt doubly foolish. She stopped. "Oh God, I'm sorry. I'll go."

He let out a breath. "It's all right. You can come if you want." He turned to her. "Seriously, come. I've got some news from Vikram, anyway. If you want to hear it. But I gotta do my thing first."

Together, they threaded their way through the graves and left the old part of the cemetery, crossing on foot underneath the BQE, then proceeded along industrial Fifty-Fourth Avenue, its packaging companies and shipping companies, a business on the corner that sold custom neon signage. Without speaking, he led her under the LIE and onto Forty-Eighth Street and back onto hallowed ground.

Newer graves here. Granite instead of slate and marble. Dwayne seemed to know exactly where he was going. His jouncy walk, his fists inside his pockets—they seemed endearingly boyish to her. Yet he'd scolded her and she knew she deserved it.

He slowed to wait for her. "Shawn was sick most of his life," he said. "He had a lung disease. But he was a fighter. Have you heard that before? It's a cliché that they use here about people who are sick—that they're fighting their condition. That's not what I mean, though. Shawn hated talking about cystic fibrosis. He was a big baby about it. He would get stuff in the mail from the hospital and just tear it up unopened, without seeing whether it was a bill or test results, or anything. I always had to get to the mailbox before him. What I mean when I say Shawn was a fighter is that he was a *fighter*. A regular scrapper. Tough guy, you know? One time, he caught me and my friend trying on his new cologne, this stuff I saw him buy on clearance at the Rite Aid. Man, he beat our asses for that. But he always kept me safe. Had my back, like a big brother should."

They turned up a sort of alley. Hel noticed a fleet of candy-pink stones to the left, their inscriptions carved in a script she didn't know. A family. "You come here a lot?" she asked.

"Never."

"Oh. How long has he been dead?"

"Years. Three years."

Hel thought about what that meant. Maybe he was right about her self-centeredness. On the day her life fell apart, the day she won the lottery and stepped through the Gate to begin a new one, Dwayne Sealy and his grandmother had been newly bereaved and grieving.

"So, what about your kid?" Dwayne asked her. "Vikram says you lost a son."

CHAPTER SEVENTEEN

Jonas didn't walk across the country. That would have been crazy. He traveled out from Western Refuge, the renamed township where he lived with his father, on a borrowed blazer. Even including the stops he had to make to scavenge for fuel and for food, the cross-country trip took under two weeks. Not bad. Not bad at all.

Hardly any of the main roads had been repaired since Jonas was a child. He had a map, but it was hard to predict which routes would still be passable. In the first years, when there was still fuel to be bought, some municipalities sent out wrecking crews to clear away the junked pods, but in other places, rusted pileups impeded passage, forcing Jonas to wheel the heavy bike along the shoulder. He knew enough, as he moved east, to avoid the cities.

He was close enough now to the Exclusion Zone that he needed to seriously consider his entry point. The highway Jonas had been following since the ruins of Buffalo now led south and east and ended right at a checkpoint. That meant that for any nonmilitary purposes, it was a dead end.

He'd been warned about this already by a stranger he met on the road. Together, the two of them broke the window of a room in a chain motel, a Du-Sleep-Inn. They took the unit on the far end, which ended up having two double beds. Jonas opened the door and wheeled the blazer inside, leaving streaks of grime on the carpet, and then he and the stranger piled the two dressers in front of the window, put the dead bolt on, and spent the night in there, taking turns watching the approach through an old-fashioned spyglass John wore around his neck under his dirty coat.

John. That was the guy's name. "I always take the end room," John said. "It's good luck."

John? Like John Gund, in the book y'all keep talking about?

No. Hiram. That was the guy's name. "I always take the end room," Hiram said. "It's good luck." He gave Jonas a fishy look. "Normally, I like to leave the door open, too. That way, I can see what's coming. Anybody comes up on me, I take off before they can bother me."

Jonas could see the logic behind the strategy. Hiram was younger than Jonas by a few years—maybe young enough to have been born Before, but too young to remember much about it—and he had a cough. He didn't seem strong. Probably chronic radiation syndrome.

"Too bad," Jonas said. He felt no pity. His mission had to come first. If anyone spotted them, he'd never be able to wrestle the big diesel bike out from where he'd propped it. The better option was to pretend they weren't even there. That meant a closed door.

In the morning, the two went their separate ways. Hiram headed west, out of the Neverlands, while Jonas continued east.

People told him he couldn't do it, and maybe he wouldn't. Maybe he would stop at the fence. But maybe not.

Neverlands, did you say?

That's what I said.

Also, is this now? Wouldn't Jonas be, like, thirteen? That seems too young to be out on his own.

This isn't now.

Oh. OK.

He's older. Why couldn't he be older? I want him to be strong. I want him to live a long time.

Jonas passed through a town as he started to lose the light. It was clear immediately that no one lived in this area anymore. Even the people who'd weathered the crisis years on their own, refusing to be evacuated, tended to stay on the outskirts, avoiding the populated areas where Homeland Defense was more likely to conduct sweeps. So this was a ghost town. And it hadn't been resettled. Everyone knew what the officially sanctioned radiation levels were, but no one knew how far you could push it. If you'd lived on the verge like this, it was usually wiser to pull up stakes. Jonas found his way to the streets in the center of the town, where the post office was and the routing station. Then, he found a house with an attached shed. He didn't like staying in other people's homes, even if they were never coming back. Even if they were dead.

That night, he curled under his two tarps. He'd had enough to eat—canned goods pillaged from a small grocery store he'd hit the night before—and so he slept soundly, without dreams. He'd heard tales of people in the Neverlands who grew their own crops and actually ate them, but Jonas would never do that. Don't take any risks, his dad always warned him. All you have is your health. Not everything his dad said was foolish; they'd seen so many get sick, even in Western Refuge, 1,500 kilometers from the nearest site, the one in Escondido.

What kind of parent would let his child—

Teenager, like I said. And I'm not saying he would let Jonas do anything. He's a stubborn kid. He would have snuck away. Raym—my ex—he would know Jonas enough to see it coming. That's all.

Can I ask, without sounding rude—can I ask what the point is, of all of this?

The next morning, Jonas found his way to the fence. He'd left the highway and was feeling his way on local roads. The map wasn't much help so he consulted his compass frequently, always heading east.

And then, up ahead, he saw it.

They'd put fences all around the Exclusion Zone. Barbed wire topped the chain-link, and charge boxes placed at intervals hinted that the fence was electrified, but Jonas doubted the current still ran. What would power it? Of course, he wasn't sure. He'd never seen an electric fence in operation in his whole life.

He wheeled the blazer to the far side of a little meadow—farther from the road than you could get, most places, without a machete or something to hack through underbrush—and laid it on its side beneath the low-bending branches of a blight-resistant crab apple tree. He covered it with his larger tarp, which had a subdued green-and-brown camouflage pattern.

Leaving the blazer didn't trouble him too much. He'd done the best he could to hide it. Either it would be here when he got back, or it wouldn't.

And he continued inward on foot, through the second-growth forest.

I was there in the hospital. I saw Shawn die, so I could never pretend that he wasn't gone. But I used to think about what he could have done in life, if he hadn't been taken from us. I still do think about that, sometimes.

Even this close, it was hard to tell that anything had happened. The trees were green and healthy in appearance. Birds called and the sun rained down fat drops of light between the leaves. Poison. It was all poisoned. After America Unida sympathizers took down the plants, the standoff was off and the USA show-ered Caracas with warheads. And after that, AU flattened New York City with its fusion-boosted fission bomb. That was the end of the war, but everything within fifty klicks was still Ex-cluded. Would be forever, the old-timers said.

He put his ear to the fence. Didn't hear any buzzing. He could risk it. He stretched out a hand to the metal links.

The closest he'd ever gotten to the place where his mother had died.

But it hurts, wondering like that. Makes you ache. It ain't real. Don't do no good. I don't think this is healthy, Helen. And having him come there, for you? Putting himself in danger?

Jonas decided. This was the nearest he would approach. He could not see her city, that mass grave. When he was a kid, he used to imagine she got out, in that lottery. Now, he knew how unlikely that was, and he could mourn. It was the feeling, here, that made the journey worthwhile. The feeling he got standing here in the Neverlands of upstate New York. Remembering a picture he'd made once, a drawing of a tiger. He'd signed it with a shaky, deliberate J. He remembered traveling by airship to meet her, long ago. How she'd been waiting when he disem-barked, just like she'd said she'd be. How she'd taken him into her arms.

You never meant to leave him.

Yes I did. Are you kidding? They called my number and I went.

You couldn't have saved him, though. There's no way. You wouldn't have done him any good by staying behind.

Still.

I don't think you should beat yourself up.

I can't help it.

Think about it logically. What do you think you were supposed to do?

I don't know.

CHAPTER EIGHTEEN

William Sleight stayed at the Califone Hotel. After his son died, he holed up in a luxury suite for weeks. Daniel, the archivist from the public library, had showed Hel a digitized copy of the hotel's registry book, found in the Brooklyn Collection. In later years, the elder Sleight never talked or wrote about the period of time surrounding his son's death, the period—just over a year—when he himself had vanished. Daniel had to do a lot of work to put together the pieces.

He had showed Hel everything he had when she went to visit him after her trip to the school upstate. "See here," Daniel had said, spreading papers in front of her on the desk in his overheated office. "First, Sleight Sr. stayed at the Califone. Here's him checking in. Then, two weeks later, he checked out, and there's no record of where he went. The big town house he owned in Brooklyn Heights that had been his primary residence, he closed it up, see? His brother Hiram worked for the Suffolk County DA, so most of his private correspondence is at the state archive up in Albany, but there's no indication that William told Hiram where he was going. Hiram went back and forth with the NorthKing Baking Soda board of directors about William's whereabouts when William first stopped attending meetings, said the family was looking for him." Daniel indicated a pile of letter facsimiles, written in a dense, ornate hand. "Hiram thought he might be traveling abroad, but I think the better bet is his property in Brownsville."

"Brownsville?"

Daniel pushed forward a deed. "Yeah, he'd bought a parcel of land out there in the early years of his marriage, when he was on the make. The cottage was old—left over from when the Dutch used to farm out there—but Sleight was probably going to knock it down and put up tenements for the influx of poor European Jews, like everyone was doing. He just never got around to it. Then, all of a sudden, about a year after his son's drowning, Sleight Sr. got rid of it. The whole Brownsville parcel. I think that's where he'd been living after he left the hotel—in the cottage there."

"The painting," Hel asked. "What about that?"

"No known connection to Sleight Sr. No paper trail at all, after 1909."

She imagined the grieving father at the Califone. Beds made up every day, but never slept in. Food on trays, untouched. Tall windows, their curtains drawn. Just like his adult son in another world, typing away with paper over the panes, William Sleight would have prevented all light from entering the suite. He would not want to be able to distinguish day from night.

How might he have grieved?

She imagined Sleight cross-legged on the floor, cards spread in front of him. Asking, where is he? Where is he now? Where did he go? She imagined him sifting through the cards, searching in vain for a picture of the tiger with red-stained teeth that he could, perhaps, feel, gnawing at his vitals.

But that didn't make sense. No Truth deck. No tiger. Those belonged to her, not William Sleight. How had he lived through those first days?

William Sleight paced. He ordered room-service meals and then left the plates of food to congeal under their cloches. He stared at the paneled walls. Poured bourbon from a crystal decanter into a crystal glass. Lit his pipe with Califone matches. He picked up the telephone receiver, put it down. Dropped the glass. Threw the pipe.

The father of the dead boy tried to convince himself that he'd done nothing wrong. He'd sent Ezra away to be educated when it became unsuitable—impossible—for him to look after the growing child on his own. There'd been no reason to suspect danger. His son wrote him tormented letters to which he'd seldom found time to respond. Since he hadn't known it would be permanent, their separation hadn't even pained him. This was William Sleight's secret shame. Only now was he sensible of what he'd lost.

And then, of all places, he'd gone to Brownsville.

"What happened to the cottage?" Hel asked. "You said he sold it?"

"No, he transferred it to a Mrs. Effie Washington." Daniel pointed out the name on the deed. "I guess she'd been his housekeeper at the big house in Brooklyn Heights. Look at the date on the deed—just about a year and a half after Ezra's death. That's when I can pick up a paper trail for William again. Like his life starts back up. It's a funny thing. You never stop feeling a death, but at some point, the pain stops being so sharp."

"Does it."

Hel imagined William Sleight in the cottage, neither comforted nor disturbed by the specter of his grown son who might otherwise have written tales of horror in that very room. William Sleight, perfectly unaware, kneeling on the boards, just as Hel had knelt on the grass between two graves—searching, feeling. And in front of William, she imagined the painting. *The Shipwreck.*

There was no record of the painting in Sleight Sr.'s possession. She was making it up, but that didn't matter. The fantasy—William staring into George Lowery's masterwork, propped up against the wall in the cottage—it felt true. His only son had drowned, after all, just like the painted sailor. Where else would he look for rescue?

William almost touching it, the pads of all ten fingers a fraction of an inch away. The big canvas, tall as a growing boy. As delicate, as wonderfully made. How senseless. How unpredictable. He might have seen the painting as a door, and wondered how it could be unlocked. In extremities of drink and laudanum and grief, he might have viewed the heavy gold frame as a gate that could be stepped through, a threshold that could be breached. Crossed.

○

"You're telling me," Wes said to Vikram, "that this old woman Lida Cristaudo was the first person to come through."

"Yes," Vikram said. "First official." He'd brought Wes to the cottage to show him *The Shipwreck*. They'd entered by the back door, into the cleaned-out kitchen. Sundown came early on the shortest days of the dying year, but a security light over the neighbor's back steps shone straight in through the dusty glass of the unobstructed windows.

Wes leaned against one of the counters. "No, wait." He let his head fall backward, striking a cabinet door with a resonant *thonk*. "I'm still trying to figure this out. You talked to this woman? And didn't mention anything about her to us?"

"I'm sorry. It was a lot to process." He hadn't thought about it at the time but really, as a UDP, Wes deserved to know everything Vikram had learned. Dwayne too, with all he'd done for them.

Wes didn't seem angry. "This is exactly what your project needed all along! It's much better than Oliveira. You need to track her down again. Other than you, has she talked to anyone about this? Been interviewed by the news or something?"

"I gathered she'd been interviewed by the government—thoroughly. She seemed kind of shell-shocked."

"Of course she would be! She's the first of our kind."

"Technically the second, if you count that graduate student Cristaudo told me about. But that woman probably ended up in a completely different world from us where the South won the Civil War or Asia colonized the Americas."

Wes stood. "Are you going to show me this painting or what?"

"Hold on. I've got to go get the light." Vikram moved with caution through the blackness of the living room, kicking out gingerly with his feet as he stepped to make sure he didn't trip. He didn't run into anything but couldn't find the battery-powered lantern where he'd left it in the vestibule by the main door. Pressing the home button on his phone, he turned the illuminated screen toward the baseboards. "Hey, I can't find Dwayne's lantern. Bring your phone and help me look."

"I don't have it with me." Wes's general shape was barely visible, silhouetted in the kitchen doorway now. "It's pay-as-you-go. I didn't pay this month?"

"Here." Vikram tossed him his cigarette lighter. Wes caught it, struck the wheel. The flickering flame showed just what Vikram's phone had: an empty place where he would have sworn the lantern should be. "Huh. I must have left it upstairs this morning."

"Maybe we'll find it up there. Man, I hate these lighters. The metal gets all hot under your thumb." Wes let the flame go out.

They climbed the stairs, Vikram leading the way, shadows dancing just out of reach all around. He felt like he did during his rounds at the warehouse. But there was no sense of isolation here. The walls of the silent house were nothing but a fragile barrier between him and everyone else in the neighborhood, everyone carrying on their own activities. Dogs barked. A nearby TV sang to them. The subway sighed on its tracks. A car alarm went off on the avenue. He and Wes were alone, but not alone. This feeling, as if the veil between him and others were permeable. Other worlds, side by side. Other possibilities, lives unlived.

Maybe that was what Sleight had meant. *Every big city has its ghosts.*

"Do you smell something?" Wes asked in a quiet voice.

Vikram did, something sharp and acrid, chemical, yet somehow pleasant. Like the smell of the fuel when, as a boy, he'd gone to the station to fill a jerrican for Sanjay's blazer. When he reached the top of the flight—the half bath and smaller bedroom to the right, the large bedroom with *The Shipwreck* to the left—he paused. Behind him, Wes said nothing.

Vikram turned left and then, for reasons he couldn't explain, he knocked on the door. Three sharp raps.

He waited for a ghost to invite them in.

After what felt like a full minute but couldn't have been, Wes pushed past him, lighter lit. With the door open, the smell came out to them stronger, a bright coffee-turpentine miasma. Alcohol. No—pine, licorice.

Gasoline.

Through the open door, Vikram saw the tumbled field of possessions, as disordered as he had left them. He saw the narrow path that led to the wall where the painting hung. It all dimmed as the screen of his phone turned off; for a moment, the only source of light was the flame in Wes's hand. "Put that out," Vikram said.

"Good idea," said a voice from inside the room.

The light went out abruptly—maybe Wes dropped it in shock—and in the pitch darkness that followed, Vikram searched his memory to identify the woman who had just spoken. Where had he heard that voice before?

It wasn't hard to figure out. This morning. Just this morning, over green tea.

"Teresa." He thumbed the button to reactivate the phone. "What are you doing here?"

There she stood, the painting behind her just discernible. Trapezoids of blue at her sides, sea and ice, and a further triangle of sea between her wide-planted legs. Sunset sky and gilded frame.

"I didn't expect anyone here," she said. She kicked at a red plastic jug by her foot. "You'd better get out. There's about to be a house fire."

A million considerations flew unmoored through Vikram's head as if suddenly set free from gravity, floating and bumping like objects in a space shuttle after liftoff. He knew that vehicles sometimes burned in neighborhoods like Brownsville— vandals set abandoned cars ablaze or joyriders burned their targets to hide evidence. But what happened if a whole house went up, so close to other buildings? All the people vulnerable to hurt: the TV watchers, the yellers and screamers, the laughers, the music players. Even the dogs.

And Hel never even got to see the painting. A tragedy.

He batted away the junk thoughts, the cobwebs. Was Wes still behind him in the dark? He didn't dare turn to see. "You want me to leave," he said to Klay. "What will you do once I leave?"

She didn't speak.

"You'll light it all on fire," he answered for her. "But if I stand here and block the doorway, you won't. You can't, because you don't want to die yourself." He was still working through it. He hadn't meant to say that out loud.

"This isn't a movie," Teresa Klay said. "There's not *that* much fuel. I was conservative. Even if I light it up while we're still in the room, I think we'll both have time to get out before the floorboards catch fire. It would depend on how long you can resist the compulsion of your basic survival instincts. The painting, though? It's pretty soaked with lighter fluid. It's already done for. So there's nothing really to save."

"Wes!" Vikram called out without taking his eyes from the blank dark oval of Klay's face. "Hey, Wes!"

No answer from behind him.

"He took off." Klay pulled something from her pocket. A cheap plastic cylinder lighter like Vikram's, the lighter he'd just tossed to Wes. This one was patterned with soccer balls. "I used to be a scientist," she said. "But it didn't make me happy. Then I discovered art. Art saved my life." The grind of the wheel and the flame.

"Happy," Vikram repeated stupidly. He was missing something crucial. "Why are you doing this?"

Klay shrugged. The Bic stayed lit. "It's like *The Pyronauts*. Sometimes you burn because it's your job. And other times, to send a message."

The Pyronauts. How would she know about that?

○

Before Vikram got his security gig, there was a period of unemployment. He sat in his apartment and watched cable television all day. When the TV made him feel like dying, he reminded himself that this was an essential part of his education. This was how all immigrants learned about America, these days.

He loved to watch people with problems he didn't share—unruly families, exotic illnesses, addictions and compulsions of all kinds. He was especially intrigued by the phenomenon known as hoarding. Vikram—who owned only the one stuffed backpack's worth of books, himself—had watched demented denizens be parted by force from the mountains of things that had rendered their houses unlivable. On the shows, a counselor would help a hoarder to sort and discard. When the victim of this help proved incapable, the counselor did the work without the hoarder's participation. Well-meaning family members rented construction Dumpsters to cart away all the rubbish.

Reality TV, this type of program was called. He watched men and women be ousted from the nests they had built, the worlds that surrounded and sustained them. Watching this moved him. He wept, and felt a secret satisfaction when they wept, too.

From his TV habit, he knew the terminology. Some hoarders left clear spaces between their clots and clogs. Others made goat paths that allowed them to move over the piles in the room. A floor's surface might be completely covered, but there were still ways of getting through that became part of the internal geography of the room. These ways were uneven and treacherous but passable.

When Hel appeared—when she entered Sleight's bedroom through the door behind Vikram—she took in the flotsam that lapped at the walls faster than he would have believed possible. Before he could speak, before Klay could speak, Hel was vaulting over the piles at a run, finding footholds and handholds, Mrs. Defoe's stuff crunching, breaking, collapsing under her weight, and yet in a blink, she'd gotten around behind Klay and looped an arm around her neck.

Vikram pressed the button on his phone to light the screen once again. "Hel."

She didn't acknowledge him. "You know I carry a knife," she said, right in Teresa Klay's ear. "You must know that about me. I'm an otolaryngologist. That means an ear, nose, and throat specialist. I know exactly what I'm doing. Put that lighter out. And tell me where my book is."

In the gloom, Vikram could just make out Hel's hands. There was no knife. Gripped tight in Hel's fingers, something utterly the wrong shape to be a weapon pushed harmlessly against the soft part of Klay's throat.

○

John Gund lay on the ground. In the distance, the lookout point outside the city's entrance loomed. He watched the guardhouse atop the scaffold burn.

This was the highest structure around, though in the stunted, blackened landscape, nothing else remained to compare. The little house—the size of a garden shed or small garage—perched atop spindly ten-meter-tall legs, reachable by a zigzag of stairs, fifteen half-flight switchbacks. It had been guarded from the waves of immolation that had passed across the earth since the aliens' departure. Once, park rangers with heliographs and passenger pigeons guarded the forest from this perch, alert for accidental fires. Now, the birds were dead, and there was no one to signal to, no one aboveground. Still, to this day, a watchperson staffed it at all times. No enemy approach would take Vic City by surprise.

John Gund watched the conflagration wreck the cabin. The tower's metal legs and platform could not be destroyed so easily. They would endure. If materials for a new shelter could not be found, future watchers would crouch out in the open as punishment for letting Asyl approach their safehold.

When he'd woken at the filling station to find her gone, John Gund felt a sense of unreality, patting the empty place next to him, sure that he was dreaming. But no—she must have left at first light. He realized he should have anticipated it. He stepped outside the tent. No more sign of her than there had been of Aitch a few days before.

Taking stock of what remained in their campsite, he noted that in addition to her bedroll, she'd packed a few days' rations, her flame pistol, and a spare tank. More disturbing was the presence of her helmet, which she'd left outside, placed deliberately over the ashes of the fire he'd made for companionship the day before. Through the clear plexi faceplate, he could make out a charred length of chair leg.

He gathered up the rest of his gear as quickly as he could, loading the essentials into his knapsack, hiding what he couldn't carry inside the old ice chest, a cache to which he could return at a later time. He lashed her helmet to his belt. It was valuable—irreplaceable—and she would need it later. When she came to her senses. If too much damage had not been done.

He began to walk. Though this section of the Never was not within their patrol area, they'd skirted it on their westernmost circuits many times, and John Gund sometimes visited Vic City on his furloughs. He climbed the ring of hills and passed down into a valley he knew, shaped like a cupped palm. On a clear, bright day like today, it was easy to imagine how pleasant these outskirts must have been Before. It wasn't long before he spotted Asyl up ahead, moving at the same pace he was. A tiny speck. His eyesight had faded as he aged; he couldn't make out anything more than a vague person-shape, but the quality of its movements told him it was she.

If she happened to look back over her shoulder, she would see John Gund. Maybe she already had. But her lead was too great for either of them to be heard over the wind; she couldn't tell him to stay back.

John Gund couldn't hope to follow Aitch's trail on his own. He didn't have the tracking skills. Had Asyl abandoned the trail in hopes of asking the sentries which way he had passed? Or was this slow descent also the path Aitch had walked before them?

The house atop the watchtower appeared on the faraway ridge, dark against a pale blue sky, like a floating castle. Soon enough, his eyes made out the threadlike scaffolding that held it up. It swayed a little, as it was designed to do.

The watchers up there would have a powerful spyglass. They would see her uniform. They would also see that her helmet was missing.

John Gund reached the bottom of the valley as Asyl arrived at the far side of the bowl. She stopped at the foot of the tower. On high, the door of the watch post opened, and a figure stepped out. Asyl exchanged words with the sentinel. Or at least, that seemed probable. The wind roared, sucking her words away. Then, the ladder he couldn't quite see must have been extended in invitation, and she began to climb. John

Gund increased his speed, trotting now, his breath fogging the face shield. Her helmet struck him in a steady rhythm as it swung from his belt. He tracked the formless mote he knew to be Asyl, moving up and up and up. She gained the platform. She stood on the deck. She entered the little house.

A full minute later, he spied the smoke. At first, it appeared pale gray, wispy, and he doubted his eyes. Though why should he have? Fires were his livelihood now. They were all men's livelihood.

(And all women's, too, Hel was sure Sleight had meant.)

Then, the smoke became dense and dark, as full of portent as a thundercloud. Black smoke bubbled out of the cabin at an acute angle, carried fast on the breeze. Any pyronaut could read the signs. Asyl had gone into the house to parley for information on Aitch. Now, minutes later, the structure was on fire.

John Gund ran. He ran until his lungs ached, until his exertions overwhelmed the ventilation system in his suit and his face shield turned opaque, ran blind until one foot landed in a hole—the abandoned den of some poor animal, extinct now—and he twisted his ankle and fell. He couldn't wait for the shield to clear. He removed his helmet. Took his first unprotected breath in years, expecting it to sting, to sear.

But it didn't. The sky domed above him, still blue, the way it had always been Before. Fingers of flame poked up through the roof of the guard post. He knew the pale yellow color of a fire fed by good fuel and plenty of oxygen. The same air John Gund took now, unfiltered, into his lungs.

One human figure, an undifferentiated blur, clung to the ladder. He or she had climbed partway down and now tarried at the level just below the inferno, as if trying to decide on a course of action, though it was clear to John Gund that the fire would not be extinguished, that no power could save the guardhouse now. The platform at the top of the scaffold glowed like a furnace. Veils of fire obscured the little house's walls, its collapsing roof. The line of smoke was an arrow in the sky, pointing it out; the open door its molten orange heart. No one trapped within could survive such a crucible.

Yet he could see only one person. Was it a guard there on the ladder? Or was it Asyl?

John Gund clutched at his ankle and thought of Asyl's God, who lifted people from the hottest of fires. Wasn't hers the shape he couldn't quite identify? Wasn't it? He would have to get closer to know, but he didn't try to rise from the ground yet.

He was a sinner, too weak to have deserved salvation—or was it his very weakness that had preserved him? That was what John Gund thought to himself just then. Or something along those lines; Hel couldn't quite remember the terms he'd used to berate himself. He was too late. He'd made himself too late.

Hel had to read it again, to know the rest for sure.

○

An hour before they would enter Sleight's house together, Hel and Dwayne stood in front of a grave, the cold stone incised with Shawn Sealy's name and the dates he had lived. There was the patch of grass that was all the real estate he had in the world.

"What do you do here?" she'd asked.

"I'm going to talk to him now. Just like I would if you weren't with me. I'm going to concentrate on what I want to tell him and I'm going to say it in my head. Even though he can't hear it. I'm not crazy. I know he ain't really here. Still, it makes me think of him, standing on this spot." Dwayne's gaze swept the nearby graves, with their flowers and stuffed toys and miniature Christmas trees. "You don't really have anywhere to go, for Jonas." He said her son's name carefully. "Do you?"

"No," she whispered.

She could put down the bouquet of poinsettias she was still carrying, right here on Shawn Sealy's grave. Their spade-shaped cloth leaves were dyed a red as bright as oxygenated blood. She remembered what that looked like, when you made the first incision. The body's protest; the most alive thing she knew of. She wanted to lay them down here.

As she started to crouch, Dwayne touched her arm, stopping her. "Please." His hand on her bicep gave a little apologetic squeeze. "Please don't. I just mean, maybe you should save those for your Jonas. Find it. Figure out where."

○

Now, Hel counted. The big man with the tattoos she'd seen on the way in had been running through the empty lot behind the cottage for the avenue, which meant that four of them now remained. Dwayne in the upstairs hallway. Vikram aghast in the bedroom doorway. Klay struggling with her here, in the small clearing in front of the painting. One, two, three, four.

The place reeked of fuel. Was *The Shipwreck* already irreparably damaged? Gas was a solvent, just like paint thinner.

Only more volatile.

"If you don't want to die, right now," Hel said, keeping her voice even, "your only choice is to put out that lighter. If you burn this house, I swear I will cut your jugular." She pushed the stem of the plastic flower harder against her antagonist's bared throat. Klay stood a few inches taller than Hel but had a slighter frame. Her hair, loosened from its tie, tickled Hel's nose. Hel heard Vikram's voice, heard that he was speaking, but couldn't focus on what he said; it didn't matter right now.

Klay did not let the Bic go out, but she didn't drop it into the widening pool, either. She groped out with her free hand, reaching blindly for what she believed was a blade, but Hel held her wrist tight, keeping it immobile, and tried not to sneeze from all the dust in this place.

The Shipwreck, somehow right here where she'd sensed it would be. "Where did you find it? Why did you bring it here to burn?"

"I didn't," said Klay, bucking in her arms. "It was here. Your boyfriend told me."

The wail of an approaching siren became audible. "They're coming for you, shitfoot," Hel said. "Stop moving." She was still thinking it through. William Sleight had owned this house. Perhaps he'd recalled Ezra's fascination with the painting and asked after it, perhaps the headmistress of the school gave it to the grieving father. Perhaps William bought it outright and the record of the sale had been destroyed. Klay's body went stiff, but Hel didn't relax her hold. "Now, the lighter. Give it to me." Perhaps William Sleight crept into the foyer in the dead of night and stole the painting—the painting that failed to save his son—and brought it back here. She was not in a position to judge.

And it didn't matter how it happened. The painting had been here, all these years, hidden from a world indifferent to its survival. Now recovered, only to be annihilated.

Hel felt Klay's pulse, its ardent thrumming, and thought of lying on the couch and holding her son. Of his small heart. The memory took over her whole being, coursed through her synapses like a wave. Jonas. His smell. The plastic flower in her hand, which she still needed to give to him, and this house, which she needed to save.

"Just so you know, I took your book," Klay said. "I burned that first thing."

"What's wrong with you?" Vikram knelt in front of the painting now, and Hel heard the anger in his voice and thought he must be addressing her, but no, he was talking to Klay.

"Let me tell you both something." Klay twisted her shoulders, testing Hel's grip. "Your so-called project? Collecting UDPs' little treasures? Your book by a dead author, a crumpled-up tract from some religion that forced all its members to stay behind and kill themselves, a bottle of wine created from a variety that doesn't exist in a vineyard that's been nuked, a dead baby's goddamn shoe? That's not educational. It's just sad."

Vikram wasn't listening. "You ruined the painting! You destroyed the book! Why would you do that, when Hel needs them so badly?"

No, Hel wanted to say. *Not just me.*

"Your world wasn't that great, just because it was yours. Who would want to put its morbid relics on display? Why not just leave them buried?"

It's for all of us. But that wasn't right. Hel had been selfish in her grief. All the while she'd reached for something that could not be touched, he'd been reaching back to her in generosity. Vikram, her lover. The two of them missing each other in the dark.

Hel found she had no anger to summon. She could only defend Klay. "She's not one of us. She doesn't understand."

"She is! She should." Vikram stood. He slapped the lighter from Klay's hand, and time seemed to stop for a second, but it was only a disposable lighter, after all. Once it was out of her grasp, the flame went out, as Vikram must have known it would. The Bic dropped to the floor with a plastic clatter. "She's a UDP too—aren't you? You worked with the scientists who built the Gate. Admit it! Here, can you turn her around? I can't see her in the dark."

It didn't make sense. There was no way to hide one's status. Special requirements had to be met. Employers had to be notified. How would Donaldson not know? "Impossible," Hel said aloud, doing her best to maneuver the smaller woman toward the brighter hallway as Klay resisted passively, relaxing all her muscles. "She would have been debriefed, she would be going to meetings like us. How would the Reintegration Education and Adjustment Counseling Authority not know about her? It's impossible."

"Not if she came through before everyone else, before anyone knew to be on the lookout. I know who she is! She's the test."

"There was a test?" Hel let go without thinking. She didn't understand.

Dwayne had found the camping lantern. He turned it on, pointed it at Teresa Klay. They all looked at her.

"I burned your book. I did. I did it." Her glasses had been pushed askew, but her eyes did not stray from Hel's. "I'm *not* one of you. I wouldn't go back, not even if it was possible. And believe me, it isn't."

A marvel, Hel thought, the ferocity of her determination to destroy all evidence of her past, when her past and Hel's were as ephemeral as anyone else's—neither to be held, nor fully released.

Now Dwayne swung the lantern toward the painting. She could see its surface, dappled and marred by streaks of discoloration where the gasoline had touched it. The desperate hand rubbed out. She saw it and wondered: Where was the impact? Staring at the place in the ocean where she knew the artist had painted that drowning sailor, she remembered how it had been for her, the first time she'd thought *The Shipwreck* gone, in the old school upstate. She didn't feel that now.

Klay by the lakeside, telling her to breathe. Klay on the bench, her arm around Hel's shoulders.

"It doesn't matter, really," Hel said, not sure to whom she was speaking. She reached out for Klay, who looked as if she were about to bolt for the stairs. She wrapped her arms around her, an authoritarian hug. In that moment, she reminded herself of Seff, comforting Hel and berating her at the same time. The sirens wailed louder now, very near. "You know, oil paint itself is flammable. You didn't need the extra fuel."

Something with hard edges poked against her stomach. Hel lifted the tail of Klay's shirt. Tucked into her waistband, a paperback.

"No! I burned it up," Klay insisted, even as Hel drew it out.

The paper cover, robin's egg blue.

Hel held it between them, in the light. After a moment, Vikram reached out, lifted it from her hands.

○

Vikram waited under the overhang by the entrance of the Home Depot in Jamaica as the snow swept down at an angle. He watched plows clear the lot, watched another inch accumulate, and watched it cleared a second time before he spotted a pickup with an extended cab skidding in from 168th Street and slaloming around the cart corral. Hel stepped out of the driver's side, bundled up in a parka he didn't recognize. The wind lifted tendrils of her black hair, sending them dancing. She beckoned at him, then got back in.

Pulling up his hood, Vikram closed the distance between them. All the way, the snow found his unprotected face like a swarm of tiny, stinging insects. He fumbled for the door handle. "What?"

"Still fifteen minutes before they open," she said. "I thought you might want to wait out of the weather."

The big cab felt small to him. The two of them hadn't been alone in a room together since Hel had come to Jerome Avenue to move her things out of his apartment, more than a year ago. They'd both agreed that was a good idea, at the time.

"Thanks," Vikram said now.

"Thanks for not cancelling on me, like everyone else."

Before leaving his house, he'd double-checked the online message-board service Hel used now to organize volunteers. There was her post: *still on!* with no comments. "Not a problem," he said. He took off his gloves, flexed his fingers. They stung as circulation returned. "Nice ride, by the way. Who does it belong to?"

"Hector. You've been to a couple of workdays—I think you must have met him. Tall Puerto Rican guy with glasses? He helped Eden do the power washing."

"It's awfully high off the ground. And that little bench seat back there? Is that really necessary?"

"I'll take what I can get," Hel said. "Can't transport a bunch of sheetrock on the subway."

After that, they sat, not talking. Air from the vents blew on them, painfully hot, and on the other side of the glass, the silent storm progressed without other human witnesses. It would have been nice to think that maybe all the Home Depot employees had been given the day off at the last minute, but Vikram was acquainted with capitalism's demands and doubted it. He was starting to worry about conditions on the roads back to Brownsville, though. The longer this took, the more dangerous it would be for Hel to drive with her load to the building the FDNY had saved and cleared.

Not that she wasn't capable. He knew she was.

Hurt, he'd stayed away. When he came to a workday as a New Year's resolution, he found a different woman, one who knew how to wire a switch and seal a corner. She seemed to be everywhere, delegating tasks to volunteers, defusing an argument she hadn't even started. Happier than he'd ever seen her. Asking for help, when she needed it.

He tried not to take it personally.

"I don't know what's going on here," Hel said. "Do you think we should leave?"

Just then, a kid in an orange vest came out and unlocked the front doors.

The cavernous store felt deserted. They couldn't find anyone to ask for directions, so they walked aimlessly. Each aisle they peered down bristled with objects and tools. Vikram wasn't sure which should be familiar and which were safely foreign. "Do you know what sheetrock looks like?"

"Yeah. I looked it up. It's like a big sheet of . . ." She waved her hands. "I don't know. Wall."

"It's big, right? I feel like it would be with the lumber. Definitely around the edge somewhere." They circled the perimeter and found it in Building Materials. Vikram helped her load four-foot-by-eight-foot panels onto a low cart, and together, they guided it toward the front.

"You normally have your class," she said. "On Thursday mornings. Don't you?"

"It's in the afternoon. Anyway, it's cancelled." He was taking a contemporary poetry class at CUNY in the Heights. It touched him so, the thought of Hel asking after him, that he stopped pushing his end. "How did you know about that?"

She'd stopped walking too. "I'm glad. I'd hate for you to miss out, for this."

I would do anything for you.

No. Not appropriate. He swallowed the words. "I know the cottage is important."

At the automatic checkout, she scanned and paid. "Have you ever heard that most couples divorce when their child dies?" Receipt paper from the machine sifted through her fingers. "It's just too much trauma. Even though they shared the experience, it tears them apart."

"Yes. I think I've read that."

She put her gloved hand on his arm. "But what happened to us was sort of the opposite of that, don't you think?"

"If that's true," he said, "what do you think it means?" All the aspects of his world and Hel's that were gone, all the people and places they would never see again. And weighing against these deficiencies, the few things they'd saved. He felt the press of her fingers. "Maybe you and I know too much about each other to ever start fresh. Have you ever thought of that?"

"No," she said. "You still love me. It's good that you know me. And I *like* that you were there with me to see it." With a heave, she got the cart of drywall moving again.

"To see what?"

Outside the automatic doors, the snow hadn't paused. It blanketed the expanse of concrete once again. It had swallowed up their footprints. Together, they stepped out into the white.

"A reversal of fortune," Hel said.

INTERVIEW TRANSCRIPT:
CARLOS OLIVEIRA, AGE 73, MANHATTAN

I don't want to talk about me. I want to tell you about a man named Jin Fan-Wen.

It's easier to think of him as two men who lived different lives. Two people: Dr. Jin and Mr. Jin. Both are dead. As a specialist in the sociology of scientific knowledge, I knew Dr. Jin by reputation. Mr. Jin, who lived and died in *this* world, is a person with whom I've become acquainted only recently. But he is the one I want to tell you about. About his fate, as it unfolded here.

Nineteen hundred and nine is the generally accepted year now, the year of the first divergences. Jin Fan-Wen was born safely just Before, in 1908, to a middle-class family in the Chinese city of Xiangshan on the western bank of the Pearl River. His well-educated parents—a laboratory technician and a shorthand instructor at a secretarial school—expected their only son to excel. Young Fan-Wen received high marks, showing special promise in the sciences. A sober-natured child, he was known to spend his leisure time not in games or sport but with a pencil and pad. I've had the opportunity to examine a few of his schoolboy drawings—made in 1918 and 1919 and saved by a sentimental mother—intricate thatches of abstract line. (No doubt his counterpart also liked to draw, in the other world. No doubt he tended toward variations of the same themes.) I find the sketches mesmerizingly creative, though I am not one to judge their artistic merit.

But by any standard, Fan-Wen was bright and obedient. He studied his lessons. All who knew him felt secure in predicting for him a brilliant career.

The fortunes of the boy who would one day become Mr. Jin changed drastically in the spring of his eighteenth year. Ineffable forces delayed the split between Communists and Nationalists, and the White Famine that ravaged my China never emerged; thus, in 1926, the political and social situation in his country remained sufficiently stable for young Jin Fan-Wen's parents to decide to send him to the newly founded National Central University, rather than shipping him abroad to be educated as they would do in my own world. In the city of Nanking, where he was to sit the examination, the streetcar in which young Fan-Wen traveled collided with a stuffed-bun cart, which had become stuck on the tracks while the vendor who owned it attempted to push it to a better spot in the shade of the buildings on the avenue. Fan-Wen and other uninjured parties helped to pull the dead and dying from the wrecked car. By the time he reached the university, arriving on foot with a torn shirt and blood beneath his fingernails, the examinations were already underway. His excuses were not accepted.

My informant in all these particulars is Mr. Jin's adult daughter, Jin Bingbing, who heard the story of this fateful day many times at her father's knee. Why would such an intimate encounter with others' mortality put a young man with talent and inclination off medicine as a course of study? Why was Jin Fan-Wen not able to take the examinations on another day or the following year? Jin Bingbing, with whom I communicate by email through a translator, does not seem able to answer these questions. When I heard his story, I wondered if perhaps he stopped to help those injured streetcar passengers precisely *because* he wished to escape the fate that, his whole life long, seemed to have been prearranged for him.

Catastrophe. The sweep of a butterfly's wing. I wonder what I would have done if it hadn't been for that booby-trapped house in San Antonio my unit was assigned to patrol. There are things a man is expected to do with his hands. After the incisions healed and they finally released me from the hospital, I would get drunk. Little blue bottles. It was a test of my dexterity, getting them open. Holding the bottle still between my knees and gripping with one re-formed arm and then the other, and then the reward. I would feel the liquor burn down my esophagus. Drunk was the only state in which I felt able to attempt the exercises set for me by my therapists. Drawing lines, as the young Fan-Wen had once done, only in my case, I pinned the pencil between two extremities that had, until the procedure, been the bones of my forearm. The alcohol that fogged my brain estranged me from the grief, the horror that I normally felt until, at last, all I saw was a problem to solve.

What can I do with these broken tools? Asking this question turned me into a scientist.

But I told you that I didn't want to talk about myself. You have tricked me!

Mr. Jin would never be a doctor. He did not attend university, not in Nanking (soon to be renamed Nanjing) or anywhere else. Instead, he took up the trade of mending appliances, apprenticing in the workroom of a small repair shop in the suburbs built up in the alluvial plains around Xiangshan, soon to become re-Romanized as Zhongshan. When the appliance shop became collectivized, he hung on. Though he came from an undesirable class background, he kept his head down and survived the Cultural Revolution. All day, he wired broken lamps and rewelded hot plates that no longer heated. Sometimes, when the case was hopeless, he advised customers where they might buy a replacement. He married a rather quarrelsome woman and when she died young, of an ovarian cancer, he got married again—more felicitously—to Jin Bingbing's mother. He was an active parent; Ms. Jin remembers him helping her with calligraphy in their one-room apartment.

And at night, he diagrammed elaborate circuits. The switches and coils, the resistors and capacitors: all drawn confidently in ink. Mr. Jin died as a very old man. He was weak and bald as a baby and utterly without material or intellectual legacy, unsung and unrecognized. But he died at home. His granddaughter cried at his bedside.

Fated by identical genes, Dr. Jin also survived to an advanced age. Just a decade after finishing his studies, he grew famous for his pioneering study of lipoprotein levels among the Chinese immigrant population in Oceania and the correlation of these levels with heart disease. He was among the first to emphasize the role of diet in promoting cardiovascular health. As an epidemiologist, he could take indirect credit for saving thousands of lives. He passed from life on a modern sofa of Indonesian design in an elegant Sydney penthouse. Many admired him; he possessed honorary degrees from institutions all over the world. Still, Dr. Jin was a lifelong bachelor. It would be days before the cleaning lady discovered the body.

There could be a third world where this man was an engineer. A fourth where he became an art teacher. The possibilities stretch into eternity, for all of us. It is dizzying.

I used the word *fate* just now. I may have said it more than once. We humans tend to see whatever befalls us as our fate. We perceive good things and bad things alike as happening just the way they are meant to. To teach us lessons, maybe. To make us into the women and men we ought to become. If one lives to be old—as I have—it's terrifying to imagine the infinite slew of choices made over the course of a lifetime. Different events. Different luck.

A politician makes a speech. A virus fails to mutate. A homemade bomb goes off. A traffic accident happens in China. Who is to say what constitutes our happiness? How can we predict? I would not take my hands back now, though I certainly would have at any time in the decade after I lost them.

So I can understand this: whether her passage through Dr. Mornay's Gate was purposeful or accidental, Teresa Klay made the best of things. She got used to secrecy and to her own singularity. Then when the life she'd pulled together was challenged, she reacted violently, trying to erase all evidence of the world she came from. Ree viewed the possibility of renewed interest in the world that UDPs like herself came from, the potential for sustained inquiry into the nature of the divergence, as threats.

I look upon the whole thing as a mistaken response. Like the faulty reaction of an immune system that attacks the very tissues of the body.

Nineteen hundred and nine is the year of the first divergences. Helen Nash has finally shown this to all the experts' satisfaction, though neither she nor anyone else can say why the multiverse should have split the way it did, or whether Sleight's death was, in fact, the catalyst for all that followed, or what caused that death. No doubt, as observers from both known worlds continue to scrutinize the brief part of the twentieth century that we all share, an earlier divergence will be found. For now, Hel's museum takes up both floors of the restored cottage, and it is called Divergence Memorial House. It runs on charitable donations furnished by the curious and the sentimental, including myself. And at my request, Mr. Jin's story appears there, alongside that of Dr. Jin.

No. My father did not believe in fate, Jin Bingbing wrote to me, when I asked this question of her. But those words traveled back and forth across kilometers of land and ocean, deciphered for me by one of my young Chinese students who helps with my correspondence. Like me, this student is a sociologist; he has no training in the art of translation. Who knows whether the rendering from Cantonese to English was done skillfully. The question remains: What *is* fate?

Another gleaning from one of Ms. Jin's emails. Less equivocal, less open to interpretation. *For the rest of his life, my father never went to Nanjing again.*

What is fate? What are its qualities? What is its nature? I think of myself as I was, years ago, giving up on my new weaker grip and biting the cap of a bottle in my teeth. I think of Teresa Klay, her little wave at the security camera.

I like to imagine a world where that footage exists. I picture a flat-screen hung just inside the door of the new museum. Ree—there one moment and gone the next. Good-bye.

ACKNOWLEDGEMENTS

I owe heartfelt thanks to a long list of people.

To Stacia Decker, my agent, for having my back and fielding a million questions. To Tony Perez, my editor, who understood the story I wanted to tell and guided its refinement. To Jakob Vala, for creating a beautiful design and to Anne Horowitz and Meg Storey, for a keen copyedit and a precise proofread. To Arielle Datz, Alana Csaposs, Sabrina Wise and everyone at Tin House Books and at Dunow, Carlson & Lerner.

To Pinckney Benedict, who told me that this idea could be a book. To other fine teachers: Scott Blackwood, Edward Brunner, Dean Crawford, Beth Lordan, Julie Rose and Paul Russell. To the W. K. Rose Fellowship Committee for a vote of confidence on which I couldn't put a price.

To all my New York City roommates, coworkers and back-in-the-day lovers. Also, to the underappreciated city of Carbondale, Illinois and the friends who kept me going during the gestation of this book, including Emily Rose Cole, Talib

Fletter and family, Me-Chelle Hall, Maria Romasco Moore, Natalie Nash, Sandra Sidi, Brandon Timm, Honna Veerkamp, and Kate Worzala. And to Ms. Patty Norris, whose warm welcome convinced me to come there in the first place.

To Mary Kate Varnau for providing a valuable example of professionalism as well as hospitality at all hours and good conversation. To Toni Judnitch, whose comeradship continually delights and improves me, even at long distance. To the many fellow writers from whose work and comments I have learned.

To my longtime ride-or-die companions, Lindsay Mac-Callum, Phillip Wilson-Camhi and especially Sabina-Elease Utley. Here's to another fifteen years.

To Libby Westie and Joel Brattin, dear parents and voracious readers. To my brother, John Brattin, who is good at sharing. To the rest of my large and loving family.

And to my strong and fascinating wife, Shaylla Chess—partner, confidante and inspiration. I dream with you.